THE DANCING

by the same author

A CAGE OF ICE
FLIGHT INTO FEAR
A RAFT OF SWORDS
TERROR'S CRADLE
IN DEEP
BLACK CAMELOT
GREEN RIVER HIGH
STALKING POINT
THE SEMONOV IMPULSE
THE KING'S COMMISSAR

Duncan Kyle

THE DANCING MEN

COLLINS
8 Grafton Street, London W1
1985

William Collins Sons & Co. Ltd
London · Glasgow · Sydney · Auckland
Toronto · Johannesburg

First published in 1985
Copyright © 1985 by Duncan Kyle

BRITISH LIBRARY CATALOGUING IN PUBLICATION DATA

Kyle, Duncan
The dancing men.
Rn: John Brockholm   I. Title
823′.914[F]   PR6061.Y4

ISBN 0 00 222940 4

Photoset in Linotron Plantin by
Rowland Phototypesetting Ltd
Bury St Edmunds, Suffolk
Made and printed in Great Britain by
William Collins Sons & Co. Ltd, Glasgow

My debt to
SIMON WOOD
is gratefully acknowledged

1

Long afterwards, when there was all too much time, Zee Quist would sometimes think about the start of it all and where the first stirrings must have occurred. With some anonymous Viking, perhaps, reeling off a longship to rob and ravish on a long-gone British coast? Or with a brave and upright Suffolk squire taking his devout band to the hardships of freedom from the king? Or maybe it was the brutal soldier a couple of centuries on? Once it was over, these were matters for reflection only.

But there was no doubt about the moment when it all started to happen to her. She was reaching the end of Hamilton's job-hunting letter when the honey-brown private telephone gave its delicate warble. She reached for the instrument slowly, still absorbing Hamilton's final sentence. 'Hello.'

'Zee? Anyone with you?'

She said, 'Not a soul,' and smiled, and then stopped smiling because in her imagination she could see the damn smile and hated the way it dragged down the corners of her mouth. This was recent, new in the last couple of months: one more small deterioration, another set of muscles going beyond her control.

'I had a call, Zee, around half an hour ago. It's begun!'

'Of course it has,' she said. 'Had to happen. Who was it? The ex-President in person?'

'National chairman. He said –'

She interrupted '– that you'd be crazy not to run, yes? He's right.'

'But I'm a very junior senator, Zee! Less than four years on the Hill.'

'Like Jack Kennedy. He won. You *have* to run.'

'Zee.'

'What?'

'Can you control it for me? How're you feeling?'

'Stiff from too much exercise,' she said, a sudden fury putting a break in her voice. She controlled it quickly. 'Sorry John, didn't mean –'

Now he interrupted her. 'Hope I'll always understand, Zee.'

'It's my damned new apartment. Thought I had it all worked out, but there's a million things I can't reach, or touch, or get to, and – Yes, John, of course I'll do it.'

He said with slow emphasis: 'I'm grateful, Zee. When I win you'll see just how grateful.'

'One small thing,' Zee Quist said.

'Name it.'

'Brother Bill.'

She heard his sigh. 'You know how it works, Zee. I talk to William about political issues, especially in foreign affairs. The organization is yours, all of it.'

'Tell Bill, huh!'

'I'll tell him.'

She said, 'I like him, you know that. But when Bacon said youth and discretion are unnatural companions, Bacon was so right.'

'I'll make sure it sticks.'

When the conversation ended, she pushed her wheelchair back from the desk and hand-rolled it over to the bright window wall that looked way out over lower Manhattan and the water. Damn, she'd left her cigarettes on the desk! But the tough little plastic trough by the chair arm held another pack, which was why she'd recently had the device bolted on, the device which all weekend had stopped her using doorways, had made the master bathroom and bedroom inaccessible.

'That weekend is over!' She said it aloud, in an endeavour to thrust those two miserable days into the ragbag of the past. Trouble was, her own past was anything but easy to forget. As she lit the cigarette and raised her head, another reminder of it moved into the edge of her vision: the photograph.

She wheeled over it, thinking: 'Now that boy is going to run for President,' and altering it at once. Not is going to – he's running *now*.

In the picture they stood one side of the net, she and John.

8

Laver and Margaret Smith were on the other, everybody smiling and shaking hands, Forest Hills twenty-two years ago, seven five, seven five, just beaten out of a mixed doubles final. Not bad for a scratch pair who couldn't total forty years between them.

Running for President! It seemed incredible. John Leyden was running for President! And Zee Quist was running, too – running his campaign. If he won – well, if he won she was White House chief of staff, that was the gratitude of which he'd spoken. They'd talked – when? – yes, Friday, after that first, airy remark on the Today programme when Carter said Leyden had all the hallmarks, his words triggering immediately about a million enthusiastic phone calls.

The tennis photograph was one of six, framed to match, marching in a line across the wall: John in a flying suit in the doorway of a rescue helicopter in Vietnam; John and Mercy on the stump in the senatorial campaign; herself with the cup after winning the inter-collegiate singles, and, on the far end, the picture *Life* magazine had put on its cover: 'Zee Quist does a stem Christiani: grace with pace as America's ski queen shows speed of turn.'

She spent several minutes smoking, looking out of the window, brooding. Chief of staff. Not bad at all. If John got there, Zee Quist would run the White House.

And Mercy Smith Leyden would be First Lady.

Everything was done with understanding and, indeed, with a smoothness that came from experience. The Wall Street law firm of Hampden and Bradford was, like Sullivan and Cromwell a generation ago, accustomed to having partners borrowed for the great offices of state, often at short notice. Well before lunch her desk was clear, her work-in-progress in other and safe hands, her letters of explanation dictated, written, signed and sent to her clients.

She took a yellow legal pad and quietly and carefully began making notes. Now, for an hour or two, she had peace. There would be no more until polling day in November – and quite possibly none after that for eight years. It was mid-afternoon when her secretary entered with a tea-tray set with fine china, poured the Lapsang Souchong, and as Zee Quist sipped and savoured, asked about the one or two administrative odds and ends remaining. Among these was the letter from young Hamilton.

He came to see her first thing next morning, having caught the baggy-eye special out of Boston at six. He was a tall, well-set-up, pleasant young man who gave an immediate impression of naïveté, but could be nobody's fool, having graduated high in his Yale law class. His family owned fourteen newspapers, six radio and two TV stations, none very large, all profitable.

Zee Quist said, 'How did you know?'

He smiled with boyish modesty. 'I guessed, that's all. After the TV it had to happen.'

'You guessed. Senator Leyden wasn't even a possible candidate when you wrote that letter. And I certainly wasn't in line to – Tell me, I'm interested in futurology.'

James Hamilton said, 'The handsome and heroic young Senator went one hundred and forty feet up a Douglas fir to rescue a little girl's kitten. On television.'

She said almost defensively, 'He didn't know about the TV.'

'Okay. But the CBS evening news was extended, the audience got to fifty-six million. There was no chance he wouldn't run. Or after that,' Hamilton went on, 'that Ms Zelda Quist would not mastermind his campaign. I wrote to you as soon as his feet hit the ground.'

Zee Quist laughed. 'What kind of work is it you want?'

He grinned back. 'Lick envelopes, order print, open doors, shake hands. Anything.'

'There's no pay.'

'I don't need pay.'

'Why Senator Leyden? There are lots of Democrats looking for the nomination.'

'Because he'll win, Ms Quist. And because he's young. And because I like what I know of him.'

'How much is that?'

He looked briefly disconcerted. 'I've read all the profiles. The autobiography, the essays.'

She said, 'Tell me about his paternal grand-father.'

'Oh God, I don't even remember the name,' Hamilton flushed.

'Unimportant.'

'Okay. Well, Leyden's an Old Dutch name – old Dutch family, in fact – and the family adopted the Senator's father. The grand-father, though, wasn't he Irish.'

'Know any more?'

Hamilton shrugged. 'Things I've read. Grandpa was a soldier, and that must have been in the British Army. He came to America round nineteen hundred, or a bit earlier, and was killed on the street by a horse-drawn carriage, belonging to the Leydens. His wife was pregnant at the time and she died soon after in childbirth. The baby was adopted by the Leyden family. I don't think there's too much more, not about the grandfather.'

Zee Quist said, 'All true. The carriage was a phaeton and Henryk Leyden was driving it himself, but that's all you missed out. Your CV mentions genealogy.'

'Family history, that's all. I spent a couple of summer vacations tracing a family tree. Trying, anyway.'

'Get far?'

'Back to sixteen-forty.' Hamilton looked embarrassed. 'Had a bit of professional help. But I'll get farther back one day, doing the whole thing myself.'

She pushed a cigarette box toward him. 'Smoke?'

'No thanks.' He looked at her in the mildly astonished way today's young always seemed to look at smokers, and Zee Quist said wryly, 'When you're stuck in one of these chairs, it isn't easy to find too many vices. This is mine. What's yours?'

'Well, music maybe.'

'Rock and roll?'

'Yes, ma'am.'

'Oh boy, that is a vice! Now listen – it is often reckoned – in my view incorrectly – that this country has twenty million people of Irish descent. A lot of votes there. And John Leyden has an Irish grandfather. So we maximise. What we need is a picture of the cottage he left behind, and the roses round the door, and the girl who looks like Maureen O'Hara in *The Quiet Man* – you ever see that movie?'

Hamilton nodded. 'Thirty times. Forty maybe.'

'She's his long-lost cousin, and she's admiring the roses. Got it?'

'Loud and clear.'

'Okay. Do this chore well and there'll be others.' She opened a drawer in her desk and removed a yellow envelope, out of which she took two pieces of faded paper and something metallic. 'This is a cap badge for Grandpa's outfit in the British Army. This is Grandpa's death certificate, and this one is Grandma's. Okay? One more thing, he was probably born in a place named Ballyhara which is apparently in Donegal. That's family hearsay and it's all there is. Can do?'

Hamilton said, 'How deep d'you want me to dig?'

Zee Quist smiled, suddenly remembered the rictus effect and cut the smile off. 'You mean if there's something scandalous? I don't think it's likely. If you think about it, he must have been a village boy; he was probably half-starved – remember how Ireland was then – and he joined the army. Not much scope for high-born bastards or card-sharping, and who'd care now, anyway?' She paused and added warningly. 'But – don't go making any decisions. Don't go suppressing anything. Any information you get – I want it, in documentary form, on my desk and at once. Use facsimile transmission, okay? Don't, repeat don't, announce anything to any reporters either. Watch your tongue at all times. Right?'

'Right Ms Quist. On my way.' He rose. 'One thing. Where do I send facsimiles – here?'

She wrote briefly on a small notepad. 'To this office. We have a Fax machine. But I'll be at campaign headquarters from tomorrow.'

Zee Quist gave a small, private nod of satisfaction as her office door closed behind Hamilton. In his way he represented everything she wanted in the campaign: youth, intelligence, a degree of idealism, willingness to work. Better still, he had the money and the time to devote to his enthusiasms, and he brought with him a sizeable hunk of assorted media to support Senator Leyden. He was a thoroughly worthwhile recruit to the campaign staff – even had the useful minor genealogical experience for the task she had given him. Also, she'd be damned glad to have old Grandpa safely documented; all through John's senatorial campaign the lack of knowledge of the old man had bothered her. What if he'd been a drunk, an illegal immigrant, or a bomb-throwing Fenian? Now, with the Presidency in their sights, it was essential to investigate Grandpa before someone else thought of doing it.

Her phone rang and she flicked a glance at it. 'How many thousand times are you gonna ring before November?' she asked, and reached for it.

'Zee?' No mistaking that voice!

'Hi, Mrs Crombie. How's the President's mother?'

'The mother of one out of many possible candidates, is inclined to caution, in public anyway. In private though, Zee, I have a suitably-large bet on his nose.'

'At good odds, I hope.'

'Excellent odds. How are you, Zee, and how's the new apartment?'

Zee Quist talked for a moment about the apartment.

'And you, Zee. What about you?'

She grinned to herself. When Helena Crombie called, she asked all the right questions and in the right order. Always. But you could never be quite certain of her primary purpose. One of two things might be about to happen, she guessed. Either Helena Crombie was about to invite herself to the apartment or she was checking whether Zee felt up to the job John Leyden was giving to her.

'I'm hopping about,' Zee Quist said, 'like one of Mr Disney's bunny rabbits, only you can't see it because it's all happening on the inside.'

'You're well? I ask because this thing will be a lot of work, a lot of stress.'

'I thrive on it.'

'Yes, dear, I know you do.' The blessing now? Zee Quist thought. But no. Not yet. 'Zee, when did you last see a doctor?'

'I have a quarterly check. Matter of fact it was two weeks back.'

'And?'

'And nothing could be finer if I went to Carolina in the morning.'

'Oh, I'm glad! I worry about you, Zee.'

'I know you do. But no need at the moment, so it seems.'

'And I'm so pleased you'll be helping John. He'll need you'—there it was: the Blessing—'and you must let me know if he really overloads you. But he's bound to, I suppose. He relies on your good sense.'

'If I have any, it's his to rely on, Mrs Crombie.'

'One more thing, Zee. Before the work load gets too horrendous, will you let me visit you in your new apartment? I shall be in New York next week.'

'Sure. Any time.'

How old was she, Zee Quist asked herself as she replaced the phone. She counted on her fingers. Probably seventy-seven. Smiling, she emitted a little *wow!* of admiration. Helena Leyden was genuinely extraordinary. She was gifted, able, rich and intensely capable. Beyond that she was thoroughly nice, generous and very clever with people. Beyond that, she had an eye like a circling hawk for every detail of the world around her. Zee Quist wondered how much money Helena Crombie had guaranteed for her son's campaign.

Before the week was out, Zee Quist knew two things more about young Hamilton: he was a mover, and he seemed able to operate. On Friday morning, forwarded with the compliments of the State Department, she received a foolscap envelope Hamilton had persuaded the US Embassy in Dublin to send on. 'I reckoned,' he said in his letter, 'that the diplomatic bag is more secure than the postal services, Irish or US, and that it is also quicker.'

There was one document, a photocopy, enclosed with the letter.

'Sorry it's not a transmitted facsimile,' he wrote, 'though in its way maybe it is. What it is, also, is an entry from the muster roll of his regiment, showing his mustering to the colours. As you can see Joseph Patrick Connor, from Ballyhara in County Donegal, enlisted in The 27th Regiment of Foot at St Lucia

Barracks, Omagh, on 2nd April 1870 and took the Queen's shilling. The probability was that he set off from home with a nearly empty belly and walked to Enniskillen in the belief that he could enlist there. But he couldn't. They may or may not have given him a mug of tea before sending him on another twenty-seven miles to Omagh. On foot, of course. Long walk for a shilling, I'd say, wouldn't you?'

'Tomorrow I'm off to Ballyhara, but without any expectation – population, I understand, is about eight.'

There wasn't much of Ballyhara. A dozen or so cottages, none of any size, and all visible from the cheap pine door of the half-derelict little church. Landlord or landowner would be over the hill somewhere, he thought, or in Cork or London. Strange to think that from this spot had come a man whose grandson was now bidding for the most powerful elective position the world had to offer. That election was next November, yet for the moment the name of Leyden was virtually unknown outside America. Hamilton wondered whether if he knocked on a cottage door, there'd be a Connor inside.

There wasn't. 'Connor? Sure and I wouldn't be knowin' no Connor. Not here.' The woman was probably in her late sixties. When she was born, Connor had already been gone from Ballyhara nearly half a century.

'You don't know the name?'

'Never heard it. Not here.'

'Tell me,' Hamilton said, 'who is the oldest person in Ballyhara?'

'The oldest? That'll be Pat Quinn. He lives over there. The dark cottage. Down the small track.'

Pat Quinn was ninety-one and spry, with beady little button eyes and, apparently, a single tooth. Hamilton wondered how, in this deadening place for all the decades, he had managed to retain his brightness.

'Connor?' He repeated the name. 'Sure, not for a long – ooh, not since I was a boy.' His face lit up suddenly. 'Miss Connor, she was, the ould divvil. In the churchyard, you'll find her there, you will. Last of the Connors, she'd say, and me dad would say t'ank the Lord for it.'

15

'When did she die, Mr Quinn?'

'What year is this – eighty-three?'

'Eighty-four.'

'I'd have been eight. Nine maybe.' He gave a cheerful chuckle. It was in the year the old Queen went. Like her, Miss Connor was. Little and fat.'

Hamilton questioned him gently but Quinn knew no more, except that Miss Connor had lived in a little dark-walled cottage which he pointed out.

Finally Hamilton rose. 'And where will I find the priest?'

'Him? Comes once in a year, over the Iron Mountains, face like flat Guinness. You'll not be wantin' him, son.'

As Hamilton faithfully reported, 'The priest with a face like flat Guinness proved easy enough to find.' Difficulty began when Hamilton opened the conversation.

'Parish register for Ballyhara you want?' the priest stood at the door of his hovel of a presbytery. 'Yes, well I attend there once a year only and devil anybody comes to mass. Should be closed so it should.'

'I'm sorry,' Hamilton said. He thought the man had a face more like an old potato and with as much life in it. 'I'm looking for the parish registers.'

'Not here.'

'Still in Ballyhara?'

'Not there either.'

They had, Hamilton discovered, been sent to Dublin. 'Sent there in – no, I don't remember.'

'I'd better be off to Dublin then!'

The priest regarded Hamilton with lumpen melancholy. 'No use. There was a fire.'

'In Dublin?'

'A bad fire it was, in 1922 at the Dublin Public Records Office. Destroyed a great number of old parish records, most of them of the small, rural parishes.'

The potato-faced priest began to explain at extreme length that the National Library of Ireland might contain references of interest. Hamilton tried to detach himself. The man said everything three times, and sometimes four, scarcely varying

16

the words. Now he was at gravestone inscriptions, going on and on and Hamilton backed away.

Departing, finally, Hamilton left a quantity of tyre rubber on the road in his eagerness to escape. Potato-face diminished with satisfactory speed in the rear-view mirror and soon, on high ground, he stopped to admire the view and to think. The absence of those particular parish records was not important. The muster rolls sufficed for Grandpa's origins. But now?

He decided to go direct to Dublin, having first telephoned ahead from a roadside kiosk. That night he installed himself at the Shelbourne Hotel and there, at the table in his room, set out what he knew so far of the life of Grandpa:

Joseph Patrick Connor

Born: 1851, Ballyhara, Co. Donegall, Ireland
Died: 1896, New York, NY. USA.
Married: Date and place unknown.
Wife: Jane ———. Name to be discovered.
Children: One known: John. (Surname of adoptive parents assumed upon adoption 1897).
Parents: Unknown and likely to remain so in view of destruction by fire of parish register. (Central registration not begun in Ireland until 1864).
Siblings: If any, unknown and likely to remain so.
History: Enlisted 1870 in 27th Regt. of Foot at St Lucia barracks, Omagh.
In 1881 the Regt. became the Royal Inniskilling Fusiliers. Since Connor's cap badge was that of the 27th Regt. it can perhaps be concluded that he left the Regt. (and the army?) before that date.
In 1871 the 27th Regt. was posted to join the Garrison at the town of Colchester, in England. I shall go there tomorrow in the hope of examining any records the still-existing Garrison may keep.

Note: All other records are at Public Record Office, London.

The brief summary, with a covering note, he delivered that

night to his acquaintance at the Dublin Embassy. It would, he was promised, be in the following day's diplomatic bag.

Next morning, Hamilton flew to London on the Aer Lingus plane.

2

Warwick Todd was a man of middle height, with a rather sallow complexion, black hair thinning a little, and he wore a short-cropped, though extensive black beard. The metal frames of his reading glasses tended to give him a somewhat scholarly air, but when he removed them, as he did when rising to greet James Hamilton, the dark eyes could be seen to be surrounded by whites of that bluish tinge that is the property only of the very fit. He was well-knit, compact, balanced, and thirty-five.

'Pleasure to meet you,' he said. 'Thanks for your message.'

'This place okay?' Hamilton asked, looking round him doubtfully. They were in Quo Vadis in Dean Street, Soho, a restaurant recommended by the porter at his hotel. He wondered if the porter might have resented the failure to use the hotel's own dining room, and have acted accordingly.

'It's good,' Todd said. 'You might be interested to know Karl Marx used to live here, in this building.' He smiled. 'What's produced here nowadays is a good deal more readily digestible. What can I do for you?'

Hamilton smiled. 'Have a drink while I explain.'

'Gin and tonic, thanks. You've been in Ireland?'

'I have.' With the drinks safely ordered, Hamilton said, 'You did fine work for my family.'

'Several years ago. A piece of genealogical research. I looked it up to remind myself after I had your letter.'

'We were very pleased. You connected Hamilton to Dalzell, which neither Dad nor I nor anybody else could manage.'

Todd laughed. 'Tenuously. I said so at the time.'

He enjoyed the lunch, eating steadily as the young man described his Irish researches and then allowing Hamilton to pick his brain.

'You've got it set out?' he asked at the end.

Hamilton gave him the detail sheet on Connor. Todd glanced through it. 'What do you want me to do?'

'Be a record agent, that's all. It would take me weeks to find anything in the British records. You'll do it fast because you know where to look.'

Todd laughed. 'Perhaps not as fast as you imagine. And I'm afraid there are fees.'

'Tell me.'

'One hundred pounds per day. Plus expenses – which I don't fabricate.'

Hamilton nodded. 'The thing – it's for a friend. Kind of a present, really. Joseph Patrick Connor was his grandfather.'

'Well, it's all very unusual,' Todd said.

'Why unusual?'

'Three generations. Four at the outside, and starting with grandfather. It's usually the other way round.'

'You have to work backwards from the present, you mean?'

'That's right,' Todd said. 'Just about everybody knows who his or her grandparents were. An awful lot fewer know anything about great grand-parents. So this Connor chappie will make a change.'

'How difficult will it be?'

Todd smiled. 'You'd think it would be easy, and so it may be. But from the 1850's onwards you're into the time when people began to travel. Before that, families stayed in the same village, and sometimes at the same cottage or the same farm, for centuries. Then came steam. Suddenly they're going from Plymouth, Devon to Plymouth, Massachusetts, or Newcastle here to Newcastle, Australia, and they're dying there and marrying there, and above all they're begetting children there. It can take a bit of following up. Do you want me to do it all, this time, or do you want to be involved again?'

'I was hoping,' Hamilton said, 'that you'd advise me where to look and let me do the searching. I kind of enjoy old records.'

'Me, too. Otherwise the job would be –' He saw Hamilton's sudden wince. 'What's the matter?'

Hamilton swore. 'It's a migraine coming on. First stab. Get it three or four times a year. Will they have aspirin here?'

They had. 'How long does it last?'

'Couple of days. Christ, I'd better not be sick in here.' Hamilton was now swallowing repeatedly.

Todd paid the bill and took him out to a taxi and back to the Stafford Hotel. 'You'll be okay?'

'Wednesday I'll be okay,' Hamilton said. 'If I can just sleep, it helps!'

'Call me Wednesday,' Todd said.

But in fact Todd did a good deal more. A piece of research he had intended for the day following – the Tuesday – became impracticable because a letter he needed failed to arrive from Canada. He therefore, with sympathetic thoughts of young Hamilton and his migraine, took a cheerful walk from his flat in Trinity Court, Grays Inn Road to Cannon Street, and thence proceeded on an underground train to Kew. A further walk of seven or eight minutes saw him in the Public Record Office, presenting carefully filled-in inquiry slips at the desk. Section W.O. (for War Office) 12 housed some thirteen thousand volumes covering regimental muster rolls dating back to the early 18th century. The one for the 27th Foot, which Hamilton inspected at Enniskillen Castle might be a duplicate or it might be a copy. The true record was here, in London.

He filled in more slips, handed them to the woman behind the desk, then devoted twenty optimistic minutes to the cross-word puzzle in *The Times*. He often found that if he got a few answers quickly while awaiting the record volumes, then the day turned out to be rewarding. If not, not. 'No going to the meeting (8)' was the clue for 1. down. Railway lines aren't, he thought. No, but they're parallel! He got six more, including, of all things, a quotation from *Cymbeline*, before the volumes were produced and he settled at his appointed table to do some work.

The muster roll of the 27th confirmed Hamilton's summary in every particular. Todd had expected it to do so, but in the matter of records was too experienced to take someone else on trust, especially if the other were inexpert. By doing so he found he avoided spending long periods chasing unnecessarily down blind alleys.

He pushed the muster rolls aside and checked the slip on the next two books. W.O.25 meant the *Description and Succession, Regimental*, volumes. Within a few minutes he was noting on his clip board: 'Trade before enlistment, farm labourer.' Soon, too, there was a physical description, noted on his pad: 'Connor had been 5ft 8″ tall, swarthy of skin, with brown eyes and black hair and a prominent scar on the cheekbone immediately below the right eye.' Even Todd was still pleasantly surprised at the extent of the detail given in old army records, and clients were usually far more so. 'If your ancestor is a civilian you'll never know whether his eyes were pale blue or brown,' he would tell people, 'but because he's a soldier, you're lucky.' Female clients were usually the more impressed, liking the notion of the hereditary hair or eye colour. Todd would explain, if asked, the reason for the army's careful recording of appearances: soldiers deserted, and their officers liked to be able to describe them accurately and also to be able to alert the law men of the deserter's likely return to home pastures.

Todd placed the volume aside and rested his eyes for a moment. *Soldiers' Documents* next, and they really were pot luck! Dublin wasn't the only Record Office to have had its fires: there'd been a nasty one years ago at the Public Record Office in Chancery Lane, with the result that soldiers' documents now exist only for men who survived to draw pensions. If a soldier died while serving, or if he were discharged before a pension became due, there would be no record. Still, that in itself could be useful.

He went to work.

An hour later Warwick Todd knew that whatever else Joseph Patrick Connor might have done, he had not earned a pension. Todd returned to the counter, briefly consulted the Guide, then filled in several more requisition slips; he was ordering muster rolls for the period after Connor's enlistment until the change in the Regiment's name – the change from 27th Foot to Royal Inniskilling Fusiliers.

Warwick Todd then took himself off to a lunch of a ham

sandwich and a glass of cider. He enjoyed both, and came close for once to completing the crossword puzzle. He returned to the Record Office with a pleasant feeling of anticipation. This afternoon, he felt, more Connor secrets would be revealed.

And so they were, though not all, and not at once. The muster rolls were often for quite irregular periods and the search had to be painstaking or things could be missed. Todd found the first significant mention of Connor in a roll which covered Christmas of 1872. 'Pte. Connor J. P. 27109, awarded two days' punishment, plus two shillings fine for fighting.'

Yes, well, he was Irish, Todd thought, and soldiers were there to fight, but only when told, and not to fight each other. Yet they did, all the time; it was fitness and frustration. Two more minor disciplinary offences followed in a fairly short time. In February of 1872, Private Connor 27109 received three days' punishment, also for fighting. He was further fined ten shillings. And in March, for threatening a corporal, Connor was fined £2 and given 14 days' punishment.

What next? Todd wondered. The punishments had steadily become more severe. Was that because the offences themselves were more serious, or because they were repeated? He grinned to himself. At the rate things were going, Connor might well be a regicide by June! But in fact it was fifteen months later, in 1873 before there was further significant mention. Connor had been drunk a couple of times, and hadn't stopped scrapping, but was still, in the old phrase, soldiering on.

In May of 1873, though, there came a further and resounding final entry relating to Joseph Patrick Connor, and it was one which made emphatically clear that Connor must have been engaged in something more than drinking a little too much porter and having the occasional swing at a corporal. The entry, initialled by the regiment's adjutant, read: 'Authority has been granted for the discharge of Private Connor of 27th Foot on account of his incorrigibly bad and worthless character, the decision to be conveyed to him wherever he now rests.'

Todd gave a little whistle, and read the entry again. Flung out! Well, they didn't fling you out for nothing, not in the 1870's. Those were the days of floggings at the colonel's whim,

23

and a fair proportion of the entire army was of incorrigibly bad character. A few years later the new Army Act changed things, but those were still hard days.

So what had Connor done? The regimental record listed all minor offences, but now no further offence, major or minor included mention of Connor. 'Wherever he now rests.' Even for 1873 that was a pompous form of military English. But what did it mean – lodgings, the local lock-up, prison proper? Wherever! Had Connor deserted? Had he gone overseas? Briefly and almost irrelevantly Todd found himself wondering in what year the French had founded the Foreign Legion, designed as it was, for people exactly like Connor. He seemed to remember it was in the 1830's. Could Connor have slipped off to the *régiments étrangers* and Sidi Bel Abbes in Algeria. Doubtful – but Todd made a note of the possibility. It would be interesting to consult Foreign Legion records, if they kept any, and if recruits gave their true names, neither of which seemed remotely likely.

At all events there was chasing to be done here. Or rather, there was if James Hamilton wanted it. A nice three-generation family tree was fine as a gift if someone really wanted to know about his grandparents, but there were people, and plenty of them, who set high store by family respectability, and would hardly be grateful for the tidings that grandfather was of so incorrigibly worthless a character that he'd even been bounced out of an army half composed, in any case, of roughs and thieves. Not the news you give to prim aunts, Todd thought; and wondered at once who the friend might be. As a rule, of course when things were sought 'for friends', the seeker wanted the information himself. But Hamilton's own family had already been exhaustively charted. It would probably be some girl he hoped to impress.

Perhaps, Todd thought, he ought to stop here, at least until he'd checked with Hamilton. Yet at lunch the previous day Hamilton had been precise and seemingly determined about his requirements, and certainly nobody engaged a record agent to make essentially frivolous inquiries. In any case, Todd thought with a twist of private cynicism, there were those who actually enjoyed having a scandal in the family provided it was a couple of generations back. Only two or three weeks earlier a woman client wearing a small, discreet CND badge had been absolutely delighted to learn that her great-grandfather, far from charging the guns at Balaclava, had been hanged for cowardice on the orders of a field court presided over by Milord Cardigan himself.

So, he might as well carry on this afternoon and tomorrow, and see what turned up, then present it all to Hamilton and leave the decision to him. But in fact he found nothing more, and went home with the long-ago phrase ringing in his mind: 'Wherever he now rests.' Todd felt the familiar bump of determination hardening somewhere between heart and stomach. He was becoming intrigued by this old devil Connor, who'd now been dead the better part of a century and still had the power to compel. Yes, well Todd wouldn't surrender to it entirely, but he'd give the records of the courts a try. His instinct said Connor must have found his way in front of some kind of judge. So let's see: Chelmsford? Yes, the County Record Office, there.

He had decided not to telephone Hamilton. The young man might well be sleeping and was certainly suffering. Instead, Todd wrote a brief note.

'Dear Mr Hamilton,
   I spent yesterday at the PRO and found something more about Connor. He seems to have been a doubtful character altogether: there were several punishments for drunkenness and violence – fighting, punching an NCO, and so on. But then things seem to have become more serious, and he was dismissed from the army because he was an "incorrigibly bad and worthless character." Just what he did I don't know. But I intend to find out.
                    Hope you're recovering,
                    Warwick Todd.'

Todd went into Essex next morning. Chelmsford was a mere half-hour out of town and the records staff there were, as he knew from experience, efficient, serious and knowledgeable.

Chelmsford sat, greyish and dull, under the leaky grey cloud it seemed always to wear like a hat whenever Todd went

through it on the train. Yet this was an ancient borough: the
Romans had found a ford, then built a fort, and a town, upon
the banks of the Chelmer; but for all its two thousand years
Chelmsford contrived to look modern, nasty, cheap and sub-
urban, with none of the pleasing dignity of York or Lincoln.

'Quarter Session records?' The girl archivist was of an
altogether better quality than the town she served: fair and
thirtyish, with glasses on the end of her nose and a wisp of
hair falling over her face. 'What year?'

'Years, I'm afraid,' Todd said. 'From eighteen-seventy to
seventy-four. Are there any gaps?'

'No.' She smiled. 'Good thing it's not the eighties you want.'

He grinned. 'Because you'd have to refuse, wouldn't you!
You go and apply your hundred years rule to someone else!'

'Takes one to know one, doesn't it,' she said, cheerfully
hoisting up the volumes. 'Are you a researcher?'

'Record agent.'

'At the PRO? Oh, my. If I give you a cup of coffee, will
you tell me how one achieves those dizzy heights?'

Todd had wondered, on the journey down, just what Connor's
offence, if any, might have been. The eighteen-seventies were
a long time ago and life had changed enormously since. In a
sense, of course, they were not so far away: indeed it was
probable that a few people still alive had been born in that
decade. But London had its stews then, and work houses and
starvation and TB and diptheria were a part of life, and boys
from the Irish bogs sought to improve themselves and their
circumstances in Victoria's service. Theft? Theft was probable.
The garrison social life would be considerable and expensive
a century ago: officers and their ladies, the occasional grand
ball and the fashionable assembly; jewels and gowns and fine
horses and ostentatious riches. Tempting for a boy on a bob a
day less stoppages. Yes, he'd bet on theft. And given Connor's
liking for hurling his fists about, perhaps with a little violence
added.

That kind of offence was certainly common at the time. The
record of Chelmsford Quarter Sessions in the 1870's showed
that theft with moderate violence was almost a national sport.

26

People went into shops, hit shopkeepers over the head, and stole a couple of loaves, or perhaps a tin of blacking. A brace of pheasant was a matter for imprisonment and hard labour. Todd had seen the like many times and was always struck by this detailed record of the troubles of another time. More than once he fell into the archivist's trap of becoming too interested and reading on. But the archivist's friend protected him – that forever inexplicable fact that the name one is looking for leaps out of a page. He was actually turning the page when Connor came zooming up at his eyes: Connor, Joseph Patrick, private soldier 27th Foot, Cavalry Barracks, Colchester, hereby charged that . . .

Todd read the charges, and thought: a present? God, it would be handing over a gift-box with a cobra inside! Still, presumably there was nothing hereditary. He asked the archivist for three photocopies, paid, and as he departed, she said, 'This the chappie you were looking for – this fellow Connor?'

Todd nodded.

She glanced at the page. 'A blessing he's dead!'

Todd caught the next train back to London.

At fifty-three, Douglas Hamilton, editor-in-chief, sole owner and publisher of Hamilton News Inc., was a man of vigour and strong physique. For many years it had been his habit to run the six miles to his office each morning, take a shower, put on a business suit and only then begin his working day, opening his mail while consuming an apple and a cup of coffee at his desk. In the late evening the procedure was reversed: he put on a track suit and ran home. Anything he needed to carry between home and office – the laundry, for example, generated by his life style, and the business papers on which he sometimes worked in the late evening – was transported by an office car.

His housekeeper became worried that morning when Hamilton having not only failed to come downstairs at seven, still had not appeared an hour later. Soon after eight, she knocked on his bedroom door and, receiving no answer, entered.

The necessary post-mortem examination was later to confirm

what Dr Hoffman diagnosed immediately upon seeing him: Hamilton was dead of a massive myocardial infarction. 'Too much goddam exercise at that age,' Dr Hoffman observed to the colleague with whom he lunched that day, 'weakens a man. Always did say so.' The two medical men then went on to discuss the announcement on the previous evening's TV news that Senator John Leyden had at last decided to seek the nomination for President, thus putting an end to a full month and more of speculation. On the whole, Dr Hoffman rather approved.

'No visible vices,' he said, busy with his Crab Louie, 'which is kind of a shame. I like to see a politician with a cigar and a broad and a bottle of Bollinger. Know where you are with a guy like that. He won't fool around with taxes. This guy Leyden's too clean, if anything. See him, last night? Oh boy! Straight out of the church choir. Those six adopted war orphans, and that movie-star wife of his. I tell you, George, it's like Jack Kennedy had married Grace Kelly and they'd adopted the Trapp family. My wife thinks J. Walter Thompson thought up the whole thing. I think he's either honest or he's crazy! No man would sentence himself to all that gleaming goodness if he wasn't one or the other!'

While Dr Hoffman discoursed, Miss Marion Hayes, secretary to the late Douglas Hamilton, was still engaged upon the distressing task of passing on the news of her boss's death to all those she felt should know at once. First among them, naturally, had been the son, James Hamilton, whom she knew to be staying at the Stafford Hotel in St James's, in London, and whom she had awakened at six a.m. London time with the dreadful news. James Hamilton, badly-shaken, stricken by grief and still with the remnant of his all-but crippling migraine, at once began making arrangements to fly home. The arrangements necessary were, in fact, few; he had only to book a plane seat, cancel the remainder of his stay at the Stafford, and order a hire car for noon. Having done all three he wrote a note to Warwick Todd giving him precise instructions on what was to be done in the matter of Joseph Patrick Connor, deceased. In essentials, these instructions were simply that research into Connor should continue as a matter of urgency

28

(the London papers had announced Leyden's candidacy boldly, and used many pictures, concentrating mainly on Mercy Leyden, the candidate's beautiful ex-actress wife, wearing a bikini) and that the resulting paperwork should go (a) in the case of bills, travel expenses, fees etc. to the Boston, Mass., offices of Hamilton News Inc; and (b) in the case of documents concerning Connor, to Hamilton, c/o Zee Quist, Hampden & Bradford, 101 Wall Street, New York, NY. His note added, 'I would appreciate it if all documents could be sent by facsimile transmission to 922–1031, which is the call number of the Fax machine at Hampden & Bradford.' Young Hamilton was by now sadly aware that in the aftermath of his father's sudden death he would be far too busy finding his way around the family business to spend any time in electoral activity this time around. To bear the cost of the Connor investigation was the one small thing he could do.

As he paid his bill at the Stafford Hotel, he asked the hovering porter to post his letter to Todd and was told there was in return a letter for him. 'Came by second post, sir. Wouldn't have let you go without it.' He tipped the man and put the letter in his pocket to read later.

He opened the envelope, when he remembered about it, on the plane, and was pleased to see Todd's signature. It was a relief to divert his mind, however briefly, from grief and the waiting panoply of death.

He read the letter with astonishment. The soldier boy from Ballyhara seemed to have changed remarkably fast and for the worse – Private Jekyll into Private Hyde. Zee Quist's notion of a little Irish cottage with roses around the door seemed unlikely to find realization. He read it again, the heavy, condemnatory words thudding like drumbeats in his mind: *dismissed . . . incorrigibly bad . . . worthless character*.

Christ – what if that got into the papers!

It was then, at that precise moment, that something clicked in his mind. He remembered how his father had always insisted: 'I'm a newspaperman first, last and all the time. Remember, Jim, news comes first.'

This was certainly news. It was the first real news story ever to come directly into James Hamilton's possession, and though

29

he was scarcely experienced in news judgements, he had no doubt this could be a big story – a very big story, played and timed right. *Worthless character . . . incorrigibly bad!* Those words were, or could be dynamite, politically.

He had just reached home when the call came: 'Jim Hamilton? This is Zee Quist. I just want to let you know how sorry everybody is here in New York. John Leyden asked me especially to convey his sympathy.'

'Thank you, Miss Quist.'

'Your father had offered his support – but you know that – and Mr Leyden placed great value on that. He was a fine newspaperman. You can be proud of him.'

'Yes, he was. And thanks – thanks again, Miss Quist.'

'I've been wondering how you've been getting along Jim. Find anything?'

He hesitated. 'A little. Sorry, I should have told . . .'

'You've been too busy, Jim. These things hurt and hurt bad. And there's always a lot to do.'

'All the same, I should . . .'

'Come talk to me, huh?'

'I will, Miss Quist. When do you . . . The funeral's tomorrow.'

'When you can. But soon. Just drop by, don't make an appointment. We're working out of two suites at the Admiral Hotel, okay?'

Nice of her to call he thought. Then the other thoughts came, welling out of the black bitterness of his bereavement. She wanted things, and that, not sympathy was the purpose of the call. She wanted to know that Hamilton support for John Leyden's campaign would continue, though she surely had more than one good reason for supposing it would. And she wanted to know about Connor, too: wanted assurance that there were no dirty, little, long-forgotten secrets that would blast the campaign into fragments. Her call wasn't a human gesture, it was a calculation, he told himself savagely. So bad luck, Ms. Quist, and damn you for your spurious sympathy. 'John Leyden asked me specially to convey . . .' He wondered if Leyden even knew of his father's death. Why should he, when there was a campaign running, a lot of votes to chase, a lot of calculations to make about TV time?

An early death frequently causes deep bitterness in a family. The bereaved ask why, and get no satisfactory answer. For James Hamilton, this was the second time that brutally sudden death had robbed him of a parent. Three years earlier his mother, her car skidding on winter ice, had been crushed by a truck. His thoughts, as the thoughts of sons often are at such a time, were full of resolution: I'll be as fine a newspaperman as he was. You'll be proud of me, dad! And the thoughts chased each other through a mind that grief was tilting out of balance, a mind that never forgot the story that could make his name as a newspaperman. He felt very alone, and increasingly vindictive.

3

The Admiral Hotel, three blocks from Grand Central Station, stood upon a site where, a hundred years before, the Leyden family had had its Manhattan mansion. Like the now-demolished Commodore Hotel, upon which it was modelled, the Admiral was spacious, a little gloomy and old fashioned, and declining. The ratio of cubic feet to dollars was, by modern hotel standards, ludicrously wrong. Vast areas were hardly used. So it was one of the last places in Manhattan where substantial spaces could be hired for long periods at comparatively low cost; as indeed they were, every time an election came around, and as had happened now. Two cavernous suites, each of five rooms, and with a connecting stair and a private elevator between them, now formed the John Leyden Campaign Headquarters and had been appropriately transformed. Hundreds of posters decorated the walls. Streaming banners – 'Now let him rescue America!' – hung across big, old rooms. The predominant colours were red, white and blue. There was a special podium, banks of lights for the vital TV cameras, and endlessly available coffee, Coke – and in the evening, beer, scotch and bourbon – for the TV crews. American politics now was no longer about issues and policies. Jimmy Carter and his bright team of Georgia Boys had changed forever the system in which the candidate's personality was only one of the factors – important, but still one – that got him elected. After Carter it was purely a personality contest, and next time around a professional actor, who had been projecting a likeable personality for forty years, demonstrated the gap between pro and amateur by beating the hapless Carter over the head with Carter's own club. One of the actor's top advisers said soon after the election, that the landslide had been achieved on the nightly news; it was there that the sympathetic, smiling man with the charm and the bright one-liners had destroyed the transparently weary President.

John Leyden had begun brilliantly in the eyes of the political professionals. Eighteen solid minutes of prime time, in which he'd been seen to be youthful, athletic, determined and romantically heroic, had been seen by a huge audience. It was, furthermore, an audience to whom Leyden was already a hero of legend: the rich young man who had had no need to go to Vietnam, who could have dodged the draft. But he'd gone all the same, as winchman in a rescue helicopter, time and again lifting the wounded out of the jungle before the VC could get to them. He'd been on TV then, too: a grimy figure in mud-wet camouflage uniform, wounded twice, decorated twice, caught off-guard by the cameras, but the most shy of heroes, deeply reluctant even to speak to the correspondent behind the lens. The picture was a famous one: one of the memorable images of the whole Vietnam war, appealing to young and old alike, for here was a man who rescued sons and grandsons. Here, equally, was a someone who, in a deeply unpopular war, was a self-evidently good man.

Leyden had refused ever since to talk about Vietnam or his experiences there. But on the night of his declaration to run there had been no avoiding the TV interviewers:

Q: Wasn't it a little foolhardy, Senator, to climb up that tree after an animal? It's been calculated you went up a hundred and forty feet to get to the kitten.

A: It's my daughter's kitten.

Q: Even so, Senator?

A: You know what happened to Jade, do you? She's boat people – only survivor of fifty. Eighteen hours in the sea clinging to the wreck, with bodies – including her parents' – floating beside her and sharks feeding on them. She was six years old, and she's seven now and she loves that kitten.

Q: Would you do it again?

A: If I had to.

Q: Even if you were President?

33

A: If I were President, I'll bet the Secret Service would put
    wire round the base of the tree.

Now let him rescue America! The slogan was Bill's, and Brother
Bill had his undoubted uses, Zee Quist reflected. She sat in
her chair in the quiet of early morning, watching the big
meeting room of the suite being cleaned by blue-uniformed
hotel staff.

Bill was due at ten. He was on his best behaviour now, in
these early days, and she wondered how long that state of
affairs might persist, because the candidate's brother was, like
the little girl with the curl, very good – sometimes. And horrid
at others.

Brother Bill. It was a name attached originally within the
family and now out and in public use. And they weren't
brothers, not really: half-brothers rather, with the same mother
and different fathers.

That was another problem, that would have to be coped
with one day soon – a problem in public relations. For Mr
Clean, as the papers were already calling John Leyden, had a
remarkably complicated background. Marriages, adoptions,
early deaths: all were a part of the tapestry and before long
the reporters would start the questions. She crossed her fingers
and offered a quiet, private prayer that Grandpa was okay.

But within minutes she knew he wasn't. No sooner had the
cleaners departed than James Hamilton came walking across
the slightly-worn blue carpet towards her. He looked thin,
haunted and somehow angry and she began to offer the routine
words of comfort.

He shook his head. 'Don't, please. I've had so much . . .'
he shrugged and quickly pulled from his jacket pocket what
looked like two or three sheets of paper folded together. 'Here,
Miss Quist.'

'Grandpa, huh?'

He nodded, and she took the papers but didn't unfold them.
'Bad. I can see that.'

He nodded again.

Zee Quist said, 'Tell me.'

Hamilton gave a little shrug. 'It looks like he was a real

no-good. Joined the British Army, lasted three years then they tossed him out.'

'Could have been bad luck, couldn't it?'

He said, 'Nope. Listen, Grandpa was bad. Look at that stuff and you'll see.'

'I'd sooner you told me.'

'Okay. He started with little things – drink and fighting. By the time they gave him the elbow he was 'an incorrigibly bad and worthless character.'

Zee Quist felt her cheeks tighten in surprise. 'What year?'

'Seventy-three.'

'Hell, he was only twenty-three years old then. Nobody's that bad at twenty-three.'

'The record says he is.'

'Why. What did he do?' Dammit, she demanded of herself, why fight it when it's true?'

'I don't know.'

'You don't . . .' She stopped, anger rising in her. 'Why in hell don't you know? You were sent to find out!'

Hamilton was glaring at her. 'My father died – remember? I'd have found out.'

'I'm sorry.' She said it at once, in quick and complete humility. 'That was unforgiveable of me. It's just that it's such terrible news. I apologise.'

He said evenly, 'I can see it's a problem. Skeletons can pop right out of cupbaords and . . .'

Zee Quist said, 'Mr Hamilton, where did this –' she hefted the papers '– come from?'

'Public Record Office, London.'

'Available to anybody, of course.'

'That's right.'

'Oh, Jesus! And we don't even know how bad it really is, right? He was kicked out of the army for being a son-of-a-bitch but we don't know what kind. Can we find out?'

'I think we'll know quite soon.'

She muttered, 'Good,' and added: 'It'll be a load off when we know, won't it!' And congratulated herself on no reaction. Feeling as though she was about to explode, Zee Quist reached for a cigarette and lighter. *The bastard had told somebody!*

Exhaling smoke, she said, 'We'll have to work out how to handle this.'

He said, 'I thought you'd want to keep it real quiet.'

Zee Quist shook her head. Nothing she'd like more, she thought. But she said, 'Dangerous to play it that way. It would come out. Then there's egg on everybody's face.'

'What'll you do?'

'Wait till we know the details. Then have John Leyden announce it himself, maybe.'

'If the Press doesn't get there first,' Hamilton said.

'You think they will?'

'I think they have.'

'Who? Oh, you mean you – James Hamilton. Well sure, but you had a privileged start. Nobody else knows, and the connection with the names would be tricky to make.'

'It's made.'

She looked up at him. From a wheelchair you always looked up. 'You thinking of publishing it?'

He shook his head. 'No.'

'That's good.'

'But I got to thinking. If somebody else gets there, I'm the one with egg on my face.'

She raised a hand. 'Okay, okay. You've got a string of papers and you've got a story you don't want to lose. Now, aside from the fact that your father offered the support of his papers to Mr Leyden, and aside from the fact that you came to me begging to be allowed to help in the campaign, and that's why you got the story, what do you want – to smash the candidacy?'

He shrugged and she went on quietly: 'It's no big deal, Jim, really. All that happens is when the announcement's made, John Leyden makes it, but he makes it in your newspapers. Okay?'

He nodded.

Brother Bill found her at her desk staring dead ahead and smoking hard. He said flatly. 'Tell Uncle all about it, Zee.'

She told him, and saw the change occurring as she spoke. Little Boots, everybody's charming boy was suddenly metamorphosed into Caligula, capriciously dangerous. Like her, William Crombie was a lawyer; unlike her, he'd chosen to serve always in public office: an assistant District Attorney in Baltimore, then in New York, and then in the Justice Department. He was very rich, as all the family were. With no need to pursue money, he'd pursued a reputation. He harried organized crime where he could, and more often, corrupt politicians. He was mentally agile in court, relentless in examining witnesses, and he bullied juries with conspicuous success. She thought him ruthless and probably without scruple, though he pretended extreme scrupulousness.

Bill Crombie said immediately, 'He'll have to do something.'

She looked up. 'Like?'

He turned quickly, making for the door, saying over his shoulder. 'Forget the whole damn thing Zee. It's past. Forget it.'

4

—◆◆—

'Who is the guy?'

The heavy man shrugged. 'Aw, c'mon. Need to know – that's the principle. All I need to know is where to find the guy for the job and I sure do know, and you're it, baby. What you need to know is the route and the time and the model of car.'

'So tell me.'

'Datsun two-eighty-zee coupe. Tag number 2KN–38438. Colour silver. Got that, Parker?'

'Check.'

'Out of the city on I-95 heading north, right?'

'Got it. Where d'you want it?'

The heavy man shrugged. 'Any place is good as any other place. Somewhere quiet, huh? Up past Norwalk, maybe.'

'How much time will I have?'

'All you want.'

'You go past New Haven maybe twenty miles, there's that piece to Clinton.'

The heavy man clapped his shoulder. 'The camber, sure. Enjoy your drive,' he said.

Parker ordered coffee-to-go and a doughnut and took them out to the rig. When he'd eaten the doughnut and licked his fingers, he sat sipping the coffee and smoking a fat King Edward Invincible – and listening to the CB radio. The heavy man had a couple of spotters ten miles back down the road. Ten miles exactly. If they stayed awake, and if the Datsun took the I-95, they ought to spot it, and ought to confirm the registration, and ought to murmur 'Heigh-ho Silver' into the CB, so that everybody listening would just think there were Lone Ranger freaks loose tonight. If anybody still knew who the Lone Ranger was; and if 'Heigh-ho Silver' could be heard above the racket some Alabama air-hog was creating on the band.

The King Edward smouldered down to its last, sodden inch. Parker still sat, silent and alert, concentrating hard upon the babble of voices in the C.B. No goddam discipline, he thought. No discipline as drivers, none as citizens, none as users of the air waves. Parker himself was a man of precise skills and judgements and the unending idiot babble irritated him. He straightened suddenly. What was that? All he'd got was '– ho Sil –,' the spotter diving into a pause as some yodelling fool drew breath. '– ho Silver!' Okay: that was three of four syllables coming over clear. Parker moved the rig towards the truck-park exit, stopped short, flung away the wet stump of the cigar, and sat still in the dark. The Datsun would be doing fifty-five/fifty-eight no more – not on this road, not with highway patrolmen every five feet manning speed traps. So ten miles at fifty-five meant a little less than ten minutes. At nine he switched on the rig's lights and picked up a pair of binoculars. Traffic was heavy, the night darkening, the Datsun would be long gone by him if he . . . No, there it was! He picked up the number from the rear tag, murmuring numerals and letters to himself, then set the rig rolling forward. By the time he'd found his gap and settled, the rig into the stream, the Datsun must, Parker reckoned, be a mile or more ahead.

Nice. Simple to catch, and no dramatics in the catching. He began to move along a little, working his way forward, handling the big articulated rig with all the easy skill developed in fifteen years of long-haul driving and fifteen more of driver-school instructing. In four or five minutes the distinctive tail-lighting assembly of the Datsun coupe registered itself on Parker's vision and he lit another cigar and settled in his seat. As the rig throbbed north past Stamford, Norwalk and Bridgeport, over the river at New Haven, he sat crooning softly around the cigar, hands easy on the wheel, observing with satisfaction the way the traffic had drained off I-95 into the Connecticut cities. He possessed, had always possessed, the ability to know what was around him; and as his eyes made their ceaseless circuits of his driving mirrors, he waited and hoped for a precise condition in the traffic. Behind him the blacktop gleamed in the lights of a Mack rig two hundred yards back. Apart from that one guy, the night was his.

'Turn off, Mister Mack,' he murmured to himself. 'There's steak for dinner, Mister Mack.'

As though in obedience, the Mack's indicator began to flash and the truck moved from mirror to mirror and away down the exit ramp.

Parker hung back until beyond Guilford, then began easing forward, rehearsing events in his mind's eye. He might have worked the thing at Norwalk, but this was far better. He'd spent the morning re-adjusting the braking – both the rig's and the dead-man's brake on the trailer – and putting a new switch in the wiring harness. Yes, he was ready.

Still the night was dark behind him. Cars came towards him, but there was no-one tucked behind. He gunned the rig forward and out, on to the passing lane, moved gradually up level with the Datsun and glanced sideways. The guy looked relaxed, just ambling in a car like that. Radio on, or a tape deck. Everything smooth and easy.

The Datsun's lights moved from one to another of Parker's mirrors, slipping back, now level with the front of the trailer, now with the middle, now with the rear wheels. Parker eased off and moved a foot, two feet right, and switched off his own tail lighting. There was no oncoming traffic on the other side of the median.

He was calm about it. The movement, when he made it, was harsh but well-educated: he braked sharply right-footed and pulled simultaneously on the dead-man's brake that operated on the trailer alone. All sudden – but brief. The trailer flicked swiftly to the right, about eight feet Parker guessed and as swiftly back again as he released the brakes. In doing so, the trailer hit the Datsun like an iron club hitting a golf ball, and with much the same effect. The Datsun was chipped neatly off the road. It smashed against the concrete base of an exit sign.

Parker waited a full minute before switching on his tail lights again. His mirrors told him there was no traffic close behind. What he could see was flames from the Datsun wreck.

In his mind's eye, he could see something else: fifteen thousand dollars was a handy fee.

Two things happened next morning. The first was that Zee Quist saw the story in the *New York Times*:

PUBLISHING HEIR DIES IN TURNPIKE CRASH

James Hamilton, twenty-two, who only a week ago inherited the Hamilton News chain of New England newspapers and TV stations on the sudden death of his father, Douglas Hamilton, was himself killed in a road crash on Route I-95 last night.

Highway police in Connecticut state that Hamilton's car, a foreign sports coupe, apparently left the road, crashed into an obstacle and caught fire. Police doubt the involvement of any other vehicle. 'It looks,' said police Capt. Kenneth Jimson, 'as though he fell asleep at the wheel.'

Hamilton News is worth an estimated $30 million. The heir is believed to be a second cousin presently living in Tacoma, Washington.

Zee Quist reacted in several ways of which the first was deep shock. She'd talked to Hamilton only yesterday, damn it, and now nobody was ever going to talk to him again! She was shaken more by death's proximity than by grief.

Soon though, the thought struck her that Hamilton's death removed a possible embarrassment. He'd told somebody he was investigating Connor but not who Connor was, and not the reasons – to do so would have destroyed his story. So now, for the time being at least, Connor was not going to appear on front pages and TV cameras.

Brother Bill came into her room soon after ten, by which time Zee Quist was drinking coffee, smoking a cigarette, and working hard. Hamilton was no longer right in the forefront of her mind. But he returned at once.

'You seen the papers, Bill?'

'Seen the –? Well of course I've seen them, Zee. Oh, you mean Hamilton?'

'That's what I mean.'

41

He said, 'It was bad luck. The worst – falling asleep at the wheel like that.' He was standing by the window, looking out, his back to the room. She thought there was something about his voice, something odd . . .

'Bill?'

He turned, smiling. That was it, she'd heard a smile. 'Bill, I'm trying to remember what you said yesterday. We'll have to do something. That's what you said.'

'Did I?' The smile was widening, now almost a grin. She felt a cold shiver across her shoulders.

She said. 'You also said, "forget it, Zee".'

He shrugged. 'What's to worry about?'

Zee Quist thought: why am I suddenly suspicious? Is there a reason? The grin was fading on his face to be replaced by – what?

He said in irritation, 'Zee, for Christ's Sake!'

'Did you, Bill?'

'What?'

'Do something?'

'Like what? Like kill him?' Irritation was becoming anger. 'He killed himself, Zee. It says so in the *Times*. What more do you want?'

'I want you to look innocent, Bill. And you look guilty as hell.'

He sat on the corner of her desk. 'Zee, this is crazy! Hamilton had a piece of bad luck. For us it's maybe solved a little problem. Does that make me John Dillinger?'

She was saying, 'Well . . .' when the phone rang.

'Hello?'

'Papers for you, Miss Quist. Sent over from Hampden & Bradford.'

'Thanks. Bring them in unopened.'

There was one foolscap envelope. It contained three sheets. The paper was greyish on its coated side. FAX paper. Sending station: London.

If the finding of Joseph Patrick Connor, soldier of the Queen, had been relatively easy, keeping track of him was not. Todd's pursuit had hit road blocks after Chelmsford. The court record had given him the charges, the verdicts. The sentence. But that was all the county records held. Todd wanted evidence, and was certain his client would demand evidence, too.

And evidence was not immediately to be had. Or not much. A visit to the huge legal record store at the magnificent Old Public Record Office in Chancery Lane produced a large cardboard box tied with tape and labelled Assizes 35, Indictments 313. It contained, among many other dusty things, the parchment slip upon which the clerk of Assize had recorded the jury's verdict.

The parchment was of a size and shape and in a condition which made machine-copying impossible, according to the rules governing the handling of irreplaceable archive material. Todd copied out the words in pencil – a new one cost him ten pence – because another rule forbade use of pens. The document which arrived on Zee Quist's desk at The Admiral Hotel in mid-town Manhattan had been copied into neat typescript and bore no resemblance to the worn, blackened parchment original.

But the words were the same:

The Jurors for our said Lady the Queen upon their oath present that Joseph Patrick Connor private soldier of the Parish of St Giles in the County of Essex, on the 25th day of June in the Year of Our Lord One Thousand, Eight Hundred and Seventy-Three with force and Arms at the parish aforesaid in the County aforesaid, in and upon Mary Eves unlawfully did make an assault and her the said Mary Eves did beat, wound and illtreat with intent her, the said Mary Eves, there and then, against her will violently and feloniously to ravish and carnally know, against the form of the Statute in such case made and provided and against the Peace of our said Lady the Queen, her Crown and Dignity.
Second Count:
And the jurors aforesaid upon their oath aforesaid do further present that the said Joseph Patrick Connor unlawfully and indecently did make an indecent assault upon the said Mary Eves on the 23rd day of June in the

43

year aforesaid and unlawfully and indecently did beat wound and illtreat her, and other wrongs to the said Mary Eves, then did to the great damage of the said Mary Eves assault and ravish and indecently assault her against the Peace of our said Lady the Queen, her Crown and Dignity. Note on verdictship (Clerk of Assize):

Puts himself. Jury say guilty on both counts. To be first flogged (one dozen lashes) then imprisoned and kept to hard labour in The House of Correction at Springfield two years and three Calendar months.

There were eleven further counts. In five of them no age was given indicating that the victim was a grown woman. But in six charges the ages were only too clear. Connor had raped, beaten, and indecently assaulted six girls aged eleven and twelve, as well as six presumably grown women.

Todd had appended to the last sheet a note: 'Useless to hunt for depositions – only retained in murder cases.'

Both were lawyers. The antique and repetitive usages were familiar. Zee Quist read the first sheet in silence and passed it across the desk. Characteristically she read each sheet carefully. Brother Bill, after an appalled survey of the first paper, did little more than glance at the other two.

She looked up at him and gave a slow shrug. 'There goes the complete goddam ball game.'

'Shit!' said Brother Bill swinging angrily away. 'Oh, shit. Oh, shit!'

Zee Quist let the bitter grin surface, the hell with the rictus. 'The worst,' she said. 'It had to be the worst – absolutely the stinking, noisiest skeleton in the goddam world. Bank robber wouldn't matter. If he were Jesse James's grandson there'd be glamour in it – didn't Audie Murphy play James? Damn it, Bill, I wouldn't care if he were Stalin's grandson! But not, oh God not two generations on from a compulsive child molester. And flogged, yet! He'd get the weirdo vote and that's all.'

'The weirdo vote I can take,' Bill said. 'And use. It's the news, the straight plain information that's the killer.' He was standing, arms folded, half-turned away. Now he swung

44

abruptly to face her. 'Unless we kill the whole thing first.'

'Kill it? How'd you do that?'

'Let me think. Grandpa's known, right? But not much. Mysterious, faintly attractive figure, run down by a horse a long time ago. Baby goes to rich fairy godfather. A fairy tale. Zee – we keep it that way.'

'Fine,' she said. 'Do just that. But tell me how!'

He held up his hands, palms facing her. 'Whoa down, Zee. We didn't know. Nobody else knew either. But we know now. And only us.'

'Nope. So does he,' said Zee Quist.

'Who?'

'Sam, Sam the research man.' She waved the FAX sheets at him.

'We call him off. Pay him. He's probably some five-buck no-hoper anyway. Or better still –' he snapped his fingers with enthusiasm.

Zee Quist read his mind. 'He knows where all the stuff is, right? So we send him round destroying it, yes?'

Bill nodded. 'Sure. Then when the Networks start searching, there's nothing to find.'

'There's a problem, Bill old Brother.'

'Go on.'

'We don't know who the hell he is!'

He looked at her aghast. 'Don't know! You must know. Somebody has to be paying him.'

She said, 'Hamilton paid. The late James Hamilton. Ever hear, Bill, of engineers getting hoist by their own petards?'

'I've never understood that,' he said irritably. 'What is a petard, for Christ's sake?'

'It's a box full of gunpowder and you lift it in the air and it goes off in your face.'

'So we'll find the guy.'

No denial, she thought. Old Man Connor the Multiple Rapist was bad news, all right. A shock, certainly. Enough to upset anybody's thought process – true. But in her brain a voice was pointing out icily, 'You just accused Brother Bill of murder and he never even blinked.'

'Find him – how?'

'There'll be ways.' He reached for the FAX sheets. 'There'll be reference numbers right here.'

But there weren't.

She had been dreaming, as often she did, of the critical moment. The dream came when pressure was on her, and she had first lain for several hours brooding and deeply concerned, before dropping into shallow and twitching slumber. Zee Quist was not a woman for ducking issues and this one was, after all, clear cut. She strongly suspected Brother Bill of murder – murder or involvement in murder, or maybe conspiracy to murder. Maybe all three! Brother Bill: William Crombie, attorney-at-law; half-brother of a declared Presidential candidate, and himself a noted pursuer of miscreants. It was barely credible. Would Bill even know where to start?

Murder! She had more or less accused him. He neither reacted nor cared. He was either so sublimely innocent he didn't even notice; or so hardened to crime he didn't care. But if so, he'd kept that side of himself very quiet.

Zee Quist had thought long and hard. Brothers were important in politics. Carter's brother Billy had half-way ruined a Presidency; Nixon's brother Donald's business dealings had seemed to cast an unfortunate side-light on the Presidency until Nixon's own behaviour put it in the shade. Bobby and Ted Kennedy, Milton Eisenhower – there were always brothers and they always counted, for good or ill. So what about Bill?

She'd known him twenty years, but never well. He was a matter-of-fact cool, an attacker by nature. A barracuda, some said, and certainly he'd taken large bites out of many people.

On the side of right? Well, that was the picture. A crusading barracuda! She had smiled to herself at the notion, and then the smile had been wiped away. Bill Crombie had hunted, had prosecuted the racketeers. He'd indicted them, he'd examined and cross-examined them. He'd talked to them as prisoners, as witnesses: many of them over the years.

So, if nothing else, he knew plenty of hoods. Perhaps he'd done favours? Failed to prosecute, dropped a charge – convenient bargaining could happen. And organized crime was respectable in modern America; it moved in top society, as Bill did. Damn it, even John Kennedy had once shared a mistress with a top Mafia hood, Sam Giacanna.

It was far from impossible! And Brother Bill could probably put in the fix if he chose.

Would he so choose? With the Presidency as the prize to be lost he'd be tempted, as anybody – and every politician – would be tempted. But would he act?

Her anxiety abruptly switched her restless mind to a new question. If there were grounds for suspicion, and perhaps there were, what should she do? Tell John Leyden, tell Bill himself, tell the police? Destroy the campaign before it got going? If she felt sure enough, she must.

Or go along.

That was the alternative.

And then, in the early hours, she found herself facing the third question. Did John Leyden know? If Bill had arranged for Hamilton's murder, had he done so with John Leyden's knowledge and approval? She lay looking up at the cool dimness of the bedroom ceiling, seeing his picture there, seeing thousands of pictures of him there, running them almost pleasurably through the projector of her mind like a picture show – and knowing as she did so that there was no possibility John Leyden would connive at murder, or knowingly commit any criminal act. Mr Clean they said, and Mr Clean he was.

But even that attractive simplicity raised other and unpleasant questions. If Bill had done it, Bill should be punished. What, then of John? Should he be punished, too? And punished brutally – humiliated in public? There was no doubt about the law's attitude. But what was right?

Zee Quist fell asleep impaled upon the horns of her assorted dilemmas, and soon was on that icy, murderous downhill again, dropping breakneck down Crossbones run at Whistler, losing her right ski pole as her left ski lifted on some sub-snow bump, cartwheeling her over the edge in a second, flicking her contemptuously into paralysis in a wheelchair for the rest of her life.

She woke then, as she always did. The half of her that could tremble was trembling. She was damp with sweat. She reached

47

for the trapeze that hung above her bed, and hauled herself up against the pillows. She lit a cigarette, smoked and thought. Two hours later, with the ashtray filling beside her, she had come to a decision: Brother Bill was an irrelevancy; Hamilton was an irrelevancy; her own sworn oath as an officer of the court was an irrelevancy. What mattered was putting John Leyden into the White House. And going right on with him!

First in Chelmsford, then in Colchester and in Colindale, Todd had been examining old newspapers. The *Chelmsford Chronicle* of the time ignored the Connor case entirely, failing even to report the sentence imposed. The *Essex Standard*, however, under a minuscule headline which read 'Singular series of assaults,' had commented that the defendant was 'a respectable-looking man' and that the trial was before no less a figure than the Right Honourable Sir William Bovill, Chief Justice of the Court of Common Pleas.

Before sending off his report from the public FAX office in Clerkenwell Road, Todd added in a note in small handwriting on the A4 sheet, that Lord Chief Justice Bovill had presided at the first hearing of the celebrated Tichborne Claimant case. (In Todd's experience, contact with 'celebrated' events was always prized by clients) and furthermore that Lord Chief Justice Bovill had arrived at Shire Hall for the Assize on horseback after riding a dozen miles since breakfast.

Todd intended the paper to provide a moment of relief for Hamilton after the cataract of horror stories. Hamilton relished the minutiae of genealogical research.

What Todd did not know was that Hamilton was dead. Todd was in the happy position of having a rich client, a good agreed daily retainer and carte blanche, near enough, to investigate Joseph Patrick Connor from here to eternity. Until instructions came to end the arrangement, Todd would continue.

5

'Tell him – tell John?' Brother Bill shook his head. 'Nope.'

She said, 'He's on the stump, Bill. He's got reporters with him day and night. It only takes one unguarded moment, one awkward question. One teardrop ruined Ed Muskie, remember!'

'Look Zee, he's absolutely clean. There isn't one goddam thing anybody can say against him. Not from childhood on. Nothing. So what d'you want him to do? Stand up some place and say "Fellas, I have a confession. My grandaddy had this naughty hobby – he used to go out and ravish little girls." Zee, it would take ten seconds . . .'

She raised a hand to stop him. 'Okay, Bill, okay.'

'It has to be said, Zee. So listen. It would take ten seconds for the first funny cartoon. Leyden crouching behind the bushes and there's this little girl labelled Disarmament, or Peace, or something walking innocently towards him. A week or two of that and he'll develop long canines and hair on his palms.

'Oh, for . . .'

'*Listen* Zee. Listen and listen good. John's out there in the white suit. One little stain destroys the whole picture. The suit's either new and bright and brilliant white or it's dirty. No half-ways. It's one or the other. And he only wins if it stays white. We see any smoke floating towards him, Zee, we intercept it. We knock down the chimney if necessary!'

He gestured towards Todd's document. 'And right now that guy's the chimney. He's worse – he's like Pittsburgh in the forties, pollution, pollution and more pollution! Lord Chief Justice, yet. That really proves Ole Granpappy was in the big league. No ordinary judge, Zee, not for Grandad – Christ, no, it has to be the Lord Chief Justice in person riding in on horseback!'

She said coolly, 'I already have the message, Bill. Tell me something. Did you have a conversation with John when he appointed me to run the campaign?'

'You know we did.'

'What was agreed? C'mon, Bill, tell me.'

'Goddammit Zee!'

'You stayed out of my hair, Bill. That was agreed. You kept yourself in readiness for consultation. You were educated in Parish, Heidelberg and Oxford and you have a good grasp of foreign affairs and you're valuable to him. But grasp at my chair, Bill, and I'm going to beat your skull flat with it.' She paused and then said evenly, 'Okay?'

'Not completely, no.' He was all earnest innocence now. 'When I see something that'll harm John's chances, I'm going to act, Zee.'

'Through me,' she said. 'That's how you're going to act. Not around me, not behind my back. Through me and through this office!'

He shrugged. 'So what do we do about this guy in London?'

She lit a cigarette and thought for a moment. 'It depends how straight we play.'

'Nothing gets in John's way, Zee. Nothing. That's how the white game gets played.'

'Okay. Then we find this researcher and we call him off.'

'And?'

'Take his advice on where all the relevant papers are.'

'And?'

'Destroy them, you mean?' She hesitated, then grinned. 'All right, Bill. We get them destroyed. It's small-scale sacrilege.'

Bill Crombie frowned. 'But that's just a toe in the water, Zee. Here's a scenario: there can't be too many researchers like this guy. If the *Times* or the *Post* or CBS News decides to unearth Grandad, they sure won't waste time with little hand books called Trace Your Ancestors. They'll go to Rent-a-Researcher and hire the best. And maybe that's this same guy Hamilton got, or his buddy, or his partner.

She looked at him in surprise. 'Do you think that's likely – a partner?'

'It's possible. You can't putz around, Zee, you really can't. You want the door locked, you have to lock it.'

In some mesmerized way she felt herself being drawn on, unable to resist. The slope was steep and slippery and her foot was already on it. She said, in limp protest: 'He's probably got a family, Bill.'

He waved a dismissive hand. 'You want to handle things, Zee, you better handle them. Lots of people got families. Question: how do we find him?'

'Hamilton's body.' Zee Quist said almost helplessly. 'Maybe there's an address in his pocket.'

He looked at her for a moment. 'Ever read a thriller called *The Day of the Jackal*?'

She nodded, and he went on: 'They know there's a killer loose, out to get De Gaulle, but they don't know who. They call in the best detective in France because all they need is a name. Get the name and everything else follows: photographs, addresses, descriptions. What we need, Zee, is a detective. A guy who knows England and can operate there. And I think I know how to find the right man.'

Zee Quist, however, did the first, simple piece of detective work, dialling the call herself, no secretaries.

'Miss Hayes?'

'Yes.'

'This is Zee Quist from New York. Did you know James Hamilton was doing some work for me and for the Leyden campaign in Europe?'

'Oh Miss Quist – your wreath was very lovely. Thank you. And no, I didn't know.'

'A piece of research. Nothing vital, but – well, it's a trifle inconvenient now. I believe he'd hired a man to do some work and we don't know who the man was. Do you imagine he'd made a note some place?'

'I'll certainly look, Miss Quist. May I have your number? I'll call you back real soon.'

Marion Hayes, however, did not find anything about the

man Hamilton had hired. Hamilton had not needed to make notes since there was only one Warwick Todd in the London telephone book. They'd met before and the name was easy enough to remember.

At the beginning of the jet age, the old British Overseas Airways Corporation ran an advertisement aimed at the rich and fashionable: 'Breakfast in London, Dinner in New York!' It was reputedly Noel Coward who added 'And Baggage In Bangkok!' Now yesterday's miracle is a commonplace, available to the package tour masses. The rich can, if they care to, take breakfast in London, lunch in New York, and be back in London again for dinner. The means is the aeronautical miracle named Concorde.

William Crombie, half-brother to Democratic hopeful John Leyden, was embarking on just such a trip when he boarded Concorde at Kennedy Airport. His only baggage was a small document case, to which the smiling girl at the check-in attached the distinctive, triangular blue-and-white Concorde swing label.

Brother Bill was met at Heathrow by a chauffeur-driven car ordered in advance from Godfrey Davis Ltd, and was driven to the Royal Lancaster Hotel in Bayswater which, for all the historic overtones ringing in its name, is modern, and much used by travelling salesmen and widowed grandmothers from Kansas. It is large and it is anonymous.

At the Royal Lancaster, Crombie had three appointments, an hour apart, with two men and one woman who had been selected for him by no less a figure in genealogy than Winchester Herald to whose room at The College of Arms in Queen Victoria Street, a cheque for a hundred guineas was already on its way. The three were all of them genealogists of skill, if not, in one case, of repute. 'I should watch out if I were you,' Winchester Herald had said on the telephone. 'This business is infested with cowboys nowadays.'

'I don't mind,' Crombie had told him, 'as long as the guy's good at his job, that's fine. I'm not writing a thesis.'

'Then I'll send you a rough rider. A kind of John Wayne among the cowboys.'

'Wayne is dead.'

'In genealogy, practically everybody is dead.'

Now, in the hotel, he picked up the telephone on the second ring.

'Reception, sir. A Captain Rabbett is here.'

'Send him up.'

Captain Rabbett was nothing like his name. There were no protruding teeth and his ears were small and tight against his head. His was, in fact, a near-perfect example of the broad, somewhat brutal, fair-complexioned English face so often to be seen under the caps of army officers. He wore a somewhat elderly Burberry raincoat and carried a brown trilby hat.

'Sit down,' Crombie said, after shaking hands.

'Thank you.' Rabbett sat, placed his hat beside his polished shoes, and waited.

'Tell me about yourself.'

'Of course. I'm a retired officer of The Royal Armoured Corps. Lifelong interest in genealogy. Took it up professionally when I retired.'

'That's it?'

'Yes.'

'I understand,' Crombie said, 'you were cashiered, thrown-out, whatever the expression is. Why was that?'

Rabbett flushed slightly and stood. 'That is my business, sir, I'm afraid. Good day to you.'

Crombie let him reach the door. 'Before I hand over substantial hunks of dough to total strangers, I like to know if they're straight.'

Rabbett turned. 'It was not a matter of money, sir.'

'What was it "a matter of"', Captain Rabbett?'

The man coughed, discreetly behind his hand. 'It was a lady, sir. The wife, I'm afraid, of a brother officer.'

'Pretty?' Crombie said, grinning.

'Very.'

'And rich?'

Rabbett hesitated, then nodded. 'That, too.'

'C'mon and sit.' When Rabbett had done so, Crombie said: 'I'm told you're a cowboy. Why's that?'

He flushed again. 'Rubbish!'

'Why do people say it?'

'Because they're stuffy. The academic types can't bear anybody who isn't academic.'

'And you aren't?'

Rabbett examined his fingernails. 'I'm thorough. I do my best. But all of genealogy is based upon assumptions – and the principal assumption is that when A says he is B's father, he really is. The nearest you ever get to proof is a piece of paper. No blood tests, you see, until recent times. Now, your over-academic researcher regards his bits of paper as sacred.'

'And you don't?'

'Not invariably. There's a lot of bastardy about. Even more a couple of centuries ago. Put it this way Mr –?' Rabbett paused, his expression one of polite inquiry.

'Sir will do.'

'Very well. If I am reasonably satisfied, and my client reasonably happy, I regard that as sufficient. I'm a reasonable man.

'Sure. Would you say you're also a discreet one?'

'If discretion is required.'

'I would require it.'

'And pay for it? I'm afraid these days the labourer is worthy . . .'

Crombie cut him off. 'A life could depend on it.' He stared deliberately at Rabbett.

'Eh? Oh, mine! Yes, I see. Well, I'm a soldier. Ex-soldier, anyway.'

'Ever been shot at?'

'Yes.'

'And shot back?'

'Certainly.'

'And hit what you shot at?'

'That too.'

'Where?'

Rabbett gave a vulpine grin. 'In the arse, as a matter of fact. From the side. Passed through both buttocks. Chap jumped about a bit.'

'I meant where did it happen?'

'Northern Ireland, that one. You're looking for a killer?'

Crombie said, 'Just interested in character. Are you a killer?'

'I've killed,' Rabbett said. 'Her Majesty's Government paid me to do it. I did it. Might it not be a good idea if we stop pissing about? I'm available for hire, complete, as I stand. Or, sit. Payment at appropriate rates. I enjoy unravelling mysteries, and secrets are safe with me. Sir.'

Crombie rose, walked to the window and walked back. 'I have to find a guy. He's in your line of business. He was doing some work for a friend and the friend died so there's no point any more. What he was doing, the man was getting married and his fiancée was orphaned young and didn't know anything about her family. He was going to present her with a family tree as a gift. You with me?'

'It's perfectly clear.'

'Okay. My friend was killed in a car crash. I saw him just before and he told me the researcher had found out the girl's grandfather was all kinds of a bastard. Now that was okay while he was alive and knew they'd both be able to laugh about it. But now he's dead and she's clinically depressed and badly hurt and that kind of information she doesn't need – not now and not ever. So I have to call off the researcher. To do that I have to find him. And I don't even know his name.'

Rabbett rubbed his hands together deliberately. 'Well, it's interesting.'

'Can you find him?'

'Have you thought of an ad in the newspapers – *The Times* personal column?'

'I thought of it. It's too public. The girl knows her grandfather's name. It could get back some way. I want the whole thing stone dead.'

'Killed, in fact?'

'That's right. There are two parts to this. The first is find him. For that you get one fee. The second is the records he uncovered. I want them destroyed – just in case. You work along the same trail he followed, whatever it was, and you get a thousand dollars for every relevant document destroyed. Okay?'

'Sounds delightful,' Rabbett said.

55

'Only you don't destroy them. I do.'

'Naturally. I remove them furtively and send them to you. It's been done before. You destroy them. But there is a problem.'

'Go on.'

'First, your mystery researcher will have copies. What happens to them?'

'He gives them to you. You find them, I'll pay him. He'll give the stuff to you.'

'Ah, yes. But if he won't?'

'That's the real difficulty,' Crombie said with deliberation. 'Captain, could I leave it to your judgment?'

'Indeed you could. And I, of course, won't take any copies.'

'Wouldn't do you any good if you did,' Crombie said. He felt profoundly relieved. This unpleasant and wholly amoral man seemed exactly what he needed. 'The name wouldn't mean a damn thing. To you or anyone else. Now – about the fees.'

'My name is Rabbett,' said the Captain, 'and so I'm all ears.'

Brother Bill comfortably caught the return Concorde flight. He took with him a note of the captain's address and telephone number and a receipt for the two thousand dollars in cash which he had advanced. In return he had given Rabbett the starting point: the name of Joseph Patrick Connor, and the number of the Regiment. If Rabbett followed in the other guy's footsteps, he'd come across all the papers first, and then he'd come across the researcher.

Unaware that a hound was being set to his trail, Todd had spent that day not too far away, trying to clamber over a brick wall which lay across his path. A further trip to Chelmsford on the previous day, during which he had examined thirty thick and dusty tomes called Gaol Books, had proved fruitless. The books were supposed to contain records of prisoners while they were under correction, and indeed did so. But some volumes were missing from the sequence and unfortunately the missing ones included that covering Springfield House of Correction in Connor's time there.

So now Todd was reduced to guessing. Connor had been sentenced to be flogged and in addition to three years' gaol. The prison gates had unquestionably slammed behind Connor, but from the moment of that slam, Connor had disappeared. He hadn't died in gaol, so therefore he had been released. But when?

The brick wall facing Todd was as high as that of the House of Correction must have been. Connor had vanished into history's mists.

And Connor must now be found.

Todd made a small list over breakfast.

1. Did he marry?
2. Australia? (arrived USA ex-Aust?)
3. Prison again?

Aware that Item Three was likely, because Connor was a natural-born recidivist if ever there was one, Todd was also and guiltily aware that the pursuit should be leading him back to Chelmsford and The Quarter Sessions and Assize Calendars there. But a glance out of the window showed it to be raining cats and dogs, and the thought of Chelmsford in a downpour two days running was not to be faced.

He began, therefore, with Item One on his list and took himself in a taxi to St Catherine's House, on the corner of Kingsway and Aldwych, where Registrations of Births, Marriages and Deaths are now recorded – the grander and more appropriate Somerset House having been taken over several years earlier by the Inland Revenue. Feeling the need for coffee before beginning the search, Todd nipped into the nearby Kardomah. The familiar and fragrant brew was excellent, as ever, but *The Times* crossword puzzle proved impenetrable. He solved only two clues in twenty minutes' increasingly desperate labour, and entered St Catherine's House moodily sure this day was going to be a dog.

In spite of that, the day did produce its information. Todd learned that Joseph Patrick Connor was married in the year 1876. He was married in Dublin, Cork, Liverpool, Dublin again, Birmingham, Bristol, Rhyl, Plymouth, Manchester and Leeds. In 1876 the world was apparently alive with men named

Joseph Patrick Connor, all of them busy marrying. He ordered copies of each of the marriage certificates, strolled down to the Cock Tavern in Fleet Street, and again attacked the crossword puzzle, superstitiously certain in his mind that triumph over the puzzle would bring him Connor's head on a plate. Triumph, however, belonged that day to the anonymous compiler of the puzzle. Returning crossly to St Catherine's House, he handed over a cheque in exchange for the ten certificates and began to go over them with care.

A marriage certificate is the genealogist's friend. The details needed to complete it are many and it goes pleasantly back a generation and signposts a generation forward. For each Joseph Patrick Connor married that year he now had: name, date and place of marriage, ages of bride and groom (though some said only 'of full age' in the 1870s). Here too were the occupations and addresses of both parties, the names and occupations of the bride's father and the groom's father, and finally the signatures of bride, groom and witnesses.

Ten of them. And none could be entirely ignored, though examination quickly disposed of several. The Joseph Patrick Connor whose father's occupation was listed as Prop: Jesmond Ship Co., and who was marrying The Hon. Euphemia Percy, daughter of Lord Henry Percy, occupation: Gent., was clearly a resident of the other England, of which Disraeli had spoken. He lived in the same country, but hardly the same world, as Connor, ex-gaolbird, ex-soldier.

Comparison, comparison, comparison. Todd compared each of the ten certificates with each of the next, and discovered a crime. The crime was bigamy, and it was committed by the J. P. Connor who married in Rhyl and Plymouth on dates six weeks apart. Details differed but not the signature.

Could this be his man? Todd stared at the certificates and brooded. He opened his briefcase and looked at his document copies again. None bore a signature. Was it possible that Connor had decided to abandon ravishment in favour of charm and persuasion? It was not only possible, it would show sense. A young man, newly out of prison and with no money and few prospects, would have been very wise to find for himself a woman with property – and both brides had property – in some place where he would not be known.

He searched the birth books for 1876 (Babies are not infrequently born within a yard or two of the vestry door) and 1877 and went to the desk to order copies.

'Having a good day?' asked the clerk at the Orders window.

'Middling,' said Todd. 'But I've found a bigamy.'

'Genuine?'

'Oh, yes.'

'Dial 944–1212,' said the clerk, grinning. 'Tell Scotland Yard. It is a crime, you know.'

'This was in eighteen-seventy-six,' Todd said. 'The man's in hell long ago.'

'That's no problem to Scotland Yard. Most of their best men are there!'

Todd smiled weakly, and looked at his watch. He could wait. Or go again to Chancery Lane and look at Assize Calendars, then collect the birth certificate next day.

He went to Chancery Lane. An hour at the Calendars showed that Connor had not appeared within the three years following his release, or not at Norwich, Chelmsford or Ipswich. He must have done one of three things:

1. Abandon serious crime.
2. Move to another part of the country.
3. Go abroad.

On the grounds that men given to violence against women do not usually stop being violent, and indeed are usually incapable of stopping, Todd decided to pursue # 3. Such a course was, in any case, a shade easier and more interesting than a pursuit of Connor through the twice-yearly Assizes in all the English counties – and the Winter Assize groupings as well. He knew that at some point Connor had gone to Australia. If it were possible to find how, and when, he'd be comfortably over the wall.

6

Captain Andrew Rabbett's interest in genealogy began on the day he discovered from a magazine article – while confined to quarters awaiting what would unquestionably be a difficult interview with his CO – that possession of a coat of arms was not the privilege only of the high-born and nobly-connected. Far from it. With growing incredulity, Rabbett learned that a grant of arms was available to anybody who had achieved prominence in almost any walk of life. The itinerant tinker might be ineligible, but the stable tailor was not, and nor were soldiers who had risen to corporal, nor sailors who sang an unusually good shanty. Eight hundred pounds or so, and there you were with a beautiful coat of arms, properly drawn-up and attested by the College of Heralds itself.

The interview with the colonel went quite as badly as Rabbett expected – the captain's seduction not of a brother officer's lady, as he had told Crombie, but of the colonel's young son, produced a puce-faced demand for his instant resignation, a demand which he met – and on his way out of the camp he remembered, and returned to collect, the magazine. It might, he thought, provide the basis for future fund-raising.

And it did. Rabbett placed 'Let Me Trace your Ancestors' advertisements in selected magazines in the United States. His charges were almost indecently low in comparison with those appearing alongside. Those commissions which looked like being hard work he rejected. ('I do apologise – sudden pressure of urgent work for the College I serve')

To the simpler ones he gave his full attention. A sample Rabbett letter might read:

Dear ——

I have succeeded in tracing your family's British roots back to 1837 and enclose a family tree and (of course) my account. Prompt payment would be appreciated.

I wonder whether you realise that by virtue of your father's grandfather's eminence as a footballer/carpenter/publican in the neighbourhood of the manor/village/town of ——, you are technically entitled to a grant of Arms from the College of Heralds?

Previous experience tells me that the cost might be somewhere between £500 and £1,000, including the necessary research and the design and production on parchment of your own coat of arms, which is, of course, unique to you and your family.

I should be more than happy to pursue the matter if you find it appealing. For the moment, I simply draw it to your attention.

Yours sincerely,
Andrew Rabbett

His writing paper bore his own coat of arms and motto ('Only to serve' – that of the Prince of Wales is 'I Serve' and the resemblance was entirely contrived).

From the start of his new career, satisfactory numbers of people rose like starving steelhead trout after his dangled fly. They got their coats of arms, and paid no more than double – or treble – his first estimate, and as a rule all parties were pleased, not least Andrew Rabbett.

Given the same starting information as that provided for James Hamilton, i.e. the name Joseph Patrick Connor, and the regiment's number, Rabbett began at once. A telephone call to the library at the Ministry of Defence told him of the 27th of Foot's transformation into the Royal Inniskilling Fusiliers, now incorporated into the Royal Irish Rangers. Within minutes he was speaking to the Regimental Office in Enniskillen and already hot on Todd's still-warm trail.

Because he was a great deal less scrupulous than Todd and more than willing to cut all the corners that could be cut, he jumped into his car the moment he knew of the 27th's service there, and drove to Colchester. Rabbett had once served in Colchester himself and imagined that fact would prove helpful. It did not; Colchester Garrison still had no records worth looking at, and the languid officer in charge of Public Relations clearly felt no interest.

'Try the MOD old boy,' he said.

'Not bloody likely, old boy,' Rabbett replied, making for the door. 'And by-the-by, your boots are filthy. Is that verdigris on the eyeholes?'

He paused for thought on the pavement outside. This was Essex. The county town of Essex was Chelmsford, twenty miles away.

'Here I come,' he muttered.

Rabbett knew, as all researchers into old records know, that Britain's local archivists tend to be of excellent quality. The rest of the country's administration may be in the hands of time-servers and worse, but the archivists know their work, their records and their responsibilities, and furthermore care about all three. They tend to propriety and discretion. No use therefore he brooded, to go blinding in and asking questions he shouldn't ask. Better to proceed in another way.

He parked his car, walked cursing through the muddy streets to County Hall, and in the record room of the Essex Record Office inquired politely and loudly of the rather pretty duty archivist whether any of the people seated around the room might be professional searchers.

She looked at him doubtfully. 'Are you sure you need a professional? The staff here can usually help.'

'I'd prefer it,' said Rabbett. 'It's a question of available time. That's why,' and he raised his voice yet higher, 'I need a professional searcher.'

From a desk drawer she took a sheet of paper. 'Several are listed here, as is the Association of Genealogists. Of course, we can accept no responsibility as to their work.'

'Thanks.' Rabbett glanced through it quickly. 'No phone numbers?'

'I'm sorry. Directory Inquiry might help.'

'Thanks,' he said, and turned to run an eye over the

people working in the room. Two of them were looking at him, one, a woman, in clear disapproval of the noise he was making, and the other, an elderly man, in equally clear inquiry. To him Rabbett gave that unmistakeable sideways jerk of the head which means 'follow me outside,' and then left. The man joined him less than sixty seconds later in the hallway.

'Er – do I gather you're looking for a profes –'

'You do,' said Rabbett. 'Listen, d'you want to make a quick tenner?'

'How?'

'Simple. There's been a fellow here – he's a searcher, too – looking into a name, bloke called Connor, and a regiment, the old 27th of Foot. I want to know who he is.'

'You mean Connor?'

'No, I don't mean bloody Connor,' Rabbett said. 'I mean the searcher. I want his name. One of the girls is bound to know.'

The man pursed his lips. 'See what I can do, but I wouldn't bank on it.'

'How about twenty?'

The man looked wounded. 'I said I'd try, didn't I?'

'Well, try hard. Where's the nearest pub?'

'On the corner. Right and right again.'

'I'll wait there.'

He had waited almost an hour, brooding angrily to himself about the difficulties put in the way of decent researchers, before his man came in, and stood waiting to be offered a drink. Rabbett didn't oblige. 'Well?'

'They don't know.'

'Rubbish. You mean they won't tell you!'

The man looked unhappy. 'Maybe that's it. They think it's all private business. They're fussy. Here, I'd better get myself a drink.'

'Go ahead,' said Rabbett stonily.

'Did you,' the searcher said a moment later, 'look at the book?'

'What book?'

'Visitors.'

Rabbett swore. He'd been so busy striding to the archivist's desk . . . 'Where is it?'

'On the left, just inside the door.'

'Okay. Hop it. I'll do it this time.'

'What about the tenner?'

'Haven't earned it, have you!'

A notice inside the door said, 'Use of pens is prohibited. Pencils, 10p each, may be purchased here.'

'Pencil, please,' Rabbett said humbly. 'And I wonder if you have a copy of the *Inventory of Monuments*, published by the Royal Commission?'

'Yes. The difficulty is to find a place at a table for you.'

'I'll stand.'

'Not allowed, I'm afraid. And you'd better sign the visitor's book.'

'Of course.' This girl had not been on duty earlier. He smiled at her warmly, but she seemed not noticeably affected.

'Date, please. Then your signature and address. And print your name in the last column.'

Rabbett wrote busily. 'You do get a lot of people here, don't you?' His eye ran rapidly over the names and addresses, whoever it was would be London-based. He turned a page back. 'Of course, family history is so fascinating.'

Mentally he noted five names: Thomson without a p; Barnett, Kaufmann (what was he doing here if he wasn't a pro searcher?), Pyke, and Todd. All were London-based. All had been here more than once.

Progress.

For the sake of appearances he read the entry on 'The Balkerne Gate' in the *Inventory of Monuments*. While apparently making notes in pencil, he was in fact listing the names and addresses from the Visitors' Book.

'Good evening, I'm so sorry to disturb you. Hope I haven't caught you in mid-dinner? Oh good. My name is Rabbett, Mr Thomson, and I've been doing some work at the Essex Record Office. Yes. Well, the other day there was some kind of mix-up; someone else's books put on my table, you know the sort of thing, and I ended up with a sheet of somebody's notes. Not much on it, but there's mention of a name. Have you lost any notes?'

'No.'

'The name is Connor. Joseph Patrick Connor.'

'Not mine. Tell you what – I'd give it to the girl on the desk. Whoever's lost it will ask there, and the girls are very good.'

'Yes, I will. Sorry to disturb you.'

Rabbett hung up. Not Thomson, then, unless Thomson was a liar.

Barnett's number, three times dialled, returned the unobtainable signal. There was no reply from Kaufmann. Pyke was in bed with influenza, said Pyke's wife; but she asked whether he had lost any notes. He said no. There was no reply from Todd.

Frustrated, but not much ruffled, Rabbett went early to bed. There were plenty of avenues left, and bright and early in the morning he would begin to explore them.

'If at first you don't succeed,' Todd told his reflection as he shaved, 'you yell for bloody help, right?' The reflection nodded. 'So who can help me find Connor?' No answer.

He felt deeply depressed. Connor had walked out of the now-vanished Springfield House of Correction, near Chelmsford, some time in 1876, and had then vanished. The previous day's searches had gradually assumed a kind of random desperation, with Todd turning from one possibility to another, only to turn away as yet another possibility occurred to him. None of them delivered.

But it came down to a single fact: at some point between leaving gaol and being knocked down in New York a quarter of a century later, Joseph Patrick Connor had made at least two long trips. The first had been from Britain to Australia – must have been because it was known that he had been in Australia. The second was – perhaps – from Australia to the United States.

In neither case had he gone by jet, or by aircraft at all, because flying machines hadn't been invented. The same went for cars. Connor didn't walk on water, either, nor go on horseback. Even trains, which had been invented and developed, remained on land. Connor, therefore, if he had gone to Australia, had gone by ship, like millions of others.

Where to find him? Get help. Where? Whom did he know who was expert on Australia? Then suddenly his reflection was grinning back at him. 'Madge!' Todd said.

She was Lady Madge, in fact. She was more: she was the Lady Marjorie van Geloven, daughter of one admiral, long the widow of another, authority on ships and the sea and author of books uncounted. An hour later he saw her where he knew she'd be: in the library of the National Maritime Museum at Greenwich, surrounded by pink and yellow issue slips and by copies of back numbers of *Lloyd's List*.

He paused at a table by the door and wrote a few words on a slip of paper, then tiptoed up behind her and placed it under her nose.

'Who?' she said. The big head turned, green-framed glasses were a little awry on the high-coloured face. 'Ah, it's you, dear, sending me little notes.' She read out 'He went to Australia. I want to find out when.'

'Coffee,' Todd said.

'Wine,' said Madge. 'Nice in the caff now, you know. Red plonk or white plonk. I'll consider your advances over a little of the red.'

They threaded their way through the galleries, past Nelson's coat with the bullet hole in the shoulder and the breeches stained with his blood, past Romsey's portrait of Lady Hamilton, past the superbly decorated Worcester china service from which they had eaten.

'Good caff, this,' said Madge. 'Got atmosphere.'

He sat her in a little booth and brought her wine. 'This bloke, Madge, was a bit of a brute. Three years in the nick for ravishment, Then he came out and –'

'Shouldn't have done it, should he? First thing he does is go to Australia, yes? Half-Australian myself – the naughty half. What else can you Brits expect when you dumped all your bad apples in that barrel? Name and date?'

He told her.

'Okay, here's the good news. There was a disaster at the PRO in the early seventies.'

'What kind?'

'Human kind, silly sod. 'Bout five hundred years they've been keeping Crew Lists. Every ship that sailed, list of the crew was kept. Then, some clever bloody civil servant he says why do we want all this bloody paper, he says. We don't, he says. Who the hell cares, he says, about the names of the crew of the *Cutty Sark* and the *Agamennon*! Who cares who sailed with Drake and Raleigh!'

'I think I've heard of this,' Todd said. 'He gave it –'

She waved an angry arm. 'Scattered it to the four winds, the sod. Seventy per cent went to Newfoundland, for the Lord's sake. Ten per cent in the PRO. Ten per cent here. The rest went to anybody who fancied it. What's his name again?'

'Connor.'

'Know anything more about him?'

'Served in the army. Infantry. Twenty-seventh of Foot. Went to gaol. Went to Australia. Died in America – after being knocked down by a carriage. And there was a tattoo on his arm.'

'Of what?'

'Black circle. The size of a grape, so the story goes – I didn't actually see it myself.'

She emptied her glass. 'Stand a little more of this, young Todd. Plonk it may be, but it's not bad plonk. Is eighteen seventy-six a true date?'

'Not before.'

She pursed her large lips. 'You're going to have to be awfully lucky, but a search can be made. *Lloyd's List* to start with. You'll need to make a list of every departure for Australia from a British port. Lots, you'll allow me to tell you. Then you can see if the crew lists are in the PRO or maybe the Director-General of Shipping and Seamen has them at Cardiff. If they're not in Britain, they'll be in Memorial University in Newfoundland, so you can go there and see. And if you still haven't found him, you can start on the county record offices, because they grabbed bits of the spare ten per cent. Okay?'

'Same every year, Madge?'

67

'Every year. Cheers, dear.'

'Any clues?'

'Let me see . . . Australia trade was funny, you know. Odd, that is, not comical. Passengers out and not a hell of a lot to bring back. Some grain, yes. Coal a bit later. But a problem. There was a company – let me see. Yes, Australia–London line. Advertised for years in the *List*. Seven or eight ships and a sailing every month or so. *Zoroaster* was one of theirs. And *Haddon Hall*. Used to sail out of the East India Dock, London. Occasionally the West India Dock. Yes, try them. If I think of anything more, I'll tell you.'

Todd smiled and thanked her. But it was with a leaden feeling that he returned to the Library. *Lloyd's List*, published every day except Sunday, printed every sailing and every arrival of every ship, everywhere. For the year 1876 there were several large, bound volumes. He sat down, opened the first of them, and began to look at sailings. There were five for Australia on the first page; more on the second. And hundreds of pages in the book.

And he hadn't the faintest idea what he was looking for – not the smallest notion which of dozens of ships Connor might have sailed aboard. To go through dozens – hundreds – of crew lists would be a huge job and there'd be every chance of missing the correct name out of sheer weariness and boredom.

Madge clapped his shoulder as she limped away. 'Working! That's the way.'

He watched her approach the counter and fill in order slips, and reluctantly bent his head again. Australia–London line had eight sailings listed in their advertisement. Dutifully he began to copy the names and dates. But he was going nowhere, and he knew it very well.

The piece of paper seemed to come from nowhere. He blinked and picked it up.

'Three cheers for the grape,' it read. He pursed his lips and thought: Madge.

He turned to look for her. She was wearing an immense sheepskin coat and leaning against a bookcase a yard or two away, meticulously miming the filling of a glass. 'Come on,

68

young Todd,' she said, in what passed with Madge for a whisper.

He followed obediently. She was carrying a book. As the door of the library closed behind them, she boomed. 'Champagne, it will cost you.'

'What will?'

'Not till the cork has popped, by God! There's a wine bar in old Greenwich down yonder has one or two niceish bottles, as I remember.'

She limped alongside him in delighted silence, immensely pleased with herself. Todd had no difficulty in controlling his curiosity. Madge knew what she was about. Heaven alone knew how, but she must have made a breakthrough. He glanced sideways at her, saw the big face suffused with pleasure.

She clutched the book tightly as the bottle was brought. 'Oh goody, Bollinger. Iced properly, I hope, waiter! Your health, Master Todd.'

Todd frowned at her. 'You'll be in trouble nicking books from there.'

'I gave it to them, dear. Gave them Pa's library, like an idiot. I was young and generous in those days.'

'What have you got?'

She held the book up. '*Clippers & Cargoes*, dear. Very nice. Men they were in those days, men! Ever hear of Bully Jack Breeze and the *Lady Eliza*? Wonderful name, eh? Lady Eliza was a ship, mind, not his bit of hanky-panky. Fifty-nine days to Fremantle. Look fascinated, damn you!'

Todd said, 'I don't even believe in Bully Jack Breeze.'

'No? If you'd sailed in his ships you'd have believed. Up with the sails and then out with the padlocks – once the sails were spread, nobody could take them down, not for gales and not for God, because he'd got the lines padlocked in place. There were men who actually went crazy with fear on Bully Jack's ship.'

'And?'

'They say rounding the Horn with him was like a foretaste of Hell.'

'And apart from the melodramatics?'

69

'No soul, young Todd. That's your trouble. Bit of an amateur doctor was Bully Jack Breeze. All the clipper masters were – had to be. He had another nickname, Bully Jack did. They sometimes called him Lampblack Jack, because that's what he used for boils and burns. Used to use lampblack on 'em. Didn't do any good, of course, but it was like tattooing, rubbing that stuff into broken skin. There were quite a few men walking round with black patches of skin. Says so, here, have a look!'

'. . . worn almost as a mark of pride,' Todd read. 'To wear a black mark was to have been a member of Capt. Breeze's crew. The sailor in the tavern boasting of a fast run was believed if he could show the mark. A habit grew up of making a small burn in the arm in order that Lampblack Jack should treat it. Even men who intended to desert at the end of the voyage were keen to carry the mark with them.'

'The *Lady Eliza*,' Todd said.

'Fill 'em up, Todd,' Madge urged. 'My info's good if yours is.'

Todd's luck had never run stronger. Crew Lists for *Lady Eliza*'s two 1876 runs were still, unbelievably, at the Greenwich museum's out-station at Woolwich. Yes, they could be sent. Today? Well, why not, there's a van leaving soon.

By five o'clock, Todd had before him two documents on which writing in a fine, copper-plate hand, was fading:

Agreement & Account of Crew
Foreign-Going Ship

Name of ship: *Lady Eliza*; Registered, Castletown, Isle of Man;
Gross tonnage 1,208; Engines, None.
Owner/Master, Jno. Breeze, Sea Hill, Castletown;
No. of seamen 45.

Todd was almost afraid to turn the page of the Crew List.

But he did. Breeze, master; Keddie, mate; Iredale, Fraser, Gutbrod, Daniels . . .

Forty-five names . . . Kerr, Bothwell, Connolly, Lewis, Lines, Connor, Hudson, Starling, Porter –
Connor! Christ, he'd passed it!

Connor, Joseph Patrick, year of birth, 1850; town or country of birth Donegal; Ship in which last served, *Carbet Castle*; year of discharge, '76; Date place of signing up, At Sea; In what capacity O.S.; Wages £1 first month, £3 p.m. thereafter. Discharge particulars: Connor had deserted at Sydney, New South Wales.

Gotcha! he thought. He rose and went over to Madge. 'Want a great big, wet, slobbery kiss?'
'Bubbly's better,' she said.

But if a somewhat dazed Warwick Todd was celebrating, and also deeply enjoying, the fluke which had just handed to him on a plate the evidence he needed of Joseph Patrick Connor's departure for Australia, no comparable luck attended the efforts – and they were considerable – of Captain Andrew Rabbett. As one trail, left behind a century and more earlier by Connor, grew abruptly warmer, another, left far more recently by Todd himself, was entirely cold.

It is fair to say that Rabbett was not always entirely scrupulous. The people for whom he produced elaborate coats-of-arms (and far less elaborate family trees) were heavily overcharged, but generally they got what they wanted. It had been his good fortune to discover and exploit an area of human vanity, using raw materials which were very cheap indeed. Few things, in fact, come cheaper to members of the public than the devoted expertise of the people who serve museums and archives. It had not, therefore, been necessary for Rabbett to seek to corrupt any of the toilers in those particular vineyards, since their very best work and efforts were available to him at nil cost.

And Rabbett did not, therefore, possess what he now needed most: a network of informants in those key establishments where searchers carry out their searches.

There was, however, one girl. Annette Hutchinson, in addition to a first-class honours degree in history from Cambridge, had an extraordinarily wide knowledge of *Middle Class Marriages of the Eighteenth Century* which was the provisional title of the PhD thesis on which she was working. She also had thick ankles, spots and a slight cast in the left eye – none of which put off Andrew Rabbett for a second.

'Find a researcher?' she said, looking at him with a mixture of regard and concern. 'Andrew, why would anyone want to find a researcher?'

'Because there's a fee if I do,' he said.

'I don't understand.'

'No? Well, you don't have to, really. All I know is there's a bloke doing a search on this character Connor and my client wants to know who it is.'

'It's a bit mysterious,' she said disapprovingly.

'Could you do it?'

'I don't know. Where would the searches be?'

'Your place, darling heart. The Public Record Office. You could look among the requisition forms, eh? Find out who ordered what.'

'But Andrew,' she protested, 'have you any idea how many there are. There are hundreds and thousands every day!'

'For me, eh?'

'Andrew, perhaps if I knew which documents –'

'Muster rolls of the 17th Regiment of Foot, in the eighteen-seventies,' Rabbett said promptly. 'Can't be too many people hoiking those out, eh? Have a look in the morning, eh, pet?'

'But the filing system's not designed that way. Anyway, Andrew, I have to go to Newcastle tomorrow.'

'Put it off,' he said.

'I can't. It's a friend's wedding you see.

'What friend?' he demanded savagely.

'From university. I promised, Andrew. Really. Look, it's only two days.'

'Two? For Christ's Sake, Annette! My God, I thought you'd at least be prepared to help me.'

'Oh, I am, Andrew.' She looked at him anxiously, a tear beginning to well in the good eye. 'I'll come back tomorrow night. Then I can look the following morning.'

He regarded her with a distaste he did not quite conceal. 'Have to do, I suppose.'

'I really will look, Andrew, honestly. I'll go in early.'

He drove her home to the little flat in Turnham Green, which pleased her, and left her at the door, which did not. But men, particularly reasonably-presentable ones in tweeds and regimental ties, did not appear often in her life, and she was all-too-aware that protests often turned into fare-wells.

Thirty-six hours later, he telephoned. It was ten o'clock and she should have put in an hour or more already.

'I'm afraid Miss Hutchinson is not in today.'

'I'm a friend. She said she'd be back this morning.'

'I'm afraid not,' said the female voice. 'Apparently it was the prawns.'

'Prawns?' said Rabbett.

'In the cocktail. The whole wedding party got salmonella poisoning. Quite serious, I believe. I could take your number and get Annette to telephone when she does come back.'

'Don't worry. I'll just keep calling.'

He did not 'keep calling', however. He lit a cigarette, thought for a moment, then telephoned The War Office Library and asked where the regimental depot of The Royal Irish Rangers might be.'

'Funny, you're the second person to ask that recently.'

Rabbett took a careful breath and said easily. 'Wonder if I know the feller?'

'You may. You may not. It was just on the phone. Didn't get the name. What you want, Captain, er –?'

'Rabbett, with an E.'

'– Is Enniskillen Castle. All the stuff's there.'

'Thanks so much.'

He telephoned Enniskillen Castle, and explained as best he could. 'Met a chap who was coming to you. He was looking, I remember, for a feller called Connor. I remember the name – Connor's I mean – but not the researcher's, and I could do with getting in touch. Can you help?'

A pause. This, as Rabbett well knew, was for the intervention of propriety. In a moment they'd say: sorry, we can't give you that information.

He said, 'He dropped a ten-pound note. Found it when he'd gone and knew it wasn't mine.'

Another pause. Then: 'Oh, I suppose it's all right. Yes, I remember the Connor inquiry well. He was an American, wasn't he. I can give you the name and address if you'd like to send the money to him. He's Mr James Hamilton, of . . .'

Rabbett noted it, then hung up crossly. Now it was one American who wanted to trace another. Thoroughly unusual, and, he thought, of doubtful profit.

Still, the client was plainly rich, and one of the iron laws that governed Rabbett's life was that the rich be not offended while there was the smallest chance of cash changing hands. He telephoned the number he had been given during his meeting at the Royal Lancaster Hotel and informed a faraway answering machine of his discovery.

Captain Andrew Rabbett then sat back at home, awaiting the plaudits and the cheque he felt his efforts had earned.

It was a full twenty-four hours, however, before William Crombie received the message. As he played it over, he first cursed Rabbett for an incompetent damned fool and then, as the first irritation faded, realised that the mistake was entirely understandable. He reached for the telephone and dialled.

'Rabbett, you got the wrong man!'

'Absolutely not,' the captain protested. 'This chap Hamilton –'

'I know about him,' Crombie said. 'There's another guy, though, a real reseacher. A pro.'

'You're sure?'

'I'm sure. Find him! And now we can help – we have his initials.'

The reason for Crombie's certitude lay in a pile of documents received overnight on the FAX machine at Hampden & Bradford, and shown to him by Zee Quist.

'What d'you think of them apples?' she asked, handing him the first.

He glanced at it. 'Marriage certificate? Joseph Patrick Connor and Elaine Mitchell-Hands. This was really him, Zee?'

She laughed shortly. 'Unless this was. Or this.' Zee Quist handed other copies across. 'Ten of them, Bill. The guy's thorough. Ten Joseph Patrick Connors, all married the same year.'

'So which?'

'We don't know. But there's something we do know.'

'And that is?'

'She pushed across the final sheet of chemically treated FAX paper. The simple, typed paragraph read:

'Connor served sentence Springfield House of Correction, Chelmsford, Essex. Am now investigating all possibilities for his subsequent movements.
W.T.'

'We know he's W.T.' said Zee Quist.

7

Returning to his flat in Trinity Court a little muzzy from the
champagne he had drunk, Warwick Todd found awaiting him
a letter bearing a New York City postmark of a week earlier.
The envelope bore also the logo of the ABC TV network –
mildly puzzling because the letter inside was from James
Hamilton, and was written on Hamilton News letterhead.

Dear Warwick,

I want to re-emphasise the great importance to me of
the commission I gave you in London. If anything it has
now increased – for reasons I cannot really discuss here
and now.

But I want to ask you to pursue it with all the urgency
you can, and to do so without regard to time or expense.
I am only too aware of the inevitably random nature of
much genealogical investigation, and it's clear that, since
Connor came to the USA by way of Australia, you may
need to consult archive material there. If you need to go,
then go. If you then need to come on to the USA do so.
I do not wish to have your researches delayed even by a
day because you feel you need to seek my permission
before incurring expense.

To make it clear, therefore, I want you to know that I
am willing to spend up to £10,000 (ten thousand pounds
sterling) on your researches and that up to that figure,
expenditure will be at your discretion, subject of course
to validation with hotel and credit card bills; all this is in
addition to your agreed fee of £100 (one hundred pounds
sterling) per day. As you see, I am writing to you from
NYC. Tonight I return to Boston. And that's how it's
going to be from here on in. I'll be moving about a lot.

There's a lot to do and a lot to learn in the business, and I won't have time for anything else.

And don't forget the need for absolute discretion. This thing is between us, Warwick. It must stay so.

Yours

James Hamilton.

Todd made himself coffee and a cheese sandwich in an exuberant mood. What a day . . . the breakthrough on Connor and then this! Invitations to spend ten thousand if he felt so inclined were rare, indeed unique, in his life. But Hamilton was right: it would be necessary to go to Australia if Connor were to be thoroughly tracked.

He stretched out long in his chair, with the coffee cup balanced on his chest, and let the questions surface.

Why the heavy emphasis on secrecy? 'I'm going to discover something really strange about Master Connor', Todd thought. 'And I suspect Hamilton has half an idea what it might be.'

Why the urgency with the subject dead getting on for a hundred years?

What had Connor done that could possibly matter now?

No knowing, he thought ruefully. But he'd bloody well find out – and quick. Nothing else to do in Britain, after all: he'd chased Connor as far as the dock gate and if urgency was the priority, tomorrow was the day he should really be Australia-bound.

Tomorrow?

Well, why not?

Later in the evening, a thought struck him and around ten, he telephoned the Lady Marjorie van Geloven at her home in Maze Hill, Greenwich.

'Madge? It's Warwick Todd.'

Her voice was stately with wine. 'Warwick? Oh, my dear boy. You know, it's hardly for me to talk about funny names, but I'm never quite sure whether you're a Tube station or somebody's country seat.'

'I'm a grateful genealogist,' said Todd grinning, 'that's what I am. And I want to know more.'

'About Bully Jack Breeze?'

'Yes.'

'Who wouldn't!'

Todd crossed his fingers before speaking. 'Madge, what became of his logs?'

She said with mock indignation: 'You're a naughty, greedy boy. You have the crew list.'

'And now I want the logs. If they still exist.'

'Not easy, Warwick Todd. Not unless you're ready to undertake a long perilous journey?'

'Go to the bloody Moon if I have to, Madge.'

'Near enough, dear. They're in Brisbane. They came up at auction a few years back but nobody told me, so this bloody retired Australian mutton-puncher sneaked in and got 'em.'

'Know who he is?'

'Course I know. I've got a little model of him here with pins stuck in it and his address is engraved on my liver. Fellow called Bruce Dooley, twenty-three Sweet Gum Road, Woolloongabba. Beats Warwick Todd, a name like that, don't it, sport!'

'Thanks, Madge. I'll give him your love.'

'Knife between the ribs is more in my line,' she said. 'You're really going?'

'Too right.'

'Then take a piece of paper and one of those pencils we all keep having to buy, and write down this name. Ready?'

Todd was at his desk. A pint mug held a vast assortment of pens and pencils. 'Ready.'

'R. van Geloven, Flat 24 Cross Street Tower, King's Cross. That's Sydney.'

'Got it. What relation?'

'Lord knows, distant. But a mine of information on registries. Lawyer, too, so keep your hand on your wallet.'

'Thanks.'

'My pleasure, dear. Everybody should have one day like this in a lifetime. Glad you've had yours. Just don't expect another, eh, dear?'

'I won't,' Todd promised.

'Especially not in Australia. Been before?'

'No.'

'Somebody wants something pretty badly?'

'You may be right, Madge.'

She chuckled. 'Or not, as the case may be!'

'Something like that.'

'Be careful, me dear lad, that you don't make any jokes about convicts or Botany Bay, not if you want to keep your teeth.'

'Okay.'

'And stop humouring me!'

'I will. And I'll send you a postcard.'

Todd was not an especially experienced traveller and this would be his first venture beyond Europe. As he packed a single bag he thought about visas (necessary, certainly, for the USA, but for Australia?), about vaccination and/or malaria tablets, about timetables (he tried the airlines' offices, all closed at midnight). His clothes were all lightweight, and washable in hotel bedrooms. He then began loading papers into a slim pigskin document case, then took them all out again and made photocopies on his small Xerox copier. One set – the copies – to go with him. The originals to stay at home. Mindful of Hamilton's letter with its insistence upon discretion, he hid the envelope containing them between the hanging files in the third drawer of the middle filing cabinet.

Two telephone calls, next morning, swiftly provided answers to his questions. Australia did demand a visa from UK nationals on holiday trips, but it could be obtained at once. And Qantas not only had a seat for its 20:30 departure that day, it was more than willing to accept either of his credit cards. He generally used two: the Access/Visa card issued by his bank, and the VisitingCard which gave virtually unlimited credit in return for a good deal of investigation. He went to his bank and, with a certain insouciance, virtually emptied his current account in order to buy £750 in travellers' cheques. He spent an hour in Foyles' bookshop, looking for specialist works on genealogical research in Australia, but found nothing. At Australia House in the Strand, a pleasant, sunburned girl told him little beyond the address of the Archives Office of New South Wales in Sydney. He noted it, to show willing, but felt certain Madge's uncle/cousin/nephew was likely to have it already.

At one o'clock he returned to his flat to shower, change and collect his suitcase.

While Todd had been enjoying a run of unusually good luck, Captain Rabbett had been in difficulty with his own researches. The unhappy Annette Hutchinson had remained flattened and worse by virulent salmonella poisoning in Newcastle for twenty-four hours more than she promised; and when, weak and pale, she did at last totter back to her duties at the Public Record Office, an abrupt relapse cost a further day. Then there was the mountain of requisition slips to go through – a task she could only carry out either surreptitiously or in her lunch hour. Finally, though, she telephoned Captain Rabbett.

'I think I've found him,' said Annette breathlessly.

'Time you did,' said Rabbett. 'I've waited long enough. Go on, girl.'

'Oh, Andrew, I've been so –'

'The name!'

She said ingratiatingly. 'You were right. About the initials, I mean. They are W.T.'

'Warwick Todd,' he barked. 'It is, isn't it?'

'I thought you didn't know! I've spent hours . . .'

'Yes. Well, you're a good girl,' Rabbett said, and hung up. A moment later, having looked up Todd's number in the directory, he lifted the phone again and dialled.

'Hello.'

'Would that be Mr Warwick Todd?'

'It would,' Todd was fresh from his bath, dressing-gowned and full of well-being.

'My name,' said Rabbett, 'is Macdonald. I'm told you're quite a man for family trees.' He pitched the level of the tempting lie carefully: 'There are four or five Macdonald clans

80

and the search would be interesting, tricky, and expensive, but not impossible.'

'I'm sorry,' Todd said. 'Can't take anything new on at the moment.'

'How soon? What if I come to see you.'

'Afraid not. I'm going abroad.'

'Too bad.' Rabbett sighed deliberately.

'May I ask who gave you my name?'

'Girl at the PRO,' Rabbett told him, truthfully. 'Going anywhere interesting?'

'Interesting to me,' said Todd. 'Goodbye.'

As Todd ate a snack lunch, and then dressed, Rabbett was in the taxi he picked up outside his flat off the Edgware Road. He got out close to Trinity Court and climbed the stairs to Todd's apartment. When he knocked, a man dressed in pullover and slacks came to the door.

'Mr Todd?'

Todd nodded.

'Afternoon. I'm from Frazer, the Double-Glazer,' said Rabbett. 'I believe you're interested.'

'Not me,' Todd was holding a suit by the hanger hook.

'You didn't fill in a reply card?'

'Nope.'

'Oh, dear. Still, I may as well tell you a little . . .' Rabbett could see a suitcase lying open on a couch. 'No? Well, I'm sorry you were troubled.'

He had to wait for a taxi further along Gray's Inn Road. When it came, the driver demanded five pounds in advance. Rabbett paid him, sat and waited. He paid and waited, paid and waited. At three-thirty, Todd emerged from Trinity Court carrying a suitcase and briefcase, and began walking briskly towards Holborn. Rabbett left the cab's shelter and followed. By the time Todd entered the London Underground at Chancery Lane station, Rabbett was near enough his shoulder to hear Todd say, at the ticket window, 'Heathrow Central, please.'

Rabbett bought the same ticket and took the same train, but he rode in the next carriage and followed Todd, finally, to the Qantas check-in.

Having watched Todd at last walk safely into Passport Control, he went in search of some 50p pieces and a blue telephone.

'Would you like me to follow him?' he asked New York hopefully.

'Nope.' His employer simply repeated the instructions given during their meeting at the Royal Lancaster hotel: 'Let me make it absolutely plain,' said the strong American voice. 'I want every piece of paper relevant to the progress through life of Joseph Patrick Connor. I want every piece found. I want it destroyed. I want to destroy it myself. Right?'

'Oh, of course.'

'At a thousand bucks a throw, right.'

'Certainly.'

'And one more thing. Could you get into the guy's apartment?'

'Burglary?' Rabbett hesitated.

'Come on. Or I'll get some other guy.'

'No, I can do it.'

'So do it. Let me know what you find.'

Two hours later, in her office at the Admiral hotel, Crombie said to Zee Quist, 'The research guy's on his way to Australia.'

'And?'

'He's still on Grandpa's track, that's obvious.' Brother Bill grinned. 'And he'll be an awful long ways from home.'

Zee Quist blinked. 'I'm still not sure I believe this.'

'I told you already,' Crombie said. 'The job is to get John into 1600 Pennysylvania Avenue. It is not to lobby support for *habeas corpus* or the four freedoms. Look at it this way, Zee; we're all descended from slimy things that crept out of the sea, right? Ours, yours and mine, crawled up on the sand a zillion years back and died, but not John's. John's crawled out yesterday, and it stank and left a slimy trail of ooze on the clean white beach. Now somebody's following the goddam trail and he's got to be stopped. Let's be practical, hm? How long – England to Australia?'

'Day and a half, maybe.'

'We have to get somebody on his tail. Can't afford to lose him.'

'Are you sure you can afford the other thing? What if you get tied in – his brother?'

He sighed. 'Zee, I'm not his brother. I'm his half-brother. Makes a hell of a difference. If I'm wicked nobody's surprised because half-brothers have always been no-goodniks. You don't believe me read *The Prisoner of Zenda*, read Shakespeare, read . . . Half-brothers are like step-mothers – the monsters of the legend! Okay, so I'm happy.'

She was looking at him with hard eyes, resentful at this willy-nilly involvement and showing it. He lit a cigar and went on: 'How's the campaign going?'

'You know damn well how –'

'Tell me.'

'Big in the New Hampshire. Bigger in Vermont. Gaining, taking votes and delegates.'

His chances?'

'Getting better.'

Crombie sat on the corner of her desk and leaned forward. 'He can win, Zee!'

'I know it. But he won't if he suddenly develops a dirty tricks department.'

'And he won't if his dear ole gramps turns out to be the first round-the-world child molester. Zee, leave this thing to me.' She was silent. 'Leave it to me. Handle the rest. I can do this.'

She took out a cigarette and flicked her lighter. 'Examine yourself for blood lust, Bill.'

'Oh, come on, Zee.'

'No, I'm serious. What do you gain?'

'Security.'

She shook her head. 'I have a feeling about this man, this – ah, Todd. He's good.'

'He's a dollar-a-day hireout, Zee.'

'But a good one. He's gone a long way in a short time. There are documents all the way. Proof. Use your head, Bill. Todd's leaving a trail, too. What if the networks go after Grandad and find he's disappeared from the records, but there was this man Todd researching Grandad and that's Todd's body right over there – the one with the bullet holes. What then, Bill?'

'What are you saying?'

'I'm saying we want him on our side. He's a two-bit hireout, so okay, we hire him. If there's more dirt to come, he finds it for us and we're prepared.'

'But he still knows, Zee. And what he knows could be enough to swing the whole election. You want a guy in that position walking round loose?'

Zee Quist said: 'John would trust him.'

'Sure he would. John's a practical saint. And when the guy dropped John down the pit, John would say a prayer for the guy with his last breath. That's why John needs to be in the White House, Zee, but I'm not like that and neither are you, and John has to be protected.'

She said, 'We'll talk again.'

Brother Bill paused in the doorway. 'This thing's going to nag away like toothache, Zee. Todd knows and we know he knows. Take out the tooth, the nagging stops.'

'I'll still know, Bill. So will you. Do I kill you or do you kill me?'

He left without replying.

In the outer office, Bill Crombie paused to put his cigar into an ashtray. As he did so, Quist's secretary fielded an incoming call. 'Oh, hi, Miss Hayes. If you'll hold just a second, I think she may be free . . .' The girl's head turned and she looked inquiringly at Crombie.

He said quietly, 'Hayes, is that Hamilton News?'

She nodded.

'Let me take it.' He took the phone from her, covered the mouthpiece, and said, 'This may be private.' The secretary slipped obediently from the room.

'I'm sorry, Miss Hayes,' Crombie said smoothly. 'Miz Quist has a meeting right now. Is there a message?'

There was. 'Miss Quist wanted me to let her know if anything came from London for Mr Hamilton and it just did.'

'She'll be real glad about that. What is it exactly.'

'Oh, just a man sending in his bill. There's a few supporting accounts – credit card counterfoils, that kind of thing. The man's name is Todd – Mr Warwick Todd.'

'Gee, thanks, Miss Hayes. Matter of fact, we got his name yesterday.'

'Well, his address is on his bill. Do you want that?'

'We have it, Miss Hayes.'

She sounded disappointed. 'Oh, well. Hoped I was going to help Miss Quist and Mr Leyden. Still, anything I can do . . .'

It would be quite wrong to include Australia among those countries in which organized crime plays a dominant role as happens in Italy or the United States. But Australians are gamblers, and gambling has long been one of the major sources of revenue to organizations like Cosa Nostra & Union Corse. The Mafia has a strong foothold among the million and more Italians who have become New Australians since World War II.

The 06:30 arrival in Sydney of Qantas flight QF2 from London via Bahrein and Singapore was met by a considerable crowd, even so early in the morning. Many of the passengers were grandparents, many of those waiting were children and grandchildren. There was a general air of excitement and happiness.

Two among the crowd, however, were neither excited nor there for a long-anticipated reunion. They were at the airport in the cool of early morning because a telephone caller from New York, a few hours earlier, had instructed them to be there.

For an hour or so, the three hundred and forty-six passengers from QF2 filtered gradually out of the exit gate. Most were swept up and away by families; some obvious business men were met by company cars; immigrant families would stand for a while, looking slightly lost, before setting off along the arrowed route to the taxi ranks.

'Dark hair cut short; dark beard, likewise. Five ten. Silver-rim glasses. Pigskin document case,' one of the Italianate watchers said for the tenth time. 'He's not here.'

'Held up in Customs or immigration,' muttered his partner, also not for the first time.

'Can't observe his movements if he's not here.'

85

'Wait here. Don't let him slip by. I'll go see what I can learn.'

The Qantas inquiry desk, busy but cheerful, gave a rapid answer. 'I'm sorry, sir, but there's no Mr Todd booked to Sydney.'

'He left London on this flight,' the man said with stubborn insistence.

'Are you sure he didn't get off at Singapore, sir? A lot of people do. It's a cheap stopover and the shopping's great!' The man was not sure. 'Or Bahrein,' said the Qantas girl. 'He may have got off there. We do make a refuelling stop at Bahrein,' she added brightly.

'Can you check for me?'

'I'll try. Just a moment.' She punched rapidly at a computer terminal. 'Just come up, sir. Yes, he left the aircraft at Brisbane.'

'At Brisbane?'

'At Brisbane, sir.'

'You got an address in Brisbane?'

'I'm afraid not, sir.' Her eyes and attention moved away. Angie Vaccaro went to give the good news to his partner.

In London, at roughly the same time, Captain Rabbett was seeking to force an entry into Trinity Court. He had tried the previous evening, but a party in one of the flats had continued until nearly four in the morning and people had trooped up and down the stairs almost continuously. Rabbett had decided he was glad he lived elsewhere.

Tonight, however, equipped with a large piece of sticky paper, a glass cutter, and some of the nefarious and athletic skills taught to him by army instructors, he was balanced on a wall knocking at the glass of Todd's sitting room window. It took ten careful minutes or so, but eventually the glass came away on the sticky paper, and Rabbett climbed in.

'Make a list,' he'd been told. 'Anything important. And telex it to this number.'

He sat at Todd's desk and began a very careful search – wastepaper basket first, then telephone pad. After that the search expanded. Rabbett had plenty of time, he was thorough, and the flat was not large. Everything Todd had not taken with him was examined. As the night wore on, Rabbett gradually completed a dossier in which most of the details of Todd's existence were noted. He wrote down numbers: insurance policies, bank accounts, National Health Insurance, policies, credit cards, driving licence, cars Todd had owned.

On Todd's Xerox machine he copied more than a hundred pages taken from the filing cabinet, including all those on Connor, but also making sure he had the names and addresses of people more generally interested in ancestor-tracing, for Rabbett believed strongly in looking to his future employment. When he at last left Todd's flat, it was after seven a.m. and, feeling he had earned it, Rabbett stopped an early cruising taxi and had himself driven to The Waldorf Hotel for a massive breakfast. Afterwards, full of well-being, he walked round the corner into Kingsway to a Telex Bureau whose address he had found in the Yellow Pages.

There, as he handed over the pages to the operator and then waited while the girl behind the counter began to calculate the charges, Rabbett's feeling of well-being abruptly evaporated.

'That's all, then?' asked the girl.

'All? Yes,' said Rabbett, reflecting that in truth it wasn't much. He'd found Todd – and lost him. He had the copy documents and therefore knew what should be destroyed. The rest – the detail – was inconsequential.

But in this he was wrong. One of those details was quite enough to put determined professional killers in a position to destroy Warwick Todd.

8

'Beautiful, isn't it?'

Todd, twisted round at the window seat, drinking in glimpses of the blues and greens of sea and reef, turned his head. 'It certainly is!'

'That's the Capricorn Group. Practically the end of the Great Barrier Reef. We're starting the run into Brisbane about now, sir.' The stewardess went smiling on her way.

Brisbane, when the 747 landed not long afterwards, gave Todd an immediate lift of the spirit. The early morning air was clear and clean, the sunlight seemed to sparkle. After twenty-four cramped hours on the aircraft he at once felt better, full of that sense of well-being that comes at the end of a long flight and is itself the beginning of the jet-lag phenomenon.

The immigration officer seemed unimpressed by the morning. 'How long you be in 'Strylia?'

'Couple of weeks.'

'Holiday?'

'Yes.'

Todd's passport was opened. The quicko visa inspected. 'You're a record agent, huh? That means records like discs?'

'I'm afraid not. It means records on paper. Historical material. Archives – that kind of –'

'Be working here?' The immigration officer's tone and manner were becoming sour.

Tired as he was, Todd scented the trap. Work required work permits. He said, 'Seeing one or two friends. That's why I'm here. And to see Australia.'

'So it's a vacation and only a vacation.'

'Yes.'

'Are there record agents in Australia?'

'I've no idea.'

'I reckon,' the immigration man persisted, 'bloke like you'd need a work permit just to go into a museum.'

'Doubt if I shall, then.'

Todd's passport was swiftly and angrily stamped. He walked out of the terminal into the day's increasing heat, puzzled by the contrast between the smiling air hostess and the sour official. 'Forget it,' he told himself, realized he'd said the words aloud, and felt himself colour.

A thoroughly amiable cab driver took Todd to a motel with a swimming pool, hard by the airport. On the way Todd described the episode in immigration, and the cabbie laughed. 'Like bloody dingoes, some of those bazzas.'

'It was just hostility?'

'More than likely it was just wind!'

It was Friday morning in Brisbane, though still Thursday evening in faraway England. Todd took his bag into an immaculate motel room and wondered what to do. He found he was more than a little puzzled by Australia, by lots of geniality punctuated by little pockets of hard hostility. Perhaps he looked and sounded too English – too much the whingeing Pom of Aussie legend. And perhaps the owner of Bully Jack Breeze's logbooks, Mr Bruce Dooley, would think so, too.

But Mr Dooley could wait. Todd spent the day alternately swimming in the pool and napping in his room, hoping to shrug off twelve thousand miles of rapid travel. He only partly succeeded, and jet lag caused his mistake. Intending to telephone Dooley during the evening, he dozed instead and had to call next morning.

'Mr Dooley?'

Grunt.

'My name is Todd. I'm here from England trying to trace someone who came to Australia a century ago.'

'Convict, eh?'

'Not that I know about. But somebody told me you had some logbooks.'

'Which.'

'Breeze. Bully Jack Breeze. Would you let me see them?'

Grunt.

89

'Sorry, Mr Dooley. I didn't quite –'

'Come, see me.'

'I'd like to. When do you sugg –'

Dooley hung up.

A swift introduction is what I'm being given, Todd thought to himself, to the gallery of great Australian eccentrics.

Number twenty-three Sweet Gum Road, Woollongabba, was a fair distance from the motel, but close by a sizeable stadium. Posters announced that Queensland were soon to play Victoria. At cricket, Todd assumed.

'Here y'are, sport.' The cab had pulled in outside a house. 'Twenty-three it is.'

Todd paid and got out. 'A retired mutton-puncher', Madge had said, and he'd thought that probably meant, stripped of Madge's hyperbole, that Dooley was a farmer. Now Todd wondered.

The house was narrow and mean-looking, the front yard straggly and overgrown. Something in its appearance reminded him of the old Hitchcock film, *Psycho*. He suppressed a grin, went up the four front steps and knocked. There was much barking, followed by a pause and then the door was suddenly flung wide. The man who stood facing Todd was very tall, six feet three or so, and both skinny and gaunt. He wore ancient jeans, a none-too-fresh vest, and several days' growth of stubble. He said loudly, 'Whyja want Bully Jack's logbooks, eh?'

'To – er – well, to consult them.'

'All the way from England, eh?'

'Yes. Will you show them to me?'

'Will I? Don't know.' Dogs appeared in the hallway behind Dooley, several of them. They stood and looked at Todd, and as they did so, a waft of a fecal canine smell seemed to belch out of the open doorway. 'Come in, if you like. Don't know if I'll show you Bully Jack's books, though.'

Todd entered cautiously. The dogs, a large black Labrador, and two sizeable mongrels, declined to give way. Dooley scattered them with his boot, and led Todd into a room which, though it contained chairs, could not with any truth be described as a sitting room. More dogs occupied the chairs.

'Siddown,' said Dooley.

Todd looked around him a little helplessly. The room stank. The dogs were under only loose control, if they were controlled at all. Suddenly he thought: to hell with this, and tipped an ancient rocking chair until its occupant, a matted spaniel, tumbled resentfully out, growling a little.

Todd sat, then, and said, 'Madge van Geloven gave me your name.'

Dooley scowled. 'Gives everybody my name. Everybody and anybody. Damn woman.'

'I think,' said Todd hopefully, 'it's wonderful that the logs are still preserved at all. Do you mind showing them to me?'

'Which.'

'*Lady Eliza.*'

'Voyage?'

Todd told him.

'Name of the bloke?'

'Connor.'

'Not aboard,' said Dooley, flatly.

Todd did not contradict outright. 'I have the crew list. His name's on it.'

'Discharge in good order?'

'He deserted.'

'Where?'

'Sydney.'

'Not aboard, that's what I said.' The eyes were dark, deep in their sockets, almost invisible in the shadowy room. Todd asked himself why the man was so obstructive and could think of no reason.

Todd said, 'You have a collection?'

'What of?'

'Ships' logs. Masters' logs.'

'Why would I collect ships' logs?'

This, Todd thought, was like Alice in Wonderland. He said, 'I understood you were a collector. I'm sorry.'

'She told you,' said Dooley accusingly. 'That van Geloven woman told you. She's damn mad I got Breeze's log.'

'Bit envious, I expect, that's all,' Todd said with a geniality he was far from feeling. 'Look, Mr Dooley, I'd be really very grateful for a look at Captain Breeze's log. And –' he hesitated. Dooley looked scrawny, ill-nourished and poor, but: '– I'll be happy to pay a fee.'

Dooley's face changed at once, and unexpectedly. Where before it had been merely unfriendly, now it was stretched into fury.

'Outa my house! Out! Out! Before I have the dogs at you. Out, out!'

Todd went. There was neither sense nor point in doing anything else: Dooley was beside himself with this sudden rage which had no discernible cause. Maybe when it had died down, he could try again.

But Dooley hadn't finished yet. 'Get him,' he yelled, and the black Labrador flew at Todd, snarling, and snapped at his left arm, but caught only the material of his jacket. Todd clouted it sharply on the snout with his right and it yelped and backed off. Quickly he slammed the gate.

'Why, Mr Dooley?' But Dooley had turned and was re-entering the house, his dogs with him.

Todd walked, sweating now as the morning heat grew damp and heavy, until he could find a taxi, and then went into the city – to the large, modern library. Yes, he was told, the library did have a local history section. A quick inspection confirmed what he had expected: the city's history was short, the available material not great.

The girl librarian on duty smiled at him. 'No good, huh?'

'I'm sure it's excellent,' Todd said. 'It's just that my needs are a bit specialized.'

'Try the Royal Historical Society of Queensland,' she said. 'Breakfast Creek Road, Newstead.'

'How do I get there?'

She grinned. 'Taxi, if I were you. But not today. Saturdays they're closed. What exactly are you after, anyway?'

He told her and she said, 'This Dooley sounds like a real drongo. Rings a bell, though.'

'What kind of bell?'

She frowned. 'He paid real money for those logs, I think. There was an auction. I think that's it.'

'Who'd know?'

'Well, the *Courier Mail* – that's the Brisbane paper. Their morgue ought to know. Want me to give them a call?'

Todd did. She spoke to somebody named Shirley, smiled at him, waited, spoke again, hung up.

'So – they have a file, sir.' She grinned, enjoying her little triumph.

'On Dooley?'

'Yup. You go on over to Campbell Street, Bowen Hills. Ask for Shirlee – that's with two e's – Barnabas.'

The *Courier Mail* had a Sunday edition and a full staff on duty. Shirlee Barnabas, busy but bright and cheerful, had the file read. 'Sit down over there,' she said.

It was a small file: The first cutting told of the sale at which Dooley had bought the log:

BID KING DOOLEY'S
$A 2000 SHOCK

The log book of an old-time sailing skipper, expected to fetch only $A2–300 was dramatically knocked down at a city auction this morning to a sensational first bid of $A 2000.

The bidder, Mr Bruce Dooley of Woolloongabba would only say, afterwards, 'I was determined to have it.'

Mr Dooley, a tall, thin, greying man in his fifties, and dressed in working clothes, startled the fashionable Brisbane habitués of art and artifact auctions with his instant bid, starting at so high a figure. While it is true that Cap. 'Bully Jack' Breeze was a famous character among sailing skippers, it is not known why the log-book should be so highly-rated. For many years it formed part of the collection of the late Mr Norland James.

Other prices of the auction . . .

The second cutting, dated a month later, deepened the mystery:

FREAK BIDDER
RIPPED
RARE BOOK:
$500 FINE

Bruce Dooley (58) of Sweet Gum Road, Woolloongabba, walked into the Royal Historical Society on Monday, asked to see a rare book, then took it into a toilet and ripped it to pieces.

Today he was fined $A500 at Brisbane Court.

Prosecuting, Mr Ken Thomas said Dooley had recently bought at auction the original of the book he tore up, which was in fact a set of photocopies bound together. 'It was a wicked assault upon Queensland's historical resources,' said Mr Thomas.

Defending, Miss Rosaly Bourne said it seemed that Dooley was determined to have the only copy of the book – the log of the nineteenth century sailing ship master 'Bully Jack' Breeze. He refused to say why. Miss Bourne added that Dooley willingly undertook to inflict no further damage.'

The other two cuttings were brief colour pieces by disappointed reporters who had visited Sweet Gum Road in the hope of an interview and come away disappointed. 'In an old wooden house in the shadow of the Gabba, lives a man as strange as the secret he keeps . . .' one reporter wrote. The other said the same thing in different words.

Shirlee Barnabas took the cuttings back and smiled. 'Got everything you need?'

'Yes, and thanks.'

'Anytime.'

Todd was beginning to like Australian girls. Not only were they apparently unfailingly pretty, and sunburned, and cheerful; they were disposed to help. Still, they couldn't solve the problem Dooley presented.

Todd found a bar and a beer and glared out across the water, watching the endless pageant of boats and thinking of the ships of a century earlier. There must be some way of prising loose the logs of Bully Jack Breeze from the grip of Bruce Dooley.

There must be a key. Todd's mind ran back over their increasingly crazy conversation. Dooley had said, first, on the phone, 'Come and see me.'

Then he'd said, when Todd arrived and when asked if he'd show the logs: 'Will I? Don't know.'

It was with mention of Breeze's ship, the *Lady Eliza*, that Dooley's attitude had started its rapid change for the worse.

Why?

And why did Dooley insist that Connor had not been aboard *Lady Eliza* when the crew record proved he had.

Furthermore, why did Dooley possess the logs? It was clear Bully Jack Breeze was an important figure of the Australia trade. His log books had come on to the open market, at auction, and there would have been competition to buy, if Dooley's pre-emptive bid had not gained instant success. Madge, for one, wanted them. As would the Maritime Museum, as would any number of historians.

So why did Dooley, who was plainly no historian, place a value of £1,300 on them – and more if the fine were to be taken into the reckoning?

Plainly the logs contained something Dooley wanted to keep secret. It was hard, though, to imagine what.

His copy of the *Lady Eliza*'s crew list was in his document case. He spread it on the table and scanned the names again. There was no Dooley. No Dooley – but a *Deeley*! Todd's eye moved speculatively over the list, from Breeze's own signature at the top, down over the others. Not the same hand.

So Breeze hadn't signed the men on. Who had? Stephens, the boatswain had the right handwriting.

How did Stephens write an *e* and an *o*? Very similarly. It was a common and familiar confusion in hand-written documents. Todd's eye moved along the line. Deeley had signed on in London as an able seaman. His discharge . . .

Deeley had died at sea.

The skipper, required to name place and cause, under 'Discharge Partics' had entered 'Off Colombo' and 'suicide!'

Todd already knew that after 1865 only logs recording births and deaths usually survive. And from 1880–91, none survives. The existence of Bully Jack's was thus explained.

Where did all that get him? To the point where Dooley must be presumed to be obsessed with a hundred-year-old suicide. Edward John Deeley had been the man's name – and he could not be Dooley's father, because he'd died half a century before Dooley's birth. Grandfather then – and becoming a father at fifty even then.

Todd found a stationer's and made a copy of the Crew List. He bought a manilla envelope, scrounged a paperclip, and attached his card to the Crew List. On the back of the card he wrote: 'Sorry if I upset you. Here's *Lady Eliza*'s crew list.' On the front he put the name of his motel and its phone number. He took a taxi to Sweet Gum Road, halted it well short of number twenty-three, and bribed the driver to deliver the envelope to Dooley.

'Okay?' he asked when the driver returned.

The man shrugged. 'He took it. Didn't say anything. Friend of yours?'

'No.'

'Good.' The driver laughed. 'Thought I'd ask before I spoke. Place looks as daggy as he does. Where to?'

Todd returned to the motel. As he collected his key, the owner's wife, a fiftyish woman with the strong remnant of a Tyneside accent said, 'Were you expecting somebody. Visitors?'

His first thought was: Dooley. But it couldn't be Dooley. Not yet. 'Perhaps a phone call.'

'No. They came here, not half an hour ago.'

Todd said, 'I'm expecting nobody. Did you get a name?'

The woman shook her head. 'Two of them in a car. Big Holden it was. Tell you the truth, I didn't like their looks much.' She laughed. 'I told 'em you weren't registered here. Naughty, I know, but I didn't want them hanging about.'

'Thanks. And no phone calls?'

'No.'

Todd went thoughtfully to his room. Two men looking for him? Damn it, nobody except Dooley and the Qantas computer even knew he was in Australia! And they were two men, furthermore, whose mere appearance made an experienced motel-keeper uneasy . . .

96

He returned to the office. An engraved brass plaque said the motel's proprietors were Tim and Jean Riley. She presumably, was Jean.

'Mrs Riley, can you tell me any more about these men?'

'No,' she said, 'I can't. I think they're new Australians from their looks. Greek or Italian maybe. But second generation, mind, the one who talked to me spoke like an Australian.'

'And they left no address?'

'Not a name either.' She looked at him sharply. 'You'll excuse my speaking out. But you've not been gambling?'

He laughed. 'Not me.'

'Because that's the notion they put in my head. There are folk like that, a lot too many, down the Gold Coast?'

'The what?'

'An hour from here. Australia's holiday paradise so they say. Maybe it is if you like gambling machines and chookie bars! You're worried, are you?'

'Puzzled. I've hardly got here.'

She looked at him seriously. 'You ought to be okay. Even if they do come back, I'll say you're not here. Unless they see you. But I'd stay out of the way of folk like that in Australia.'

Todd said, equally seriously, 'And you can tell?'

The stern look vanished. 'You go out of business if you can't tell, Mr Todd. We get 'em all at an airport motel. I can tell if they're married or single, and most of the time what they do for a living. Most of all, I know if they're honest!'

'So what am I?'

Jean Riley laughed. 'Pretty honest, a scholar, and single – though a man your age shouldn't be!'

'Tell me how you know.'

'You're too naive to be a businessman, not cheeky enough to sell, your room's full of papers already, and you haven't asked the cost of a phone call to England.'

Back in his room, Todd flopped on his bed and tried to make sense of it. Two heavies after him, why? Even given Hamilton's insistence upon discretion, there was no great secret involved. Old Joseph Patrick Connor was a bad hat, but he was long dead. Hamilton cared, but no-one else. No, it couldn't be Connor. Maybe they wanted his money, but it seemed unlikely; there wasn't too much of it, anyway.

Therefore, what? Todd felt not the least desire to tangle with these men, or even to speak to them. He was conscious that to go was somewhat cowardly. On the other hand, to stay was perhaps foolhardy and almost certainly pointless, since it seemed unlikely in view of Dooley's lunatic behaviour, that a sight of Captain Breeze's log would be forthcoming.

So. So – Sydney. If by some miracle Dooley relented, he would return to Brisbane; if not, not. Meanwhile, Sydney was where Connor jumped ship, it was where the New South Wales records were kept. Sydney made sense.

He packed quickly, booked a seat by phone and paid his bill. Jean Riley herself drove the courtesy car to the airport and he gave her his card with Dooley's name on the back. 'I'll telephone in a day or so. If this man has called me, could you let me know?'

'Can and will and glad to help.' She shook his hand firmly as he got out. 'Queensland has its share of drongos, Mr Todd, but we've no monopoly. Sydney has more and worse.'

'I'll remember.'

'Yeah. Mind how you go.'

He bought a Frommer guide before boarding the evening TAA plane for the 600-mile flight south. Arriving in Sydney, he took a cab to the Texas Tavern in King's Cross, checked in, had a cooling beer, then looked up R. van Geloven in the phone book.

'Hullo.' It was one of those clipped, brisk women's voices that make hello sound as though it ends in *ope*.

'I'd like to speak to Mr Van Geloven if he's in,' Todd said.

'You know him?'

'No. I was given his name.'

'Wish somebody'd give me his name! Who gave it to you?'

'Madge Van –'

'Uh huh. And Madge didn't tell you.'

'Tell me what?'

'That I'm Robin van Geloven. I'm her niece. How is she?'

'Fit. I saw her less than a week ago.'

98

'Okay, what do you want Robin van G for?'

'It's better discussed face to face,' Todd said. Madge's niece sounded attractive, amused and fun.

She said, 'Over a beer, you mean?'

'Be nice.'

'You're half-Australian already sport. All right, come on over.'

'Now?' He glanced at his watch. Nine p.m.

'Now.'

The Tower wasn't really a tower. Her flat was on the sixth floor, though, with a big wide window that looked out over a sea of lights to the harbour and the bridge, glittering in the warm dark like an elaborate diamond brooch on a black velvet cloth.

Robin van Geloven wore velvet, too – jeans of velvet and a shirt of blue silk. She had sunburned skin and hair bleached by the sun; she had a smooth forehead, level brown eyes, an excellent figure and a challenging grin. She handed him a can of Foster's lager. 'Object to the can?'

'Saves washing glasses,' Todd said. 'And Madge is an old crook!'

Robin laughed. 'Why?'

'You're not what – you're unexpected.'

'Why thanks, mister. Unexpected. Now there's a real piece of Pommie elegance. What did Madge say about me?'

'That you're a lawyer and I should keep my hand on my wallet.'

'True. Anything else?'

'Good at records and registers.'

'You're one of those?'

'Depends. One of what?'

Robin laughed again. 'You pore over ancient papers. And you're ship crazy.'

'I do. But not ships. Except this time. Want to hear the story now?'

She nodded, and listened in silence as he told her, giving the narrative concentrated attention. At the end she said, 'Why?'

Todd shrugged. 'I suppose I'm not so different from a

lawyer, really. Clients hire me. Hamilton has a girl he wants to impress, that's what I think.'

'Rubbish,' Robin said briskly. 'Money's being spent – that's the infallible clue. Money to buy money.'

'In what sense?'

'Could be a will somewhere, and a lot resting on provenance. Want another tube of Foster's?'

'Thanks. But surely not a will. The man died in 1896.'

'One moment, please, Mr Pom.' She went smiling off to the kitchen and returned quickly with the beer cans. 'Let me explain about wills. Once upon a time there were big chunks of land available for nothing, or near enough nothing. People got them, then died and left wills that never emerged. They can still be valid though. Half Sydney believes it has an ancestor who once owned Hyde Park but the will went walkabout. But your cobber Connor's going to take tracing. How much do you know about Australian records?'

'Not much.

She rose and went to another room and returned with a book. 'Borrow this. It's in paperback nowadays so you can buy your own tomorrow.'

He looked at the title: *Roots and Branches*, *Ancestry of Australians*.* 'Thanks. I'll read it overnight.'

She said thoughtfully, 'And you could go to the Registrar-General's Department in Bridge Street for a start.'

'Good. I thought I'd have to go to Central records in Canberra.'

'I have news for you, Mr Pom. Australia's Federal. Ain't no central records. Everything's done on a state basis.'

'Including births, marriages and deaths?'

'Yup. Get your bushwalking boots out. You'll need them before you've done.' She paused, then said cheerfully, 'Give you a thought, Mr Pom.'

'What?'

'Small ads. Let me see. "CONNOR, Sydney solicitor wishes contact anyone descended from –"'

'I doubt if there is anyone.'

* Fontana $4.95

100

'Okay.' She nodded. 'How about "anyone with knowledge of the late Joseph Connor –"'

'Joseph Patrick,' Todd said. 'Narrows it down.'

She shook her head. 'Keep it wide. The folks who answer will tell you all about second names and birthplaces.'

'How do you know.'

Robin winked and laid a forefinger against the side of her nose. 'Money, Mr Pom. Put that ad in the personal columns of the main dailies and it'll be universally understood that a solicitor is looking for descendants of someone who died intestate. We ought to add something, though. When did he die?'

'Eighteen ninety-six.'

'Goodoh. "Joseph Connor, died 1896". That'll convince them there's a century of accumulated interest. Sweeten the pot. All the dailies have Sydney offices, so it's easy enough. If you like you can have the box number replies forwarded to my office.' She reached for her bag and produced a card. 'Here's the address, but don't put it in the ad, for God's Sake.'

He took a pull at the beer. 'This is good. Any more advice?'

'When did he land in America?'

'Ninety-five or ninety-six.'

Robin pursed her lips. 'You're going to have problems, Mr Pom. But I reckon there's one thing on your side.'

'Go on – cheer me up! What is it?'

'Connor was a real brute, yeh?

'Yeh.'

She laughed delightedly. 'The Australian dilemma for you, eh, Mr Pom. I say "yeh", so do you say "yes" and sound stuffy, or do you say "yeh" out of politeness and make a pig of it? With you, manners won. I quite like that.'

'Yeh,' said Todd.

'Enough already. And that's New York-Jewish-showbiz.'

'I'll stick to Pommie. Especially now.'

'So Connor was a brute,' Robin said. 'By the time he's twenty-three, he's been fined, flogged, sent to gaol and drummed out of the licentious soldiery. Off to Australia where it seems likely, though we don't know, that he spent the next twenty years.'

'Gaol records you mean?' Todd said.

'Well, he didn't spend twenty years doing bloody embroidery, did he? Not the Connor kind of article, not him. He'd be in the Bridewell, some of the time. Maybe all.'

'Where are they – the records?'

'Tell you something to gladden your heart, Mr Pom. Convict-records-in-Australia-can-be-bloody-good!'

'I'll drink to that.' He raised his can.

'You can drink to this as well. The Archives Office of New South Wales isn't far from where you sit, and I have friends there. Unfortunately –' She frowned.

'Pray continue,' said Todd, frowning too.

'No. It's serious. There came a time when shelf space was short and nincompoops in control and lots of old records from county courthouses were burned. So it's a bit uneven. But put your trust in Patsy.'

'Who?'

'Patsy. My old schoolmate in the Archives Office. I'll phone her in the morning to expect you.'

He returned with regret to the Texas Tavern. Further hours in the company of Madge's niece would be no hardship at all. In his room, he used a sheet of hotel writing-paper for a brief progress report to Hamilton.

We know Connor deserted his ship in Australia, but not why, though probably it's just behaviour in character.

He thought for a moment. No point in mentioning the Breeze log if Dooley wasn't going to part with it. A hint though? Why not.

There's an outside chance I may be on to another useful avenue, and meantime I'm told that records of convicts here are excellent, so I'm hopeful about tomorrow, at the New South Wales Archives Office.

Enclosed, I'm afraid, are more receipts. Believe me, I'm trying to give some real return for your outlay. If only the ould divvil had stayed still!

Yours,
Warwick.

'You look like your dog just died,' Zee Quist said as Brother Bill Crombie came into her office in the campaign suite at the Admiral Hotel, New York City. 'Smile. John's doing well. You see the *New York Times* – CBS poll? Proves everything our private polls tell us – just two weeks later, that's all.'

'Sure I saw it. He can win. You know it and I know it. One week more and the front runner's running second and John's running first. So okay, Zee.'

She stared at him in exasperation for a moment, then lit a cigarette and sighed on the exhalation. 'It's that guy Todd?'

'It's Todd,' he agreed.

'I told you what to do. Hire the guy.'

'First you find him, then maybe you hire him!'

'He's gone?'

Brother Bill said, 'You think I'm crazy, don't you?'

She looked at him coolly. 'Bill, I know this thing's important. Let me ask you again: he's gone?'

'It all looks casual if you look at it one way. He's going to Sydney. I'm having him met, but he gets off at Brisbane.'

'Perhaps he has friends in Brisbane.'

'If he has, he's staying with them, because I've had every hotel and motel checked and he's not staying in any of them.'

'It would be natural enough.'

'Look at it the other way, Zee. Old Man Connor's yielding plenty of dirt. Todd's hot on the trail in London. Then suddenly he jets off to Australia, he gets off the plane unexpectedly, and he goes to ground. Why?'

'Sun and sea, Bill. Why not? Australia's nice this time of year.'

'Zee, I just don't believe that. He's on to something. I don't know if I'm extra-perceptive or just paranoid. But my instincts say there's trouble boiling up. Todd has to be found!'

'And your goons can't do it?'

'I haven't any goons.'

'But you have friends and they have goons,' Zee Quist said. 'Still I actually do believe in instinct, Bill. And presentiment.'

'It's what I feel, Zee. I see the picture.'

'Tell me.'

'There's a guillotine blade and it's labelled Joseph Patrick

Connor. And standing by the guillotine is Todd, with the release rope in his hand. And on the guillotine is John Leyden, probable President of the United States, Zee. I could draw it like a cartoon.'

'I can see it like a cartoon. Want a thought?'

'If it helps, Zee. Not otherwise.'

'Your British goon – the one with the comedy name?'

'Rabbett.'

'In his burrowings,' she laughed, 'turned up quite a lot, didn't he?'

'Not much that was a heck of a lot of use.'

Zee Quist gave an emphatic shake of the head. 'Wrong, Bill, dead wrong.'

'What do you mean?'

'I want a promise first.'

He laughed. 'You got it. Anything.'

She looked at him grimly. 'No politician's promises, Brother Bill. I want the hand-on-heart guarantee.'

'Of what?'

'That you're not going to have Todd killed. What you do is retain his services. Okay, destroy all the documents if you want to, I don't care. But no killing.'

'So sworn, counsellor. Now tell me.'

Zee Quist picked up a piece of paper. 'At Hampden & Bradford we had Crockerbank as a corporate client.'

'I know you do. So?'

'So why are they linked with Banque Leblanc in Paris, with Freedman in London, with Yomotomo in Osaka.'

Crombie snapped his fingers. 'VisitingCard! How in hell did I miss that?'

'Todd uses it.' She waved the piece of paper. 'You know much about cards?'

'I sign and pay. What's to know?'

'Let me tell you. VisitingCard is a charge card. You apply for it. They check you carefully, because credit is nearly unlimited. If they take you, all you do is pay your bill every month. No interest. But oh, boy, they're careful. Charlie Kemp who runs their operation pushed me round it one time. It's in Greensboro', North Carolina – they got their big IBM

104

computer there ticking over waiting for billing inputs. Somebody goes into a store in, say, Rome or Singapore. Or a hotel. Maybe an airline. The person looks suspicious, so the clerk punches his or her own terminal and the question goes up to the satellite down to Greensboro' and the answer goes up to the satellite again and back to Rome or Singapore. It says Brother Bill's a crook, or behind with his payments, whatever. Elapsed time measured in seconds.'

'What's suspicious about Todd?'

'You are asking me? Just listen, Bill. The card companies issue a list, weekly or monthly of their top ten wanted cards – that's the ones that are lost, stolen or strayed, and being used. There's a nice reward for the store clerk who spots one. So we get Todd's number put on the VisitingCard list.'

'Can we do it?'

'Charlie Kemp is a Leyden man.' Zee Quist grinned, remembered the rictus and thought: the hell with it. 'He's Republican, but he's a Leyden man. He'll do it for John, if not for me.'

Crombie picked up the telephone. 'Call him, Zee.'

She held up a delaying hand. 'I'll call him. First, though – if you want to find Todd in the interim, I'd say he was bound to turn up at the record office, whatever its name is. Brisbane now. Sydney sooner or later. Park one of your friend's goons outside.' She picked up another of the phones on her desk. 'Help yourself. Call your pal.'

'Thanks,' he said with, she was amused to see, mild embarrassment. 'I have to go. I'll call from my office.'

9

—•—

If you use a credit card – Diner's, American Express and VisitingCard are the commonest of the more exclusive of the charge cards – the procedure following your transaction is something like this:–

You sign a small pad of matching forms, so that there is one top copy and two carbons. The customer usually is given the bottom, blurred copy; the shop or hotel or car hire agency retains the middle copy; the top sheet goes off for payment, and for calculation of various sums involved: the card company's commission, the foreign exchange transaction, etc. In the case of such establishments as big department stores or airport booking offices very large sums are involved and despatch riders are often employed to deliver the form to the card company's office so that computerised billing and crediting be not delayed.

The Airport Sunset Motel, Brisbane, however, employed nothing so dramatic as despatch riders. Jim and Jean Riley, doing the accounts each evening, simply sorted the various credit card counterfoils into little piles, according to company, put each pile into the appropriate envelope, and posted them off to Sydney. In due course the money would come through, minus an average four per cent commission. They resented the lost percentage, but were realistic enough to know that small hoteliers cannot fight international banks. Not, at any rate, and win.

The card counterfoil bearing Todd's signature accordingly made a comparatively leisurely journey. From the Brisbane sorting office it went to the airport; it was then flown to Sydney where it was again sorted, just in time to miss the day's final delivery.

In four days the slip arrived in the Sydney office of Visiting

Card, where seven girls at seven terminals sat punching inputs into storage, ready for the brief routine transmission burst which, twice a day, fed a mass of inputs into the Greenboro' computer.

There, as soon as Todd's number registered, a red light began to flash and the name and address of Jim and Jean Riley's motel was printed out at the desk of an executive selected for his alertness. Within less than a minute the terminal on the desk of Charles Mason Kemp was displaying the news and Kemp was already lifting the telephone.

'He was at the Airport Sunset Motel in Brisbane,' Kemp told Zee Quist.

'Was?'

He said patiently, 'Zee, people use charge cards to settle bills.'

'And to eat in restaurants,' she said.

'So maybe he wasn't eating out. Or maybe he was at Mac-Donald's like everybody else. This card paid a hotel bill.'

'Just the one?'

'There'll be more. I'm maintaining the top ten listing of the card. Who's going to pay the sixty bucks to the girl who eyeballed the number – you or me?'

'Regard it as a contribution to the Leyden campaign, huh?' she said sweetly.

He laughed. 'There'll be more, won't there?'

'I'm relieved to hear it, Charlie!'

There was a sequence. Quist called Crombie; Crombie, too made a call. So did the man who received Crombie's call. All were brief. Zee Quist gave the hotel's address and reminded Crombie of his promise; Crombie gave the hotel's address and passed on the message: no killing. So did Crombie's contact. But he was a gangster. To him the words no killing did not mean what they meant to the others. To him they carried an entire extra layer of meaning. The message he passed to Australia was, 'Don't kill him.' It was understood, however to mean 'stop short of termination.' It was like the message famously passed up the line in 1916 on the Somme: 'Send reinforcements, we're going to advance'. Passed on by word of mouth it became 'Send three and fourpence, we're going to a dance.'

Replacing the receiver in the twin room they shared at the Metropolitan Motor Inn, Angelo Vaccaro turned as his partner Carlo Crespi said, 'What's the news?'

'The news,' said Vaccaro, 'is he stayed at the Airport Sunset Motel.'

'We went there,' said Crespi. 'They said they didn't know him.'

'We went twice,' Vaccaro agreed, 'and they said it both times. And now he's left.'

'Where's he gone?'

Vaccaro shrugged. 'We have to find out. Maybe they'll know at the motel.'

'And maybe they still won't tell us.'

'We'll persuade them.'

'Oh, like that?'

'Just so long as we don't knock 'em off.'

It was the quiet time, between two and three in the afternoon. Last night's guests had left, tonight's had not yet arrived; the rooms were cleaned; the staff were off duty until evening.

Jim Riley, in the office, saw the big Holden car roll to a halt and called, 'Looks like they're back, Jeanie.'

She was in the dining room, folding napkins. 'Who is?' she called back.

'Your gangster pals.'

She came through to stand beside him and look. 'Yes, that's them.'

The two men walked in a leisurely kind of way towards the office. One had a brief-case. When she'd described them as 'quite sinister', Jim Riley had been inclined to disbelieve his wife, or at least think her guilty of exaggeration. Now he believed her. 'Go through the back,' he said. 'I'll handle it.'

She didn't argue. Jim was good at handling difficult people; forty years in the hotel business had taught him how.

He stood at the little counter and watched the door open slowly. They came in. They wore drills and floral shirts and white cotton sunhats like holidaymakers, but they came, he thought, direct from an Edward G. Robinson film of the Thirties. Immobile faces, black eyes.

Crespi said, 'Where's the woman?'

'The lying bitch,' amended Vaccaro. 'Where's the lying bitch?'

'I don't quite fol –' Jim Riley began. The stomach punch dropped him in a gasping, wheezing, agonized heap on the office floor.

Jean Riley heard it all. She was two rooms away but the doors stood open. She heard the thud of the punch, and Jim's dreadful grunting now as the air was driven from his body. He'd had an operation eighteen months earlier; gall bladder. That punch . . .

She had a little gun in the broom closet, never used. Years before a tiger snake had appeared on the lawn by the flagpole and she hadn't seen it until she was five yards away and she was terrified of snakes. The gun was tiny – a 20-bore, less than an ounce of shot, the kind country boys get for ninth birthdays, Jim had said.

Then the voice. 'Come out, you bitch, or we kick this wowser to pieces.'

Jean Riley slipped in the little cartridge and walked towards the office, softly on the thick carpet. All the way she could see Jim writhing and hear the awful sounds he made. But she couldn't see them, either of them.

As she went through the door, Crespi took the gun. He was standing behind the door and all that was needed was a quick reach and pull.

'Safety catch on,' he told Vaccaro with a laugh.

She tried to go to Jim, then, but they stopped her. She was made to sit in the desk chair and one of them hit her, very hard, his fist crunching at the corner of her mouth. She felt the bridgework go and the blood begin to flow.

Vaccaro said, 'You had a man here. Warwick Todd. English. I asked you and you said no.'

She spoke past blood and broken teeth. 'He wasn't. Not here.' She didn't know why she denied it. The man had gone, after all.

Vaccaro said, 'He was here. Where is he now?'

She thought, 'I don't know and they don't know – how can I harm him?' She said, 'I don't know.'

Crespi kicked Jim hard, toecap under knee. Jim screamed. She said: 'Sydney. He went on the evening TAA flight.'

'When?'

'Night before last.'

'Where's he staying?'

'I don't know,' and Jim got kicked again. 'I don't know, I tell you!' Another kick. 'I don't!' She screamed the words.

Vaccaro looked at Crespi. Crespi nodded. They recognized the truth that emerged via pain.

'Who did he phone?' Vaccaro said.

'We don't charge for local calls,' Jean Riley said. 'He didn't call long distance. See, the sheet's by the phone.'

Vaccaro picked up the record sheet by the switchboard. Number, town, room number, time of call.

'What room did he have?'

'Twelve.'

'Twelve called Rockhampton.'

She remembered. 'That was last night. Not him. Somebody else.'

'He get any messages?'

Jean Riley, tear stained, blood running from the torn lining of her mouth, in horror at the damage to her husband, was far beyond the notion now of defending a pleasant stranger. 'No' was spoken in some kind of reflex born of hate and fear, and it brought Jim another kick, this one on the outside of the thigh, at the sciatic nerve.

'His name's on this paper pinned here,' Vaccaro said. 'It says Dooley called. Who's Dooley?'

She took a breath. 'A man he wanted to see,' she muttered.

'Why?'

'I don't –' She saw the foot drawn back and screamed. 'No – leave him! I'll tell you. He wanted to see this man and the man phoned to say all right, but that was after Mr Todd left.'

'Does he know?'

Almost past speech, now, she simply shook her head.

'So how were you going to tell him?'

'Said he'd call up from Sydney.'

'Has he?'

'No.'

Vaccaro stared at her. The room was filled with small, desperate sounds of Jim's agony. Vaccaro said, 'Your car in the garage?'

She nodded.

'The English Jaguar?'

'Yes.'

He nodded to Crespi. Crespi opened the briefcase and took out a bottle of Booth's gin. He took off the cap and stood the bottle on the counter, and then removed a clean handkerchief from the case. Jean Riley tried to understand, but could not. Why would they want gin? What would they do with it? Something to Jim?

But then the odour reached her. Not gin – petrol!

Crespi jammed the handkerchief in the bottle neck and she knew at once. She was of the generation taught about Molotov cocktails in case Hitler's panzers had come to Tyneside.

It was done in a moment: a shake of the bottle to moisten the wick, a flick of a lighter, a swing of an arm. And Jim's beautiful Jag, that he'd dreamed about, was burning. And the garage was burning.

And Angelo Vaccaro had seized her by the ears and was saying, his mouth inches from her face, 'Tell the police and the whole place goes up, and him, your man there, goes too. When Todd phones, tell him about Dooley. But no warnings, or we're back to you, okay?'

She nodded and they were gone, both of them, the Holden smooth and silent. Afterward she cursed herself for failing to get its number. But how could she when she was on her knees beside Jim?

Mrs Holmes said: 'She does it to annoy, because she knows it teases.' She was thirtyish, cheerful and tanned and more or less a carbon copy of Robin van Geloven, except that she was dark. 'What does Robin call you?'

'Me?' She seems to have christened me Mister Pom.'

'Yes, well she christened me Patsy because she said I was one. It was all a long time ago and my name is Barbara and you can use it since you're a friend of hers, Mr Pom. What's more I can help you, I think. Robin rang me up as the dawn cracked this morning, so I've had time to think.'

'She told me the convict records were first-class.'

'So they are, most of the time, but there are gaps like chasms. Look, this bloke you're tracking was a no-good, wasn't he? What I thought was – the *Police Gazette*.'

Todd said, 'Good thinking, Holmes.'

She laughed. 'Elementary. He was a ship's deserter, pound in his pocket, two maybe. And he's crooked to start with. So what did he live on?'

'Crime. You're absolutely right.'

She parked him at a large light-wood table with a heap of bound volumes on it. 'Sydney and New South Wales, starting with eighteen seventy-six. Good luck, cobber. Yell if you need help.'

He said, 'You're the first person I've heard say cobber.'

Barbara Holmes grinned at him. 'The last, too. I've never heard it used in my life. But I'm giving you a little local colour.'

The pages were yellowish at the edges, where air had got to the paper and white in the middle where the pressure of the heavy binding excluded it. Todd, always happy with the past and its records, read steadily on, fascinated by the patterns of crime. Just before leaving London he'd heard a talk on the morning radio in which a policeman offered a theory. Old-time crime, the bobby said, had been to do with survival: theft of a loaf of bread or a chunk of coal. Nowadays it was all gratification and status: sex murders, car thefts, airline fraud. Todd thought at the time that old Joseph Patrick Connor failed to match the policeman's rules. In Sydney in the seventies there were pick-pockets, whores, racing swindlers and a fair amount of violent robbery and assault. Plus drunkenness, plenty of drunkenness, and in Sydney, as in London, top hats, hanson cabs and growlers. The year the Sioux killed Custer and Bell invented the telephone. And –

'Like some coffee, Mr Pom?' said Barbara Holmes.

He said 'No!' very sharply.

'Okay, I only –'

'Just a second!' Something had leapt off the page at him, and then, just as she spoke, had leapt back again. He hunted hard, nostrils pinched and she stood silently behind him understanding and willing him on.

Suddenly he laughed and picked up a pencil.

'No marking the paper,' she said, warningly and certainly not playfully.

He laid it with care on the page. 'There you are!' She bent and read:

Severe physical assault August 27th on May Christie, spinster, theft and rape at Victoria Street: Arrested and charged: Joseph Pat –

Todd said. 'The line turns on to the next page. Hold your breath.' And turned it over.

– rick CONNOR. Common labourer. No fixed abode.

Barbara Holmes gave a long low whistle. 'You ever try walking on water, Mr Pom?'

Todd grinned. 'Coffee, I think you said.'

'Come through to the office or they'll all want coffee.' A few minutes later, looking at him over the rim of a steaming cup, she said, 'How often are you this lucky?'

'Not often. But twice so far on this search.' Todd shook his head in a kind of wonder. 'The odds against are gigantic. Funny thing is that both these flukes attach to the name Van Geloven. Robin's aunt gave me the first – the ship. You gave me the second.'

'All I did was suggest the *Police Gazette*.'

'Don't be self-effacing.'

'Well you found it.'

Todd said, 'With help. Now – trial records. What would have happened?'

'To Connor?'

She gave him the Australian grin: head back, teeth white, all good humour. 'You've come to the right person, Mr Pom. We Australians know all about convicts, mainly because we've all got a couple in the family history. Mind you, some of us keep quiet about it. Very quiet, some of us.'

'But not you?'

'It's still a hot issue in Australia. Highly emotional. Once upon a time it really was necessary to keep a convict ancestor secret because you'd never have got a job. Nowadays people are often proud of a great grandad who was transported.'

'Depending on what they were convicted of?'

'Oh sure. Nobody'd go round boasting about a bloke like yours. But if great-grandad stole a sheep from the Duke of somewhere, that's socially okay.'

'And what would become of Connor?'

She frowned. 'Something unpleasant, I trust. But I doubt it. He was just in time for all the reforms. By the late 1870s Australian prisons weren't the free-for-alls they'd once been. Convicts went inside and stayed there for a good while.'

'But where – that's the question?'

'Ah well. It should all be available. But you have to understand the picture, Mr Pom. For years all Australia was near enough an open prison. More convicts than straight citizens. All Tasmania was a convict kingdom – lawless really, it was terrible. But then came reform and prisons were built – just in time for your pal. If he was found guilty, he'd go first to a place that practised cellular separation – what's nowadays called "solitary." After that, hard labour for years, and after that, the ticket-of-leave, and release.'

'This coffee cup,' said Todd, 'is empty. Where do I pick up his trail?'

'Court records. No problem at all.'

In an hour he knew the penalty. Connor had been sentenced to seven years at hard labour by the judge in Sydney. 'He'd be on road gangs or laying a railway,' said Barbara Holmes. 'Hot, hard work.'

He escaped in 1880. The record of convict Joseph Patrick Connor's running away was in the *New South Wales Government Gazette* for November.

'Luck?' said Todd to Barbara. 'He went to America in eighty-ninety-five, or thereabouts. So he was on the run for fifteen years. Where was he? And where in God's name do I start looking?'

'Does it matter?' she said. 'You know he went to America.'

He thought about it. 'Strictly speaking, probably not. But I'd like to know, all the same.'

It was still only 11.30 a.m. Todd spent the rest of the morning visiting newspaper offices to arrange for the publication of the advertisement composed by Robin van Geloven in major towns throughout Australia. He was still at it when his stomach began to nag. He drank some cold beer, and ate a sandwich, and resumed afterward. Sweat was running down his back as he tramped the hot streets. With the temperature well over ninety, he found he could barely think. All the same, he found himself wondering about Barbara Holmes's question. Did it matter that Connor had effectively vanished for fifteen years? No, it didn't – provided the trail was picked up again. And he already knew where to pick it up: New York's streets, where Connor came to his end.

Okay? So why shouldn't it be okay? All the same, it didn't feel right.

At mid-afternoon he sauntered damply back to the Texas Tavern and took a shower. The water, as he turned it from warm to tepid to cool, re-activated his baked brain, and with a towel wrapped round him, Todd picked up the phone.

'How're you doing, Pom?' Robin van Geloven said. 'Getting anywhere?'

'Could I tell you over dinner?'

'Tonight? Well, yes, all right.'

He realized suddenly he hadn't the faintest idea where to take her. Simultaneously with that realization she said, 'The Opera House.'

'Dinner, not culture.'

'Pom, it's your first evening out in Sydney. Take the lawyer's advice. Meet me at eight in the foyer at the Opera House.'

Delighted, he hung up, and asked the hotel switchboard to get him the Brisbane number of the Airport Sunset Motel. Dinner with Robin van Geloven was, he found, an immensely engaging prospect.

'Hello.' A woman's voice.

Todd said, 'Is that Mrs Riley?'

'No, she's not here.'

He gave his name and asked if there was a message. There was. Dooley was willing to see him.

'Thanks.' He hung up. It was good news – very good news, and he knew it. But it didn't make a great impact on a mind full of the notion of dinner with Robin. He frowned at himself in the mirror and found himself grinning back.

In New York that morning, Grandpa Connor occupied only a corner of Brother Bill Crombie's mind and Zee Quist wasn't thinking of him at all. Suddenly the John Leyden campaign which, to that moment, had been all sweetness, had hit a bitter moment. Only a few days earlier, after the two runaway victories in the Illinois and Florida primaries, Leyden had begun to look unstoppable for the Democratic nomination.

'Leyden's,' a veteran political commentator had written in *The New York Times*, 'is a bandwagon running over a rainbow, all goodwill and light. The rest are simply trailing.'

But on this morning, and on the *Today* show, of all places, John Leyden had spoken of the wide sweep of American policy in the Far East, had matched the words with a wide sweep of his arm, and had knocked a glass of water all over his fellow guest, a movie queen who from behind her water-soaked dress, gave him a look of concentrated disgust with which every woman in America could sympathise.

The incident had been recorded and had just been played back for the fourth time in the privacy of Zee Quist's office.

'I don't understand it,' Crombie said despairingly. 'He's not clumsy. He's never clumsy. Damn it, he's delicate as a cat on his feet!'

'He goes on no golf courses, not now,' Zee Quist said. 'And I wish to God we could keep him off aircraft steps! Look at Gerald Ford. He was a sweet mover, too. The most athletic man ever to go into the White House –'

'But pull out a camera and he fell down the stairs. Sure, I know.'

'So there John is on his hands and knees trying to dab Collins's dress dry with a Kleenex!'

'Why in hell,' Crombie demanded, 'couldn't the director cut away!'

'Would you, in his shoes?'

'I guess not.'

'And that's not all,' Zee Quist said.

'How's that?'

She said grimly, 'We have another, well, I guess you might say it's a smaller misfortune. Not much smaller.' He waited. 'They've stolen the song,' she said.

Crombie stared. 'The campaign song – *Hi there?*'

'The very same.'

They had had a top Broadway composer/lyricist working for weeks, looking urgently for something to match the 'Hello, Lyndon' of LBJ and Sammy Cahn's rewrite of 'High Hopes' for Jack Kennedy. Days earlier the man had produced a variation in the words of the old Woody Guthrie classic. It now went: 'Hi, there, it's real good to know you!' and was to be played endlessly in a string of Leyden TV ads showing the candidate shaking hands with the people. Leyden was Eastern Establishment and his whole camp felt the Western touch a brainwave.

'Who's stolen it?'

Her lips twisted. 'Who'd you reckon?'

'You mean the Veep – the ex-Veep.'

'The very same. I had Hopkins on the phone from Houston. First ads went out on the local news this morning. Be some union boy stole a recording from the studio.'

'Shit.'

'Absolutely shit. We have a problem, Bill.'

He said suddenly, 'How about running the same film and using that Beatles song – you know the one . . . er . . . "I want to hold your hand".'

'Go down great with the gays in San Francisco,' she said. 'Otherwise it's a turkey. What we have to do is get the *Today* people to say it was all their fault. Clumsy studio hand, piece of cable in the wrong place.'

'Won't work, Zee. It was a clean backhand drive.' Crombie laughed suddenly, and when she scowled, said, 'Goddammit Zee, it was funny. Half the water in her hair and the other half down her cleavage!'

'Hysteria,' she said, 'laughing at a thing like that.' But she smiled. 'You get five seconds to laugh, five to stop – then get to work repairing the damage.'

'It's impossible.'

'I know it. But we have to try.'

At roughly that moment, half a world away, the moment to which Todd had looked forward turned out, as such moments often do, to be not quite as he'd imagined it. He'd seen dimmed lights and heard soft music; seen and heard them, anyway, in his mind. The reality was a crowded foyer, and Robin van Geloven in jeans saying, 'C'mon, the cafeteria's over this way.'

So he stood, the wooden tray in his hands in the self-service restaurant at Sydney Opera House, waiting to load up with the distinctly ordinary-looking food he could see several yards ahead.

She laughed at him. 'Best dinner in Sydney, Mr Pom. Not the food maybe, but the ambience – look at it!'

He looked and was unimpressed, but laughed back, and she said, 'Just trust me.'

A few minutes later he was eating a cocoction of melon and shellfish, while gazing out from near sea level at the wide expanse of the justly-famous harbour, and at the ships gliding by like lighted castles in the night. 'This is an experience,' he conceded.

'Every tourist should see it. Tell me about the old con Connor.'

Todd described the day's successes, and at the end Robin said, suddenly, 'I'll fly you to Brisbane, sport.'

'Fly me?'

'You are looking,' she said, 'at the holder of a commercial pilot's licence. As of six weeks ago. You are also looking at the owner of a quarter share in a syndicate which owns a Piper *Apache*; and one, furthermore, whose turn to fly comes around this weekend. You pay the fuel and maintenance and I turn into dare-devil pilot.'

'I couldn't put you to the trouble.'

'Oh, you couldn't! Listen, I want to be put to the trouble. I want to fly. I'm looking for an excuse to go from A to B for a purpose, instead of stoogeing around. We fly to Brisbane on Saturday. Is that clear?'

'It's clear.'

'Meanwhile, tomorrow morning and no later, you have a task to perform, Mr Pom.'

'An important task?' Todd asked.

'Certainly. All the states have societies of one kind and another devoted to genealogy. You write to the secretary of each and every one and you ask whether, in that state, the name Connor means anything.'

'Why should it?'

'Because in Australia lots of things are named after people: farms, bridges, hills and valley.'

'Like Ayers Rock?'

'Would be, yes.'

'Who was Ayers?'

'Dunno, Mr Pom. Come to think, it was discovered by a fellow called W. B. Gosse, who described it as "an immense pebble", and it certainly is. It's five miles around the base and eleven hundred feet high! But these letters are a good idea. There may be a station or a creek called after Connor – you never know.'

After that, although both Todd and Robin van Geloven made occasional references to him, Connor edged off into the metaphorical shadows as their conversation became even more quiet, personal and interrogative and tinged often with surprise. Something was happening. Both of them knew it, though it wasn't mentioned. They ended the evening in the champagne bar giggling like teenagers over Australian bubbles. And, again without discussion, went to their separate lodgings in separate taxis.

At eleven-thirty next morning, having written the letters and addressed them to all the societies listed in *Roots & Branches*, plus one or two more, he was in the hotel lobby posting them when the desk clerk said, 'Phone call for you.'

He took it in the booth and Robin said, 'Why aren't you in your room writing letters?'

'Just posted them all,' he said smugly.

'In that case, can you swim?'

'Yes.'

'For that you get a cool, cool beer. Can you name any of the Sydney beaches?'

'I think so. Bondi. Manley.'

'You win an afternoon off. I was due in court this afternoon and it's postponed a week. Pick you up at noon.'

Robin drove an elderly Morgan sports car in racing green. In the back was an insulated box at which she jerked a thumb: 'The promised cool beer, Mr Pom. And some fruit and bread and some pate.'

'Sounds good,' he said, past the wide smile that felt fixed on his face. He wanted to say 'Looks even better,' but thought he'd better not. But he did, a second later, when the impulse grew irresistible and she said, 'Thank you,' and on the same impulse he added, 'I don't just mean today.' The implications of that kept them both fairly quiet as she threaded her way out towards the start of the southern beaches.

'Can you surf?'

'No.'

'Clovelly it is then. It's no fun being bruised by surf if you're not bruising it back.'

'Surf doesn't worry me. Sharks do.'

'Don't worry. We have nets and lifeguards and watch towers to spot 'em and surf boats to chase 'em off. You'll be all right here. Just don't fall in Sydney harbour itself – that's where the sharks like to lurk.'

They spent an idyllic afternoon. The beach was quiet, the sun hot, the water perfect, the conversation beguiling and easy. The thing that was happening continued to happen. Neither wished to complain.

By evening in New York, after spending hours watching old TV recordings and film, Brother Bill Crombie at last felt he had something good, and he transported it and the small Ampax machine to Zee Quist's office at the Admiral. ABC/NBC/CBS had been happily unhelpful and unresponsive to his approaches.

When the Media director of the Leyden campaign called

the show's producer to protest, he said, 'The candidate was sabotaged.'

'He was what?'

'You have a Republican studio hand, who put the glass too near Mr Leyden's hand!'

'Any more good ideas, Harry?'

'Has to be something like that. Maybe the guy's an Alabama Democrat.'

'Harry, we had cameras running the whole time. Leyden picked up the glass from a yard away. He drank. Then he put it down right where he hit it easiest.'

With that avenue closed, Brother Bill began searching for something he remembered from long ago: John Leyden in the year he won the Inter-Collegiate Singles, pulling off a cross-court finesse on the backhand with all the delicate foot-work of a Gene Kelly and the sweet touch of a Rosewall.

Zee Quist watched it run. Then she said, 'He was twenty years younger. Even on him it shows.'

'If we show it enough nobody can say: Clumsy.'

She said, 'Bill, it's worse. Think of the contrast. People would say: Look at him then – what the hell happened!'

'One minute, Zee. There's more.' He moved the switch on the screen, a man jumped out of the crowd and shook Leyden's hand. 'Hi there, it's real good to know you,' Crombie sang.

'I got the message,' Zee Quist said. 'You planning on doing the voice-over, too?'

'Zee, I'm trying –'

She said firmly, 'He goes on another show and he makes a joke of it. He does a neat trick with a glass of water.'

'What kind of a trick? John doesn't do tricks.'

'We find a magician to teach him. But it's got to be laughed away – it can't be obliterated. The image stays – we just have to make it a nice easy memory of a nice guy.'

'Epitaph for a campaign,' he said savagely.

'Cool it, Bill. It's just a hiccup, so long as we play it cool.'

It was late that evening when Drew Turnbull, Washington man for the *Atlanta Constitution* strolled in to the suite, accepted a drink and said, 'Quiet word, Zee?'

'Sure.'

He closed the door. 'You've heard what Inko's doing?' Inko. An abbreviated form of incumbent, was the buzz-word this time round for the ageing President whose hair remained mysteriously black as ink.

'He's made his horse a consul?' Zee Quist suggested.

'He's going to visit the Ould Sod.' Turnbull said in heavy mock-Irish.

'Takes one to know one. I didn't hear. When was it?'

'I came down on the shuttle with Clemens of his staff. Zee, your boy has Irish blood, hasn't he?'

She nodded. 'A trace of it.'

He looked astonished. 'Zee, a grandfather's more than a trace, for heaven's sake! He's a full quarter Irish. When's John Leyden going over?'

She felt the small shudder pass across her shoulder blades. It was here. Amazing, really, that the question hadn't come to her before. She said, 'It's not that important.'

Turnbull took a long pull at his glass, and moved his chair closer. 'Zee, I won't quote you on that. We're old friends, you and I. But don't ever say it again, not in anybody's hearing.'

'Drew, it's not.'

'Twenty million Irish voters with Irish grandparents, and you say an Irish grandfather's not important. Statement like that could literally cost millions of votes.' He looked at her shrewdly. 'Unless . . . Zee, one thing you're not is a fool. You're smart, always were. So how come you have to say it? You don't believe it – you know Irish blood counts in American elections. Always did, always will. Got something to hide?'

She managed to laugh. 'You mean it? John Leyden? Something to hide!'

Turnbull said, 'Strange things happen. If he's not going to Ireland, tell me, and tell me why.'

'It's simple, Drew. And you're looking for things that are complex. Did you know your grandfather?' Turnbull nodded. 'How old were you when he died?'

'Seventeen. Eighteen, I may have been.'

'So he's important to you. Gave you your first cigar. Took you to see the Braves. John's grandfather died thirty-something years before he was even born. He not only never saw him, he's never seen a photograph. So he's not really very interested.'

Turnbull laughed. 'Never thought I'd see the day, Zee. A Presidential candidate not interested in the Irish vote.'

'The vote, yes. The background, no. Come on, Drew! You know John Leyden – he hates that kind of phoney hype. Wouldn't touch it!'

He nodded. 'You're probably right, Zee. 'Bout that, anyway. Leyden wouldn't.'

She felt the beginnings of relief easing the tension inside her head. 'So he won't go over. That's why.'

He chuckled. 'Nice little story all the same. First candidate in a century not to woo the Irish vote. Yep, I may do that. Tell me, where's he stand on Northern Ireland?'

The relief evaporated instantly. Turnbull was serious and influential. The piece he wrote would appear and be noticed and quoted. Zee Quist said, 'He thinks the best hope lies with Europe.'

'With the Common Market – the six?'

'I think it's ten now, Drew,' she said delicately.

'And the North as a separate nation, sovereign status. All leading to a US of Europe?' he said.

'It's a bloodless solution. He thinks too much has been shed.'

'He's not the only one. And his grandfather died how many years before he was born?'

'Thirty-odd. I'll phone you the number. Matter of fact, I think it's in the handouts.'

'Sure,' said Drew Turnbull. 'And we have a good stringer in Dublin. I could put him on it.'

10

The paint-job on Robin van Geloven's little plane shone bright red in the sun at seven a.m.

'Actually, she's blush pink,' Robin told Todd, 'to match a lipstick. And her name is Raelene – after Raelene Boyle who was also a sweet runner.'

'You said a syndicate of four. Do they all wear blush pink lipstick?'

'Only the girls. Two of us, two of them. The men wear blush pink baseball caps.'

Todd and Robin were at a smallish airfield north of Sydney and she was unhooking the plane from its ground ties. A few minutes before, Todd had accompanied Robin as she filed a flight plan for Brisbane.

'Mudgee and Narrabri? Bit out of the way,' said the controller.

'Got a Pom here,' she grinned. 'Have to show him a bit of the outback.'

'If he whinges, leave him there, eh?' the controller said jovially. Then he became serious. 'You're single-engined. Are you equipped?'

'Twelve gallons of water. Salt tablets. One week's supply of emergency rations. Flares, smoke bombs, medical kit, emergency transmitter, anti-venin.' She ticked them off on her fingers. 'Knife, fork, spoon, twice. Matches and fire extinguisher, stove and paraffin blocks for it. Spade, hatchet, cigarettes. Bottle of medicinal brandy. Tent, burn cream, insect repellent. Inflating splints.'

He raised a hand to stop her. 'Your little Piper lift all that stuff?'

'All that and us, plus a couple of blokes as podgy as you!' she said.

Soon they were climbing on course and as she throttled back at eight thousand feet and adjusted the trim, Todd said, 'Anti-venin?'

She glanced at him, eyes merry. 'If it wriggles or crawls, we have it in Australia! Tiger snake and taipan are as deadly as anything in the world. We have a couple of tricky spiders, too. Ever hear of the funnel web?'

'Faintly.'

'Killer,' she said. 'You get bitten, you'd better have the serum quick. Otherwise . . .' cheerfully she mimed a cut throat. There was a pause. 'Mind you,' said Robin van Geloven, 'I've lived here twenty years and never seen any of 'em, except in zoos.'

'That's a relief.'

She laughed. 'Rule is, careful what you pick up, and careful where you sit down. What do you think of this flying machine?'

'Well, it's smaller than the 747.'

'It's an upgraded Piper Cherokee,' she said. 'Real hot rod. Constant speed prop with variable pitch. Continental flat six engine – plus something special to appeal to all Poms.' She waited.

'I have to ask. What is it?'

'That's the way the dialogue's written. This here continental engine is built under licence by Rolls-Royce!'

He tooted an imaginary trumpet. 'You a Pom, too?'

'No, Mr Pom, I'm not. My dad married Madge's sister. He was Australian, she wasn't. I was born here. Went back to England as a kid, then came out for good twenty years back.' She pointed down. 'Look.'

For a moment he could see nothing; then he spotted the movement as a large bunch of kangaroos hopped away from the plane's flightpath, obviously disturbed by engine noise.

Sydney to Brisbane is a little more than six hundred miles. Their posted route added a few more. Just before one o'clock she called the control tower and began losing height. At five hundred feet some kind of bird flew into the prop and dissolved in a cloud of blood and feathers. It was all too rapid for either of them to identify the bird, and Robin was plainly upset. 'Damn it,' she said. 'I hate doing that.' And a moment later. 'Pitch is jammed.'

She got the Cherokee down comfortably enough, taxied to a parking stand, then got out quickly to look at the propeller. 'Have to get this seen to,' she told Todd. 'Mind going alone?'

Todd had already arrived at a state of mind in which going anywhere alone was a great deal less pleasurable than going with Robin. 'Yes,' he said.

'I'll wait for you here,' she said. 'Try not to be long.'

He took a taxi to Woolloongabba.

Hearing the taxi stop and the door slam, Crespi crossed quickly to the window, hiding himself behind a dusty net curtain to watch as Todd paid the driver, opened the gate and approached the door. When Todd knocked, Vaccaro answered, pistol in hand, keeping it half-hidden behind the door.

'Come inside. Stand over there. Hands raised.'

Todd, astonished, obeyed.

'What's your name?' Vaccaro demanded.

Todd said, 'Where's Mr Dooley?' It was his first sight of a handgun in a hand prepared to use it. 'I'm here to see Dooley.'

'Name?' demanded a second voice.

Two men. Two men had sought him at the Airport Sunset Motel – two men whom Mrs Riley had said looked Greek or Italian and gangsterish. This pair certainly fitted the description.

The man behind him jammed something against Todd's spine and said, 'Stay still.'

The other began fishing in Todd's pockets. The first, the breast pocket, yielded one of Todd's cards.

'It's him,' Vaccaro said to Crespi.

'Good. I'll make the call.'

Todd angrily demanded, 'What the hell is all this about?'

He received no reply, until, abruptly, Vaccaro said, 'Turn. Keep the hands high.' He was made to move towards the old hardwood staircase. 'Stop. Open that door. Now down the stairs.'

It was pitch dark, but behind him a light switch clicked and a bulb came on. Clearly he was descending to some sort of cellar. From somewhere he heard dogs barking and wondered how the two men had managed to subdue Dooley's mangy pack. A door faced the bottom of the stair and Todd was instructed to open it and go through. Behind him, as he did so, the door was quickly closed, and he heard the noise of bolts sliding home.

'It's you,' said Dooley's well-remembered voice.

The old man sat on his haunches in a dark corner of the cellar, and Todd said, 'What's all this about, do you know?'

Dooley cackled. 'Said they won't hurt me. Don't know about you, though. You're the one they want.'

'But why?'

'Who knows. But they've been here waiting for you three whole days. And I've been down here three days, too.'

'I don't understand at all,' Todd said.

'Kept me down here three whole days!'

'Didn't tell you why?'

'Said they were waiting for you and did I know you?'

'So the message to come here came from them?'

'Nope. From me. 'Spect you know why they're wanting you. You just aren't saying.'

'Not true,' said Todd. 'I haven't any idea.'

'Maybe they want the same as you.'

Todd said, 'The log, you mean?'

'Well you want it. Enough to travel a thousand miles and more to get a sight of it. Why wouldn't they want it?'

'Because they don't know anything about it.'

'It's valuable – and they're crooks,' Dooley said reasonably. 'Said they'd feed my dogs. Don't know if they have.'

'Plenty of barking,' Todd told him. 'But distant.'

'In the yard. I've a wire pen out there. Can't hear 'em down here.'

Todd said, 'Have they asked you about Bully Jack Breeze's log?'

'Nope. Never mentioned it.' He gave an odd, cackling laugh. 'You want the log. They want you!'

Gently Todd asked, 'Why didn't you want to show it to me?'

'Didn't? Don't is more like it.'

'Obviously it's important to you. I understand that. Will you tell me why?'

'No.'

'It's important to me, too,' Todd said. 'There's a name, a member of the crew. I sent you the list, you remember – the Crew List.'

Unexpectedly Dooley said, 'It was good of you, that was. Surprised me, after the dog ran at you and all.' After a moment, he added hoarsely, 'There's things I can't let you see.'

Todd looked at him. In the dim light, a tear glistened in the corner of Dooley's left eye. He said, 'I'm only interested in one person in that crew.'

Dooley nodded. 'Connor. You told me.'

'You said he wasn't aboard.'

'Didn't want you here,' Dooley said. 'But you sent me the Crew List, didn't you. You've got me under an obligation now.' There was a kind of rusty catch in his voice, and as Todd watched the shadowed face the tear detached itself and slid downward into the stubble of Dooley's cheek.

'Who was the man Deeley?' Todd said softly. 'Was he your great grandfather?'

'Grandfather,' Dooley murmured. Then his manner changed. 'How do you know about him? I said, how do you know?'

'It's one of the names on the Crew List. I thought the names were similar – Dooley and Deeley.'

Dooley was silent for long moments, his eyes flicking this way and that. Todd let the silence hang. Finally Dooley said, 'You won't, will you?'

'Of course not.'

'You promise?'

'Promise what?'

'Won't tell nobody!'

'About Deeley?'

Again the long pause, as Dooley's mind surveyed some inner conflict. This time, of all things, a sob punctuated it, and then the words came. 'Said he was poxed,' Dooley said. 'Right there. In the log. Poxed!' That swine Breeze. Nobody ever knew, you see. Dad didn't. Mum didn't. I don't.'

Todd said, 'It said suicide. That was entered in the Discharge Particulars. Suicide – off Colombo.'

'Drove him to it,' Dooley said. 'Must have drove him, way I see it. There's three entries. First says "Have examined Deeley and believe him infected with the pox." Second says: "Am confining Deeley to quarters for fear of spreading pox." The third says: "A.B. Deeley jumped over the side at 11 a.m. in full view of deck crew. Must have been crazed by pox."' Tears were running down his cheeks. 'My dad was in Dublin then, a year old. It takes a long time for a man's brain to be affected. They went to doctors, but they were poor people and nobody ever confirmed it. My dad came to Australia out of shame, and I've lived here in shame.'

'That's why you had to have the book, then – so no-one would see?'

Dooley nodded. 'Won't matter when I've gone. It can go to the museums, then. You see, don't you?'

'I see,' Todd said. 'And you have my promise. And I'm sorry it worked so badly for you.'

Dooley drew a handkerchief from his pocket. It was grey with grime; he wiped away his tears, his own face looked greyer. He said, 'Bad voyage, that. A bad one.'

'For others?'

'Four died,' Dooley said. 'Four. One a woman. The luck was bad.'

'Where's the log now?'

'Upstairs. I have it in the pedigree room.'

'Your breed dogs?'

'Used to. Daren't breed kids so I bred Airedales. I gave it up, finally. Airedale's properly a big dog. Big as a German Shepherd. But the show people keep wanting 'em smaller, so I gave up. Take in strays now, that's what I do. Got sixteen, now, one kind and another.'

'Will you let me see the log where it refers to Connor?'

'Let you see the whole thing if they ever let us out.'

Todd looked round the cellar.

'Don't trouble yourself,' Dooley said, understanding. 'No way out of here except the stairway.'

Todd said, 'One of them two said he'd have to phone somebody else.'

'Makes sense. Blokes like that must work for somebody. Don't work at jobs, not blokes like that!'

Reasonable again, Todd thought. Dooley was certainly odd and more than a little crazy, but he was nobody's fool. It was simply that a few words written a hundred years back had unhinged him. Strange, the power old records sometimes had. Here was a case of the sins of the fathers visited upon the children and Dooley was the promised third generation.

But why did the men upstairs care? Not about Deeley/Dooley. They seemed unconcerned about him, but about Connor? If it was Connor they cared about. Perhaps it was Todd himself! But he could see no justification for it – no possible, no conceivable reason, however remote. His head was stuffed with random bits of information, but it was difficult to see how any of them could matter to the point of firearms and kidnap and incarceration in cellars.

He wondered when somebody would come to ask him questions – there could be no other purpose in holding him than to question him, surely? And presumably their questions, when they came, would answer his – must answer his, indeed, because then such questions would signpost the nature of the bloody mystery. As he sat brooding, it occurred to him suddenly, that he was not scared, and had not been scared even when he first saw the gun. The absence of fear worried him – a little, at first, and then more. Could they, even now, be going for Robin?

Four hours after Todd's departure, Robin van Geloven had flight-tested the newly repaired pitch variation mechanism, had eaten lunch by herself in the airport restaurant, and had waited an hour for him, leaning against the Cherokee's fuselage. Gradually her foot had begun to tap irritably at the concrete hard standing.

It couldn't take three hours, surely, to look at a few pages of Captain Breeze's log. Such books, and she'd seen plenty, were not as a rule very lengthy.

'So where are you, Todd, you drongo?' she spoke aloud and blushed, unnecessarily because nobody was near enough to hear. Come to think, she didn't know where he was. Woolloongabba, he'd said, and that was near the cricket ground, but . . .

Hold it, she told herself, this time keeping the thought firmly inside her head, hold it, he is an adult; he can look after himself; he'll come along in a taxi in a few minutes.

He didn't. An hour went by. No Todd. Miss him, she thought, almost angrily. He's not here and I miss him! But I can hardly start looking for him. Or can I? Man wouldn't like that, would he? Any man. So what do you care about men's feelings, Ms van Geloven? She smiled to herself. In the case of Todd, it seemed, quite a lot.

She listened absently, still smiling a little, as the over-loud tannoy in the terminal pumped its announcement in echoes across the field. An AVA flight in from Adelaide and Sydney. As she listened her eyes followed a small white van driving towards the departure entrance. The words Airport Sunset Motel were painted on its side. That, she thought, is where Todd got the message. She set off, walking briskly across the terminal, and there approached the waiting driver. He was about twenty, a big, healthy cheerful youth who shrugged and said, 'Don't know, ma'am, I'm only temporary till Mr Riley's back on his feet.'

Something in his tone made her ask, 'What knocked him off his feet?'

'Mrs Riley said he ran into a door,' the lad said. 'Maybe he did, but he must have run into it fast.'

First, two men had come to the motel looking for Todd, she thought. And now the owner had run into a door. She said, 'Can I have a ride to the motel?'

The lad grinned. 'That's what the courtesy bus is for, ma'am. But I have to wait for passengers off this flight.'

She nodded. The three came through quickly, businessmen with pilot bags of the kind that slipped under the aircraft seat and cut out the wait for baggage. Within twenty minutes she was at the motel talking to a patently-nervous Mrs Riley.

'I can tell you nothing,' Jean Riley insisted. 'He just walked into the edge of a door.'

'Just the address,' Robin said. 'The one you gave Mr Todd.'

131

She saw the fear that suddenly appeared in Mrs Riley's eyes, and said, gently, 'You told him. He told me.'

Mrs Riley blinked at her. 'But they said –' and she stopped and clamped a hand over her own mouth, staring at Robin.

Robin said, 'You gave it to Mr Todd. I'm his –' and hesitated – solicitor? 'I'm his solicitor' would sound like a suit for damages coming up. She said 'his girl friend.'

Mrs Riley blinked again, then nodded. 'If anyone asks, he told you – Mr Todd did.'

'That's right. Tells me everything.'

A wan smile. 'Oh no, he doesn't. They never do. It's on a bit of paper pinned to the wall in there.'

She returned to the airport in the courtesy bus, tipped the protesting boy and went in search of a policeman. It was a thin tale to tell, but she'd just have to be convincing. She was sure something was wrong.

'Somebody called Bondi, Mr Crombie.'

It was a codeword. The Australian contact, calling direct, as promised.

Brother Bill snatched up the phone. 'What is it?'

'The man you wanted us to locate, we located him.' The voice was soft and quietly-spoken, yet clearly audible over all the miles.

'Where is he?'

'Guest, at the moment, at a house in Queensland.'

'Will he see me?'

A quiet laugh. 'You can be sure of it.'

He hung up. It was a hell of a trip to make, but he'd long reconciled himself to the need. When they pinned Todd down, Crombie wanted what Todd had got: all of it. Todd was a walking bomb as far as the Leyden campaign was concerned.

Australia, though, was a full twenty-four hours' flying time away – a little more, given the change of plane necessary to get into Brisbane. Crombie buzzed his secretary.

'Yes, sir?'

'I'm going to be away for seventy-two hours. Maybe a day more, okay? And get me Continental Airlines.'

'Can I make the booking for you, Mr Crombie?'

'No thanks. I'll handle it.'

'Your address while you're gone?'

'I don't know. You don't know. Remember that.'

'Yes, sir.'

Continental's service was into Denver, change planes, and out again to Honolulu and onward.

In anticipation of need, a visa had been obtained three days earlier, quietly, from the Embassy in Ottawa for William Crombie, aged 46, bank employee resident New York City, on vacation to see friends. The cynicism of that stated purpose did not strike him. His mind was on Leyden, who that day was neck and neck in a newly-published Harris poll, with Lewis S. Jackson. Not a point separating them as front runners for the Democratic nomination in July. His brain was anchored on Leyden – and on Todd.

'You prove any of this?'

Robin van Geloven shook her head. 'All I can prove is that I'm an admitted solicitor. You'll have to take my word for the rest.'

'Look,' said the policeman. 'Why don't I get someone in a car over to the motel to make inquiries?'

'Because they won't talk. They've been threatened, I'm sure of it.'

'They talked to you.'

'Mrs Riley let me have this address, that's all. Very reluctantly.'

The policeman scratched his head. 'Don't see how I can help you, Miss.'

She nodded and abandoned him in favour of a phone box. Yellow Pages . . . the list of solicitors . . . whom did she (a) know, and (b) know to have genuine clout? Her eye ran down the list. Bruce Franklin, that's who – her contemporary at university, Bruce played international class amateur golf, some of it with the Prime Minister! But Bruce would now be out on the course; this was a Saturday afternoon.

She was right: Bruce was on the golf course. Accompanying him was a radio phone attached to his golf cart. Robin was speaking to him within three minutes, though she had to hold a further three while he played his shot.

'Sorry to keep you, Robin. Had a nasty, tricky chip.'

'Play it well?' she asked.

She heard his laugh. 'Sank it, me old darling – and won twenty dollars. What can I do for you?'

He'd charge a hundred and fifty an hour in consultations, she thought. More, probably. She explained the problem.

'What d'you want?'

'A police car and one or two men to knock on the door.'

'You're not imagining things?'

'No.'

'And you're in full possession of your senses?'

'As much as I ever am.'

'At the airport?'

'That's where I am.'

'Stay there.'

Time was going. Still no sign and no word of Todd. Even if he returned they'd be flying back in darkness, not that that concerned her much. The real problem of darkness was that it would shroud Sweet Gum Avenue, too. It was ten minutes before a police patrol car came, but it was giving solid evidence of intent with flashing lights and siren going.

At the end of Sweet Gum, another car awaited them: no flasher, no siren, but the paint-job unmistakeable. Robin van Geloven felt she was taking part in a scene from a movie, the whole thing uncanny.

The cars moved down the road and stopped. The two men in her car got out, opened the gate, climbed the few steps to the door, knocked and waited.

Nothing happened. No reply. She saw them shrug.

The other crew went round the back. She had been instructed to remain in the car, but had the window down, to hear.

'Seems deserted,' one man called.

A busy neighbour arrived, intrigued by the police presence. He reported a Holden parked at the back for three days, and departing a few minutes earlier.

Robin said, 'Break the door down. He's in there.'

The police crews declined.

She said, 'I'm a solicitor; I know the law and I'm prepared to face the consequences. Lend me a prise bar.'

'Why?'

She grinned. 'I've a nail in my shoe.'

'Well in that case . . .'

She marched up to the door, jammed the bar tip between door and frame and began levering.

'Hey, miss, that's breaking and entering!'

She nodded. 'The bloke who gave me the crow bar is an accessory. Let's find Mr Pom.'

'Who?'

'My boy friend,' she said. She found the door came out easily, this time; and a few seconds later she also found Todd and Dooley in the cellar.

The house was otherwise empty, apart from the sixteen dogs out the back.

Charges? said Todd. Yes, he'd lay charges if the men were found. And yes, he'd recognize them. No, he had no idea why he and Mr Dooley had been held prisoner. What did the two of them have in common? Why, just a mutual interest in the voyages of a nineteenth century sailing skipper. He'd only called upon Mr Dooley to look at the sailing skipper's log.

Half an hour was more than enough for the reading of 'Bully Jack' Breeze's log. Few names appeared in its pages: primarily it was an account of sea miles covered, with Breeze's pleasure shown when the number was high, by an exclamation mark, and when it was low by a black asterisk. But there was inevitably, references to discipline and death. Among the former, Connor's name equally inevitably figured:

'Cargo hatches off for ventilation,' Bully Jack reported. And the next day:

'Three men drunk on reporting for duty: ABs Roberts, Heseltine and Connor. No liquor issued since Tilbury. All deny being drunk.'

And the next day:

135

'Had the drunken ABs up before me. All continue to deny having taken drink. But I have evidence of eyes and nose and they were plainly intoxicated. Ordered each tied to Spanker Boom by irons four hours.'

A week later, Connor was ill with diarrhoea and Capt. Breeze 'gave him castor oil and laudanum though I don't like wasting good remedies on scrim-shankers.'

He gave the same remedy to an unnamed female passenger a few days later 'and no better for a second dosing, poor woman. The look of her is not good.' She then got a different treatment 'as the diarrhoea turned to dysentery I dosed her with ipecac. No improvement.'

Meanwhile Connor was back on sick parade 'with a small rope burn. Applied lampblack and sent him aloft. A loafer, Connor.'

Then came the first of the deaths:

'Passenger Jane Taylor died today of dysentery. Read burial service and committed her body to the sea.'

Lady Eliza was off Ceylon when Breeze recorded Deeley's misfortune and death, 'Turned the ship to search,' Bully Jack reported, in a hand clearly shaking with rage. 'Lost four hours sailing in good winds. No trace found of A.B. Deeley.'

A seaman died in a fall from the high spars, another was swept overboard in a storm. *Lady Eliza* reached Australia, and Connor deserted, presumably cured of diarrhoea, but forever marked by Bully Jack's lampblack.

It was a small enough contribution to Todd's research, but he noted it all and thanked Dooley. 'You reckon those blokes'll come again?' Dooley asked him as they waited for a summoned taxi to arrive.

It was Robin who said, 'Mr Dooley, you could give the log to the Historical Society, sealed for the remainder of your life. If they ever come again, and if they want the log, then you haven't got it and they can't get it. How about that?'

Dooley smiled the first smile Todd had seen on that lean gaunt face. 'It's safe like that?'

'As houses,' Robin said.

'Nobody can see it?'

'Not if it's sealed. Mr Dooley, I'm a lawyer. I'll draw up the conditions.'

Dooley's smile vanished. 'I can't afford lawyers!'

She said, 'No charge.'

They did not talk about the day's drama until they were in the Cherokee and alone at eight thousand feet in the velvet night. Then it was talked through and through again.

'What I don't understand,' Todd finally said, 'is how you guessed anything was wrong.'

She said, 'I didn't guess.'

'What do you mean?'

'I knew.'

'What did you know?'

She laughed. 'That you were in trouble.'

'I'm always in trouble of some kind.'

'Not that kind. And you don't often have me around, either.'

'That,' he said flatly, 'is a pity.'

She turned her head and met his eyes. 'It is, rather.'

'We'd better do something about it.'

'True.'

'Soon.'

'Yes.'

Below them the Pacific fussed at the eastern edge of the continent; a narrow and continuous band of surf that shone up towards them like a white and luminous string, glittering at intervals with clusters of lights. She named each little town as the Cherokee overflew it. Even with the Rolls-Royce Continental Flat Six hammering away on the other side of a flimsy bulkhead they were in a private world, sharing a relaxed and easy companionship.

Robin broke the spell. She said suddenly, 'There's New-castle!'

He stared at her. 'So?'

'Newcastle,' she said patiently. 'Go on – ask me!'

'I'm asking. Tell me.'

'I'm not Madge's niece for nothing, you know.'

'Tell me, for heaven's sake!'

'What do you know about Newcastle?'

'It's a port,' he said. 'Coal mines?'

'Coal mines, yes. And a dangerous harbour when the wind's wrong. And – come on, beg!'

'I'm begging.'

'And a coal trade with California in the eighties and nineties of last century!'

'Connor went to California from here?'

She nodded. 'It's likely. Regular traffic, regular ships to Portland and San Francisco.'

'Australian ships?'

'In the main, yes. The coal trade didn't last because the Americans found coal in the West, but for a while it was busy.'

'Crew Lists?'

'You'd better look and find out.'

'Coming with me?'

'Try and stop me.'

'It's Sunday tomorrow.'

'We'll have to do something else!'

'Why,' Todd said, 'am I wearing this idiotic smile?'

'You, too. Must be lack of oxygen.'

'Or something.'

'Something,' she said.

The euphoria persisted through the landing, through the several-times-interrupted process of securing the Cherokee to her tie-down rings, and through a car ride kept decorous by heavy traffic.

At Robin van Geloven's flat a bad blow fell. Robin played back her answering machine and learned of a cable. Madge had suffered a severe stroke.

She telephoned at once and spoke to Madge's harried house-keeper. 'How is she, Bess?'

'Conscious, but there is quite extensive paralysis. And, Robin, the outlook isn't good.'

Robin said tightly. 'Look after her. I'm coming over.' She hung up and turned to Todd. 'She's all I've got and I'm all she's got. I have to go.'

'Poor old Madge,' Todd said. 'Give her my love. And if she can drink it, give her champagne from me.'

138

He phoned the airport while she packed a bag. British Airways and Qantas flights both left mid-afternoon, but there was a late departure from Auckland, New Zealand and a connection if they moved quickly. He booked her on it. Hell of a flight, he thought: Fiji, Honolulu, Los Angeles. Possibly quicker to wait for Sunday's direct flight. But Robin would sooner be on her way.

At the airport she said, 'Three things. First, use my flat. Here are the keys. Second, don't forget Newcastle.' He waited. She was looking at him in a strange way.

'What's the third thing?' he said.

'This.' She kissed him once, hard, and walked quickly away.

11

—◆◆—

Carlo Crespi knew the Texas Tavern. He did not know its phone number, but he did know now that Todd was staying there.

Or had been staying there, because when he phoned and asked for Todd's room number he was told: 'I'm sorry, sir, Mr Todd checked out.'

'Oh.'

'But he's due back.'

'When?'

'Tomorrow, sir.'

'Thanks,' said Crespi. Someone else was also due tomorrow: the top bloke from the States was flying in, and he wanted Todd. Why tomorrow, damn it? Crespi demanded of an unfair Providence. Why not tonight?

In fact Providence was being especially unfair, for Todd returned shortly afterwards to the hotel rather than to Robin's flat, and was soon busy on the telephone. In the hour or so since he had left Robin at the airport he had decided the time had come to at least try to unravel the mystery, and to find out what the hell was going on before somebody decided to kill him. Accordingly he had placed a call to Hamilton News Inc. in Boston, USA.

'Person to person?' asked the operator.

'Yes. To Mr James Hamilton.'

He listened to assorted clicks and clunks as the circuit was completed via cables and satellites. Then the operator was back, voice wary. 'Mr Hamilton is not . . . er, just a moment.'

More clicks, then an American voice. 'Who is calling Mr James Hamilton?'

'My name's Todd. I'm doing some work for him.'

'Oh yes. Mr Warwick Todd?'

'That's right.'

'I'm sorry. I'm afraid I have to tell you that Mr Hamilton is dead. I'm Miss Hayes, the chairman's secretary.'

'Dead! When?'

'Last month. He was killed in his car.'

'But I had a letter . . .'

'He received your letters, too. Except the last one, Mr Todd. I have that here.'

Todd said, 'I'm very sorry to hear it. But the job is half done. Should I continue?'

'If that was his instruction, Mr Todd. And if you wish to.'

Todd hesitated. 'Tell me, Miss Hayes, do you know if anybody else is involved in this inquiry?'

'Why do you ask?'

'Because some strange things have happened. Very strange.'

'I'm not sure. I could try to find out.'

'Thank you. If you could, I'm staying at the Texas Tavern Hotel in Sydney, Australia.'

With the call finished, Todd went to the bar for a beer, and sat brooding over it. Hamilton dead! No, not just dead, killed – in his car. Hamilton killed, then; himself a prisoner, and, if not a prisoner for long, at least under threat by armed men. Armed man, moreover, who knew his movements; who knew he was staying at the Airport Sunset Motel; who knew he'd be at Dooley's house in Sweet Gum Avenue; who . . .

Christ, would they know he was here – at the Texas Tavern. Could they know?

No point in standing still to find out. He abandoned his beer and went to the desk.

'I'm checking out. Could you give me the bill, please.'

'Yes, sir. Oh, Mr Todd – did you get the message?'

'No.'

She glanced behind her, and took a slip of paper from the key rack. 'Yes, here it is. There was a call late this afternoon from a Mr Hamilton in the United States.'

Todd felt his mouth drop open. 'From Mister Hamilton?'

'That's right. He said he wanted to see you over there, as soon as possible. Not to telephone, he said. He won't be there for a day or two.' She looked up, smiling. 'You all right, Mr Todd?'

141

'Yes.' With difficulty Todd hoisted up his lower jaw. 'Late this afternoon?'

'Yes. Must have been six or so. Took it myself.'

Todd paid his bill somewhat absently, his mind trying hard to comprehend: about Hamilton, about his presence being required in Boston, about a bunch of thugs who seemed always to know where he was. It had long been clear that there was more to Joseph Patrick Connor than met the casual eye. The question was what it was? And he'd think about that somewhere else.

The trouble with Robin's flat was that it was all Robin, and seemed to mourn her absence and ache for her return. Dominated, as it was, by a large and immaculate desk, and by long shelves of books, many of them legal volumes, the flat was not especially feminine. Yet she was, and for all its practicality the place reflected her personality in many ways. Feeling like a cross between a burglar and a peeping Tom, he looked at her books, her records, the pictures on her walls. In his mind's eye he saw her sitting at the desk, standing at the window, putting on a Sutherland record or looking at a Nolan print. The feeling of criminality returned as he helped himself to a beer from her refrigerator. Her kitchen walls bore pictures of ships.

Finally he plonked himself in what was clearly Robin's favourite chair, and tried to think. The trouble came down to two things: first, who; secondly, how? An hour of hard speculation got him nowhere, though it must have set cog wheels turning somewhere because he awoke smartly at four o'clock in the morning, climbed off the couch on which he was sleeping (to sleep in her bedroom would have involved a degree of intrusiveness of which he was not capable) and took his document case to Robin's desk.

'Marriage certificates,' he muttered, hunting through the stacked papers. 'Specifically . . .' The name thrummed in his head. There was one Jane, possibly two . . . but a Taylor? And where else had he seen . . .?

Now he had them. Joseph Patrick Connor marries Elaine Mitchell-Hands . . . No . . . marries the Hon. Euphemia Percy . . . emphatically no . . . marries Mary Ellen Emmett, Dublin . . . No again, because the man was a barrister-at-law

. . . Marries Jane McLeod . . . at Rhyl . . . that was the bigamist . . . could it be? . . . married *Jane Taylor*, Bristol!

'Gotcha!' Todd said aloud, reading greedily at the marriage certificate. Jane Taylor, spinster, of the parish of Filton, had married Joseph Patrick Connor at Bristol Register Office, November 2nd, 1876.

And been buried at sea a few months later, by Bully Jack Breeze in person! No doubt it was with the ship blasting along, all sails set and padlocked in place, that they dropped Jane over the side, neatly sewn up in canvas.

Zee Quist, watching the early news on TV knew that suddenly the game was opening up wide. 'The President has just announced that in the summertime, and on a date just before the Republican convention, he is to visit with his cousins in Ireland at the birthplace of his Irish ancestors, the tiny village of Kilroran in County Cork.'

She gritted her teeth and heard it through, complete with its characteristic one-liner about the Irish tourist in Washington who asked a Democrat the way to the White House, and the Democrat said 'More Government spending, more . . .' There'd be a zillion press and TV men over there, following the President, and they'd do a deep, deep dig into John Leyden while they were about it.

She picked up the phone and called Brother Bill Crombie. Not here, said his secretary.

'Not here? Where is he? Has he seen the morning news? You don't know, for Christ's sake! Okay, get him to call me. Yes, it is Ms Quist. And it's urgent.'

She slammed down the phone, then stared at it thoughtfully, and called again. 'When you say, Joanna, that you don't know, do you seriously mean you don't know where he is?'

'He's away for a couple of days, Ms Quist.'

'Is he though? He didn't tell me he was going away. Did he tell Mr Leyden?'

'I don't know Ms –'

'Joanna, what is this? What did he say, exactly?'

'Just he was going away for a couple of days.'

'A couple. Today the first?'

'He said three, maybe four, Ms Quist.'

'Where?'

'He didn't tell me.'

'Joanna, has he got some girl stashed –?'

'I don't think so.'

Zee said suddenly. 'Did you book the air ticket?'

'No, he did it.'

'Right.' She tried his law secretary (Joanna was his somewhat grandly named political assistant), then she tried one of his partners, one of his sisters and was tempted to try his mother but decided against it. Involving Helena Crombie might cause family embarrassments for John. His mother would want to know all. Instead Zee Quist finally telephoned John Leyden himself, campaigning in upstate New York. He didn't know either and said merely, 'He's a big boy, Zee. If he needs a couple of days off, it's his business.'

'Sure,' she said. Instinct had a grip of her. It told her Brother Bill was up to no good. Instinct further insisted, perhaps because of the morning's Presidential news, that it had something to do with Ireland, with Grandpa Connor, and probably with the genealogist – Todd.

She wheeled her chair over to the picture window and smoked a cigarette. What could have happened that she didn't know about? Todd's new material always came direct to her via Hampden & Bradford's facsimile transmission machine, and there'd been nothing there. Todd's bills and credit card payments?

A minute later she spoke to Miss Marion Hayes.

A minute after that, she spoke to Charles Mason Kemp at VisitingCard.

'Sure, I'll talk to the airlines,' he said. 'Anything else?'

In an hour she knew Brother Bill was Australia-bound, flying Continental.

What she didn't know was his purpose. Todd was there already. Was Brother Bill, on his sneaky, secret trip, going to try to bribe Todd, or simply have him killed?

Captain Andrew Rabbett reasoning that his American employer, willing as he was to pay $1,000 for every original document referring to Connor; and demanding, as he did, that all documents referring to Connor be destroyed, and by himself at that, was requiring more than could possibly be delivered, had developed a gadget.

Certain official record documents could undoubtedly be stolen. Others could not. Photocopied yes, stolen, no.

Which left destruction. And the trouble with destruction was that if it had to be done in the archive, Rabbett had to do it. Not the American gentleman. So no $1,000.

Ah, but . . . Rabbett had reasoned further. Suppose I were to produce for him a photocopy which demonstrated clearly that the entry, if not the document, had been entirely destroyed, or rather eradicated. Then he would surely be satisfied.

Rababett went to a chain stationery store and asked for a bottle of ink eradicator, a product he had used with success as a boy on school reports.

'We don't stock it now,' he was told. 'Don't get a call for it.'

Another stationer agreed, and thought, in fact, that ink eradicator was no longer manufactured. Tippex was suggested. Rabbett said no, and fell back upon his own not inconsiderable powers of invention.

He obtained a large, felt-tipped marker pen, prised it apart and washed all the ink away. He then applied the felt tip to a sheet of clean, white paper until no colour showed. At that point, he used a pipette to refill the pen's reservoir with a much diluted sulphuric acid.

At that point, the pen dissolved into a small puddle of hissing plastic.

He began again. This time with hydrochloric acid. This time his little kitchen was swiftly filled with vile and heavy fumes.

Nor was nitric acid any more suitable; not, that is, until he switched pen manufacturers and employed the metal body of a Japanese-made marker. This time a dilute solution of nitric acid proved very satisfactory.

Having spent much of Sunday morning trying to work out what was going on in what seemed to be an increasingly convoluted world, Warwick Todd began to think about sea water and sunny beaches. He also thought about Robin's car

– the elderly and clearly-beloved Morgan in British racing green. To drive it would not be right, he told himself firmly, and rented a baby Ford from Hertz. He drove south until he found a place to park, then changed into swimming gear, bought some anti-burn lotion, anointed himself, and stretched out in the sun.

'Jane Taylor,' said something in his head. 'Jane Taylor. Jane Taylor. *Jane Taylor!*' He sat up, frowning.

Poor Jane had been Connor's wife. Dead long before Bully Jack and the *Lady Eliza* came to Australia. Dead at sea. Travelling, though, not as Connor's wife, but as a passenger, while her husband worked as crew. All that was simple enough; as was the fact that such an arrangement would save a lot of money.

Jane Taylor . . . Jane Taylor . . . Jane Taylor.

He stared at the thudding surf. It seemed to drum the name at him as it hit the sand and rattled back. *Jane Taylor.*

There was something, must be something. His mind was trying to make him bridge two pieces of information, but the bridge wouldn't build.

Too damn much of that, lately – thoughts that hovered tantalisingly and then backed off. His head needed clearing, that was what it needed. If someone would keep an eye on his clothes . . .

Someone would: a cheerful family busy five yards away with a barbecue.

Todd came out of the water twenty minutes later feeling refreshed, but still baffled. He reclaimed his possessions, checked his watch and wallet when he decently could. And thought: money okay, credit cards okay.

Credit cards?

Christ, yes – credit cards!

Realization came swiftly after that. Whoever was on his trail was able to bend the rules in big banking corporations. Which meant powerful influence.

And he'd used his VisitingCard at Hertz today.

He returned the car, walked fast through the hot, quiet streets into the park, and there dodged about to shake off any possible followers before returning to Robin's flat. He found

146

the makings of a salad sandwich and brewed some tea and tried to reason it out. Only two things emerged: he must stop using the credit card, and he must get out of Australia.

Neither should offer difficulty; he still had traveller's cheques and his airline ticket.

But there was still Newcastle. He'd intended to go to Newcastle next day.

And still could, damn it! He had a feeling about Newcastle, just as Robin had had an intinct about him. Perhaps she had some special gift that was rubbing off on him?

Which was a pleasing thought.

In far off New York, that Sunday morning there were no cheering thoughts for Zee Quist. A restless night's contemplation had further convinced her that Brother Bill Crombie would stop at nothing to prevent Todd's researches interfering with John Leyden's chances of becoming President. Had he really arranged for Hamilton to be murdered? He had never denied it, or even seemed to care about her allegation. And his whole demeanour on the question was *wrong*. If John went into the White House and Brother Bill accompanied him, there woud be an instant flavour of a decade ago, a brimstone taste of Nixon and Dirty Tricks and Plumbers. Maybe not everyone would taste it, but certainly Zee Quist would.

She'd once teased Crombie that he'd even kill her, just for knowing. In the bleak hours of the night, even that seemed not impossible. Brother Bill's face often had its brutish moments. And there was absolutely nothing she could do to stop him! He had the contacts, the ruthlessness – and a mobility she couldn't begin to match. No way Zee Quist could go zipping off to Australia.

Was there nothing she could do to stop him?

Her mind felt leaden and unresponsive. She used her father's old trick to jolt it, taking cubes from the icebox and rubbing them on her wrists and elbows and the back of her neck, finally dropping them down her back inside her nightdress. Think, damn you, think! Ask the questions and answer them. Start at the beginning and keep it simple. The melting ice sent a shudder across her shoulders.

Okay, question one. Why would Bill commit murder?

Answer: to keep a secret. How about that?

Why keep the secret? Answer: if it gets out it damages John Leyden and his chance at the White House. Right? Right. How much damage? Not as much as a murder if that got out. Can the secret be kept? Maybe. Lots of sweat and suspense. Permanent danger, and Murphy's Law applies in full. If the damn thing leaks, it leaks inevitably at the moment of maximum embarrassment.

Next question: Is defence the only answer? Can we attack? Only in Bill's way – only violence. You sure of that, Zee? Instead of zonking with the queen, how about a little move along the side with pawn or rook? How about a flanking movement? Well, great, if there's one to be made. Is there? Her gaze wandered, seeking help among the familiar objects of her home, passing, and then returning abruptly to a framed cartoon on the wall of a nineteenth century gentleman with a large nose and a tall hat. She looked at him seriously: this one was the one who whipped Napoleon. 'Publish and be damned!' – that's what Wellington would have said. *Had* said, in only slightly different circumstances!

Ridiculous! You couldn't say publish-and-be-damned in America today, not with the rampant media, not in the middle of a Presidential election, you couldn't. Could you?

Statement: if everyone knows the secret, well, there's no secret any more. Right?

Right.

If she leaked it . . . what then? Well, then, Brother Bill could actually stop being paranoid and take a constructive part in the campaign!

And John? What of John Leyden?

Ruin, probably. Political disaster. Or an end to the threat? Pay your money – take your pick.

She wheeled herself to the bathroom, worked her way by various handbars and a seat that slid, until she was sitting in her special, high, tailored tub, and letting the warmth of water soothe her as she considered the piece of treachery she had just devised.

It would hit John: hit him hard. Mercy, his wife – it would hit her, too. Forty years and not a stain on his life. Nor on hers. Never a speck on the white suits.

He could stand one speck, surely. For the sake of stopping Bill – and stopping, therefore, what could develop.

It took half an hour to implement the decision. Half an hour of clumsiness and difficulty to get out of the tub, dry her wasted body, powder it, put on the dressing gown.

Then she was writing. On plain paper.

The letter was only two paragraphs long, and it was not signed. She made a copy in her own hand.

The envelopes she addressed to:

> Senator Lewis B. Jackson
> The Capitol,
> Washington, DC

Jackson was joint front runner. And to:

> The President of the United States,
> The White House
> Washington, DC

It was just possible, she thought, that one man or the other would refuse to stoop to this kind of trick; that one or the other would be too honourable and idealistic.

Not both. Oh no, not both.

'Last thing we knew, he was where?' William Crombie asked bitterly.

'Cheap hotel in King's Cross.' The contact was a businessmen of American-Italian ancestry, the son of an American soldier who had settled – and prospered greatly – in Australia after World War Two. 'He was there twice. Checked out twice.'

'Could be back.'

The contact shook his head. 'He knows now. We had him in Brisbane, and had to let him go when the cops showed up. He's alerted now. He'll be hard to find.'

'The card,' said Crombie.

'If he uses it.'

'Why shouldn't he?'

'He'll work out how people know his movements, and he'll stop using it.'

'Maybe he can't,' Crombie said. 'Maybe he has to use it. Either way, I want Todd found.'

'We're doing our best,' said the contact.

Todd caught the early train on Monday morning from Sydney for the hundred mile journey to Newcastle, with its quarter-million population, its steelworks, its dicey harbour, and its library in the War Memorial Cultural Centre. The library, though excellent, handed him one disappointment.

Newcastle's old marriage records were in Sydney, as were births and deaths.

But when it came to shipping . . .

'Portland or San Francisco,' he was told. 'Usual stops at Fiji or Honolulu.'

'Why stop?' Todd wanted to know.

'Because it's a long way,' the librarian said. 'These were coal-burning ships. Not fast – and it's more than six thousand miles to the West Coast of America. At six knots or so that's six weeks at sea. All the sixes, that's what they used to say. So men got tired, specially the men stoking the boilers. Ships used to put in for a rest. Just a day or so.'

Todd returned to Sydney early, took himself off to the New South Wales Registrar-General's offices on Bridge Street, and began a search of the marriage records for 1894, 1895 and 1896. Connor had arrived in America probably in '96 as a married man. By the end of the day, however, it was clear he had not married in New South Wales; the quarterly records did not include the name of Joseph Patrick Connor.

With a wasted day behind him, Todd returned to Robin's flat, switched on the Recorda call machine, as he'd promised he would, and found a message from her office that some box-number mail had arrived in response to the newspaper advertisements. It had been posted and should arrive at the flat next morning.

'So,' Todd thought, 'the day wasn't wasted after all.' Mail

meant there was something positive, otherwise there'd be no point in writing.

He telephoned Robin at Madge's home in Greenwich, thinking as he waited for the call to connect, how uncannily the world had shrunk in a hundred years. Six weeks to America then, a couple of minutes to London now.

'Hello?'

'It's the Pom. How are you, and how's Madge?'

'I'm fine. Bit tired. Madge is hanging on. Not much to be done, though – it's all drugs and patience.'

He told her his theory about credit cards and she chuckled. 'Get rid of it, Mr Pom. Hey, put it in the post to Des Bigley – his address is in my book in the desk.'

'Why?'

'He's a dirty little drongo. I defended him twice and he won't pay my fee. Got him off, too. He'll never be able to resist the temptation. He'll go out on a bender with it.' Then she said, 'But it's time you got out.'

'I will when I've picked up the mail tomorrow.'

'Somebody answered?'

'So I gather. Your office left a message.'

Robin said, 'I'm waiting on in London. See you when you get here. Okay?'

'I'll be along.'

'Make sure it's soon.'

In his characteristic way, the President dispensed poison with a smile of utmost geniality. At his weekly Press conference, providentially-timed, he sang a couple of lines of Mother Machree, knowing every TV station coast-to-coast would play and repeat it. Then he said, 'I can't tell you all just how proud it makes me to know that I come of good, solid, honest Irish stock.'

The White House Press corps, knowing him well, did not miss the slight but definite stress upon the word 'honest.'

'Sure they were honest, Mr President?'

'Sure enough. There's people – candidates, even – be glad to have my ancestors instead of their own.'

'Who, Mr President?'

'Now, boys.' He raised his hands shoulder-high and grinned in the familiar posture. 'That's enough. I can't say more.'

'Which candidate, Mr President?'

'Well, he's a Democrat.'

'Lewis Brewster Jackson?'

'Now, you know as well as I do,' said the President in mock remonstrance, 'that Senator Jackson comes from a dozen generations of Virginia gentlemen. Plantation owners, they were. Fought for the South'. 'The words 'slave owners', unspoken, nevertheless hung in the air.

'Leyden? How 'bout John Leyden, Mr President. He had an Irish gran'pappy as I recall.'

'Did he?' said the President, suddenly businesslike. 'The name I'm thinking of is Connor – Joseph Connor. A dangerous, wicked Irishman. There aren't many like that, thank God. And none in my family. But he was a bad one.'

'What did he do?' It was almost a chorus.

'Terrible things,' said the President, 'things that I don't care to have soil my lips.'

He was alone in that. Within hours, Connor was on everybody's lips and John Leyden was being interviewed on a special simultaneous hook-up to all three network evening news programmes.

Zee Quist waited through the introduction, through a repeat of the President's casual hatchet-job. Since the story broke, there had been time only to talk a little on the phone, to give Leyden the rough outline of his grandfather's life, as far as it was known.

'. . . and so tonight,' the moderator of the TV question session intoned, 'we come to a position unique in this country's political history, in which the traditionally-loyal Irish Democratic vote could be swung by this revelation to a Republican, to the incumbent President, himself claiming strong family links with the Irish Republic.'

And then it began.

'Senator Leyden, what do you know about your grandfather?'

Leyden in a mid-grey suit, blue shirt, blue tie, sober and

tidy, neat but not dressy, said, 'Until today all I knew was that he was a soldier, that his name was Joseph Patrick Connor, and that he came to this country as an immigrant.'

'Did you know him.'

'No,' Leyden said. 'He died thirty years before I was born.'

'You know he went to prison?'

'I didn't. I've now been told.'

'And you've been told why?'

'Yes. Ladies and gentlemen, let me say this. I don't know the source of this information, but like you, I heard today that he was guilty, in Britain a century ago, of dreadful crimes.'

'First you heard of it?'

'It certainly is.'

'How did you feel when you learned that your own grandfather was a convicted rapist and child molester?'

'I'll tell you,' Leyden said. 'The first I felt was a kind of indignation. I mean, that kind of news shouldn't come as a surprise, not to a man my age. Not about his family. The second thing I felt was worry –'

'About the election?'

Leyden shook his head. 'About heredity. All those Bachs were musical. You get gifts passed from father to son. I wondered about that kind of behaviour. But my father was okay. So am I. I've arranged for copies of my last medical report to be available for all news media.'

'Drew Turnbull, Atlanta, Mr Leyden.'

'Yes, Mr Turnbull?'

'If you don't mind my saying so, you're kind of a mystery man.'

'In what way?'

'We've all of us known you for twenty years and more, Senator. We remember you as a tennis player, we remember you in Vietnam. We've seen you in the Senate. But your background is still remarkably obscure.'

'Obscure?' Leyden frowned. 'Never occurred to me, but okay, maybe it's fair comment.'

'Will you explain to this nation about your family? I meant, it's not just your Grandfather you didn't know?'

'No,' said Leyden, 'it isn't. And yes, I'm glad of the chance and happy to explain. Gets a little complicated, but here goes:

153

'My grandfather Connor came to America with his wife in 1896. Came from Australia. As far as I ever knew, until this morning, anyway, he was supposed to have landed somewhere on the West Coast – San Diego, Los Angeles, San Francisco, Portland, maybe even Vancouver, BC. Nobody knows, because there's not too much in the way of immigration records out in the West Coast.

'He came from Australia. We know that. Before: well, he was born in Ireland in 1851; he joined the British army, then he went to Australia. That's all I knew.'

'You're prepared to swear you had no knowledge of his criminal record?

'Absolutely none at all, I promise you. If I'd known, I'd have told you. You know me. I believe in disclosure.'

'Why are you concentrating on the Connor history – what about the Leydens, that's a complicated story, too, isn't it Senator?'

Leyden smiled a little wearily and raised his hand. 'We'll come to them, I promise. Let me tell you about Connor:

'He came east to New York. Again we don't know how. By train, probably. But really it all starts here in New York, in 1896. Connor and his wife were crossing Fifth Avenue at 41st Street, when they were hit by a runaway carriage – a phaeton and a pair of horses. The driver of the carriage was Henryk Leyden – he apparently liked to do his own driving.

'So – Grandfather Connor was killed. Until this day, ladies and gentleman, it has been thought of by my whole family, as a tragedy. Now it seems that if ever a man deserved God's retribution, he did. Nor was that the end – there was further tragedy to come. His wife was pregnant, and she, too, was very badly injured, so badly indeed she was barely alive after the accident. Labour began almost at once, and she died in giving birth to the baby who became my father.

'Police inquiries later held that Henryk Leyden was not guilty of any offence, or indeed, of any negligence. The official report of the incident says that the horses shied when a firecracker went off, and that they then bolted. But Henryk Leyden ever afterwards felt an enormous burden of guilt. What he did was arrange immediately for the adoption of the baby. He already had four children of his own, the youngest of whom was a baby three months old.

'The adopted baby was given the Christian names Joseph Connor, after his father, at his baptism. He grew up to be Joseph Connor Leyden.

'And if I am to be ashamed of my grandfather, I want to tell you I am proud to be my father's son. But *his* story is well enough known. I must spend time now retelling –'

'Senator, there will be millions of Americans who have no knowledge at all of your father.'
Leyden blinked several times.

'Okay. Briefly, he joined the US Army when America entered World War One in 1917. He was three times wounded and three times decorated. After the war, he studied law at Harvard and graduated cum laude. He also rowed in the Harvard boat against Yale, and in the US boat in the 1922 Olympic Games. He was elected to the New York State Legislature in 1924, aged twenty-eight, and to the United States Senate in 1930, aged thirty-four.

'In that year, he married my mother, Helena Leyden, the baby of the Leyden family into which he had been adopted.

'He was killed in a crash of a Ford Tri-motor aircraft in the Colorado Rockies in 1934 – the year I was born. So I never knew my father, just as he never knew his.

'And that, as I see it, is as far as my mysteries go. My mother married again, three years after my father's death, and she is still married to William Jerome Crombie who is also a lawyer, and was a widower with young children. So I have a half-brother, Bill Crombie, and two half-sisters, Jane and Alice.'

155

Zee Quist, watching the faces of the assembled reporters as the TV cameras roved among them, sensed the tension webbing from the occasion. John Leyden had begun to relax a little as the story was told, and his manner was, as always, so transparently open and honest, that it was all entirely convincing. But it wasn't over yet. She crossed her fingers and muttered: 'God, have I done the right thing?'

On the screen, a woman was on her feet. 'Senator, do you realize how nauseated all women everywhere will be by the news that your grandfather was a sex criminal of the vilest kind?'

Oh, Christ, Zee Quist thought. Much of this and we're in the garbage can.

Suddenly on the screen Leyden's face showed huge. The cameras had zoomed in to very close focus to catch the play of emotions upon the candidate's face. Damn that woman!

Leyden said softly: 'Look, ma'am, if it could all be reversed, I'd reverse it. If by not being born I could spare all those girls what my grandfather put them through, then I'd chose not to be born. But I can't – how can I! Is there a way I can make it up to people who lived a century ago. Only, surely, by trying to ensure a better life for those who will be born a century from now!'

Zee Quist thought: 'Well done.'

There was a pause, and then a youngish reporter was up and grinning. 'LeBlanc, *Agence France Presse*, Senator. Now we know about you, will you tell us please about your wife?'

'Leyden smiled. 'What do you want to know?'

'Is it true she is to make a new film?'

'No.' Leyden said. 'It's not true. She retired to look after the kids – and that's what she intends to continue doing.'

'Where is she?'

Leyden's smile broadened. 'Out the back, waiting for me.'

'Bring her on!' said several voices.

Mercy Leyden was a perpetual favourite: the gifted young American ballet dancer who'd become a movie star almost by accident, and had given it all up after two years to marry John Leyden. Their six children were all adopted, all child victims of war: Arab, Jewish, South-East Asian, Nicaraguan.

They made him go and fetch her. She came reluctantly, and

was asked the standard TV question: 'How did you feel when . . .'

Mercy Leyden said, 'I felt he was horrified by the news. Tell you what else –'

'What?'

'I felt lucky to be married to him. I always do.'

On screen the moderator was cut into shot, hand raised for silence, head cocked a little to one side. It was apparent that he was listening to something being said over his earplug. He nodded after a moment, and then said into camera: 'In the last few minutes all three major networks have received hundreds – and across the nation perhaps even thousands – of telephone calls. So far they average fourteen to one in support of Senator Leyden.' He turned to Leyden. 'Maybe Grandpa Connor is good news for you after all, Senator?'

But Leyden was frowning, 'I've done nothing,' he said, 'except tell the truth. I should have found out long ago. All this should be in the record. And there's no way Joseph Connor could be good news for me or humanity.'

Exit John and Mercy Leyden.

Cut to black.

'Hello, Ford's new Mercury . . .'

Zee Quist punched the key pad to end the broadcast, then lit a cigarette. The media world, she reflected, as she often did, was infinitely treacherous. John Leyden had got away with it – yes, clean away, and the 'phone blitz proved it. And then that idiot confession: 'I should have found out . . . it should be in the record!' The one thing a candidate never admitted: failure to act. *I should have, and didn't.* She sighed. In the President's camp, and in Senator Jackson's, they'd be working already on this free gift. In her imagination she could hear the President's professional line: 'Dilatory. That means he didn't bother to do what even he admits he should have done. Dare we face the Russians with a man who can't even be bothered?'

They were all on a tightrope. John Leyden's great strength was his honesty. But honesty, in the modern world, made a man desperately vulnerable.

12

The morning mail, when it arrived, included a ten by eight manilla envelope addressed to the absent Robin. Breaking Federal law without hesitation, Todd ripped it open and found three more letters inside. All were written in response to an advertisement which had appeared in the *West Australian*, the old-established daily newspaper in faraway Perth.

Todd sat at Robin van Geloven's immaculate desk and slit open the envelopes with an antique brass paper knife. Two of the letters concerned a claim at Kalgoorlie during the great gold strike of 1893. The claim had been won and lost in a game of 'two-up' (two coins are placed one each on the first and second fingers of the right hand, and are then tossed into the air. They can come down two heads, two tails, or one of each. This gambling game is as popular in Australia as craps in the USA) played between a man named Frommer, known as the Dutchman, who won the claim, and one Joe O'Connor, who lost it. The two letters agreed on all details, including the fact that more than £100,000 in gold had subsequently been mined from the claim by Frommer. There seemed no doubt the loser's name really was O'Connor; both letters said he was buried in Kalgoorlie and his name had once been readable on a gravestone there. It no longer was.

The third letter, written in a still well-formed copperplate and by a hand that age caused to tremble a little, read:

Dear Sir,
My father, the late Henry Tremlett, of Perth, W.A., told me when I was a girl many years ago of a man he had encountered on a journey he made, a hundred and more miles inland from Dampier on the north-western corner of our great continent. The man lived among a

tribe of aboriginals and said he had done so for many years. He further claimed he was their king and had several wives and many children. My father said there were several pale-skinned children in the tribe.

My father said also that the man's name was Connor, and that he boasted to him of being a convict runaway. He was possessed of a firearm, and used it to rob my father of all his tobacco and money, and much of his food.

My father said the man called himself King Konna, but told him his name was truly Joe Connor. He knew nothing of the recent discovery of gold; and when told of it said he must travel to Kalgoorlie and get his share.

My father was himself a strong and self-reliant man of little learning though a prospector he was accustomed to a hard life out of doors. But even he said of Connor, 'I never saw such a rough. He'd kill a man for four pence.'

I have no evidence of any of the above, though my memory of my father is strong. I hope this is of assistance to you.

Yours truly,
Elizabeth Wallis

Todd read it a second time, scarcely believing the words. The memories of old people can be, often are, among the genealogist's most fruitful sources, but they usually need to be delved into with much care and taken with a pinch or two of salt. To receive an item like this one virtually out of the blue gave Todd a prickly sensation somewhere between his shoulder blades. He had an increasingly strong superstitious feeling that in his investigations into J. P. Connor (dec'd) he was using up several decades of luck. In pure gambling terms, there never was even the smallest chance of learning what had happened after Connor-the-convict escaped. Todd thought: I wouldn't have bet a penny against a thousand pounds that anything at all would have come to light. Yet it had. Connor, rapist, child molester, convict . . . Connor had left more and deeper footprint's in time's sands than most men ever do, even if some were in obscure places. In a way, Todd felt as though he were looking at a great tapestry, with history in every scene

159

and Connor in every scene, too. Connor taking the Queen's shilling, Connor the bad soldier, Connor lurking in bushes and springing out at terrified girls, Connor flogged, Connor in gaol, Connor aloft on Bully Jack's ship as the sails were spread . . . it went on and on: Connor the convict, the escaper, the King of an aboriginal tribe. Ending with Connor bound for America – yes, and bound, too, for his grave, via the hooves of runaway horses.

Todd had left Robin's flat and was walking down the stairs towards a breakfast in some fast-food joint or another, when a thought struck hard at him. Connor in America had had a wife. Connor in Australia had not – apart, that was, from a handful of aboriginal women whose standing in law would provide problems for a bench of judges in the unlikely event the matter came before them.

So Connor must have left his tribe and gone to the gold fields. He must have met a woman there and married her. There, too, he must have accumulated enough money to pay for a passage for two to America.

On a boat that sailed from Newcastle, New South Wales?

And Connor was in Perth, three thousand miles away, with a wife and a need to travel across the continent to catch the coal boat! Also the journey would take him into areas where he was a wanted man, a dangerous convict, still on the run for all his years of freedom.

What's more, Todd thought, half-admiringly, Connor must actually have managed it. Connor would have been a bastard in just about every sense of the word, but he was indubitably a resourceful bastard.

He bought a newspaper from a little shop as he hunted for a place to eat, settling finally for the coffee shop at a large and so defiantly anonymous a hotel that the menu bore the name *Coffee Top*, but no indication at all of which hotel it was part.

Defeated by the mystery, and waiting for the waitress, Todd opened his paper, and took in that Broken Hill Pty Shares Reach New High, that West Indian Quickies have Australia Reeling Again, and scandal of Candidate's Convict Grandad.

His eye moved on, and swiftly back. Convict grandad? He scanned the story. *Connor*!

Christ! Connor was the grandfather of Senator John Leyden. And Senator Leyden didn't deny it.

'What would you like?' asked the waitress, approaching noiselessly across the carpet as Todd gaped at the paper and tried to cope with the questions that instantly massed in his mind.

He glanced up at her, thinking: I'd like to know what it's all about. But he said, 'Coffee, rolls, fruit.'

In a suite in the Boulevard Hotel, midway between the business district and the night club area of King's Cross, William Crombie, half-brother of Senator John Leyden, was also ordering breakfast. In his case it was from room service.

Like Todd, having ordered, he opened the *Sydney Morning Herald*.

Like Todd, he was instantly and profoundly startled by what he saw. He was also appalled. He was horrified. A moment later he was furiously angry, vowing vengeance – aloud – upon whoever had leaked the secret.

Who was it?

As he read the story again, his brain seethed with his fury. Somebody had crapped on the whole campaign! Well, somebody was going to pay.

Who? Hardly anybody even knew!

Himself or Zee. Hamilton, yes. But Hamilton was safely dead. And Rabbett.

Knock, knock. Come in. Your breakfast, sir.

He poured coffee for himself and strode about the sitting room, cup in hand, almost beside himself with rage.

But Rabbett didn't know! Rabbett had never known who Connor was. Rabbett knew only that records of Connor's existence were to be erased. As far as Rabbett was concerned, Connor was merely somebody dead a hundred years, an inconvenient ancestor, whose existence had to be denied.

He picked up the phone, gave the number and waited, gnawing restlessly on a roll.

'Zee?'

She was not yet in bed, not yet asleep, but anxious to be both. She was sitting in her wheelchair, a large Scotch whisky in her hand, trying to summon up the strength to begin the horribly difficult and awkward process of changing from day to night wear, of washing herself, of getting to bed.

She was exhausted to the point where there was a danger of falling asleep in the wheelchair; not that it was dangerous to fall asleep – just that a day of pain followed, as previous and bitter experience had several times demonstrated.

'Zee? Zee, is that you?'

Bill, she thought wearily. 'Hello, Brother Bill.'

'Are you okay? You sound plastered!'

She said, 'Spoken with characteristic charm and concern. I'm tired, Bill. It's been a hell of a day.'

'Jesus, Zee! Have you seen the papers?'

'Seen 'em, coped with 'em, wished 'em goodnight. Thought I'd wished everyone goodnight. But I might have known, might I not? There's always dear old Bill – I should have remembered. You mean you've just seen it?'

'In the morning pap –'

Zee Quist laughed sardonically. 'Morning papers, Bill? Been a day and a half in bed, huh? Who de chick?'

'I'm in Australia, damn it.'

She said in a bright, social voice, 'Are you really, Bill? Must be so nice now, all the sunshine and everything. Do bring me a stuffed koala!'

'Who did it, Zee?' His hard voice came carving through the chatter. 'Who was it?'

With equal harshness she said, 'I haven't had time to find out. Too busy picking up the pieces. Alone, may I say, because Senator Leyden's distinguished adviser, his distinguished brother, the authority on foreign affairs, is walking on the ceiling with some broad in Australia!'

'Cut it out, Zee.'

'The arguing? I'd like to. I want to sleep, Bill, more than I want anything. What is it you want?'

'I want to know who told the Press.'

'The President,' Zee Quist said baldly. 'And before you ask, I don't know who told the President. The FBI, maybe, or the

CIA, or NSA, or the Secret Service. Or maybe it was the IRA or Charlie Chan. If I have a minute tomorrow, remind me to run a check!'

'Knock it off Zee. This thing isn't funny. We may look like we're standing up but we're dead!'

'You may be standing up. I'm sitting, the way I always sit.'

'It's over, Zee. Like I said, we're dead!'

'You mean John's dead? Senator Leyden. The next President of these here United States? That who you mean, Bill? Because I'd say he's very much alive. I'd say he did damned well on TV last night, and the last I heard, the phone-ins were fifteen to one in his favour. He made one hell of a substantial ghost. Good night, Bill.'

'Look, Zee –'

She said, 'Come back, my hero! It's time to wave farewell to Miss Australia and help carry the goddam load!'

The click in his ear was very final. Final and frustrating, for the rage still boiled inside him and it needed an outlet.

Todd! he thought. That's who told the President, the Press, everybody. Todd – the architect of the troubles! Todd who couldn't be found, Todd who was here, somewhere quite close by, probably. He could be the guy who'd tried to blow John Leyden out of the water.

And failed. That was the amazing thing. If Zee was right and John Leyden had got away and was running free again, it was one of the modern miracles.

The hell with you, Todd.

Except . . . Todd didn't know! Like Rabbett, Todd hadn't been told, right from the start. And nothing Todd had sent back had indicated that Todd had the remotest knowledge whose slimy trail it was that he trod in so relentlessly.

Meanwhile, what game was Zee Quist playing? Bill Crombie had walked wide of Zee since his youth. In those days she would beat him level on the tennis court, in the classroom and down a ski slope, for all his extra weight. So could half-brother, John Leyden, and she was John's girl, then – engaged to be married, the two of them, and Zee had insisted she didn't want the marriage, not as a cripple. John Leyden hadn't wished to end the betrothal, but had had no option. Zee had announced from her wheelchair that it was over, announced it to TV cameras and assembled reporters in a famous quote. 'I won't be his burden, I'll be my burden.'

But Crombie had always wondered. Zee was strong, tough-minded, competent or better at everything she did. Always challenging. Had that public statement been yet another challenge – had she really meant: over-rule me – don't take my 'no' for an answer?

Leyden, ever the parfit gentil knight, had conceded gracefully, remained single for a dozen years, and only then married Mercy.

So – Zee Quist as traitor?

He pondered it only a second. She'd served John Leyden constantly over the years. Friend, support, counsellor, bridge player, critic. Betrayal now? Not in a zillion years.

Come to think about it, maybe it didn't matter. Given Leyden's easy, natural relationship with both the TV camera and the audience beyond, it was perfectly possible that he'd come out of this sewer smelling of roses. And if he could work that kind of trick, the White House was there for him.

Brother Bill decided to go home. Todd could do no further harm. Nor could Rabbett. But Zee could. Zee could say to John: 'Guess where Bill was when the flit hit the turbine blades?'

'At work, I imagine.' John always imagined the best of people.

'No. He was in Australia, of all places. With a girl.' (To John, you didn't use words like chick or broad.)

Surprise from the candidate. And forgiveness enough to set teeth grinding. And a doubt, forever rooted, and about reliability.

Back. Before Zee poisoned the well. He sent a telex to his mother's private office to let her know he would be back from his 'vacation' in a day or so.

It was a matter of purest coincidence, but also of record, that while seat 9B in the first-class cabin of the *Air Pacific* jet was occupied by Mr William Crombie, US citizen, place of residence, New York City, seat number 28C in the rear tourist cabin was being sat upon by a Mr Warwick Todd of London,

England. Had the former known of the latter's presence on board, there would have been a dangerous rampage down the aisle and much angry interrogation. As it was, both men travelled undisturbed in their differing degrees of comfort.

Todd, justly nervous now of interception, had decided to avoid the British Airways and Qantas flights. If somebody was on the lookout for him, those were the planes that would be watched. A simple telephone inquiry told him that his Sydney-London business-class return ticket could be readily exchanged for a wide variety of tourist-class flights via all sorts of unlikely places, from Tokyo to Bali to Noumea and Honolulu.

'Air Pacific go into Los Angeles,' said the girl's voice on the phone. 'You could stop over in Fiji and Honolulu. Or just the one. Or neither, if you're in a hurry.'

'Fiji and Honolulu?' Todd said.

'Yes, sir.'

'I'd rather like that, thank you.'

So Todd, gazing down now at the grey Pacific was thinking idly of very large, very muscular men, their heads topped with clouds of frizzy black hair, who played Rugby football fast, excitingly and barefoot. He reflected, too, that the coal ships from Newcastle NSW to California had called at Suva in Fiji.

He intended to do the same.

When the *Air Pacific* flight dropped gently on to the tarmac at Nandi Airport, on the Fijian island of Vikti Levu, Todd found that, though both taxis and buses to Suva were available, the distance to the capital – 132 miles – made the journey slow, expensive and impracticable compared with the twenty-nine-dollar shuttle flight over the central highlands.

Within an hour and a half he was checking into a downtown motel with a tempting name: The Courtesy Inn. The pretty Indian receptionist smilingly lived up to the name and pointed him in the direction of Victoria Parade and the Government Building. Ships dotted the harbour, big and small: inter-island schooners, fishing boats, trading ships, and among them a great white P & O liner, making a call on its round the world cruise. Fiji, he reflected, was little more than a speck in the vast spread of the Pacific, but like Connor, it had left famous footmarks on history's beach. Tasman had been here. After the *Bounty* mutiny, Captain Bligh had navigated through in his open boat, not landing out of justifiable fear of cannibals, but heading on to more long weeks of privation.

But Connor – had he been here?

'Can you operate in London?'

A soft laugh. 'London? You kidding – in London everybody's a crook.'

Brother Bill gave the name, the address and the instructions. He was in Los Angeles, with only minutes left before his New York flight. He caught it easily and with a sense of relief.

Captain Andrew Rabbett found that in practice the device he had invented worked beautifully. He was rather proud of it – and of himself, too, for thinking of it. All that was necessary was a slow pass of the acid-filled pen across either page or parchment, and then a little patience. Soon the paper (or parchment) and, of course, the words appearing on it, began to vanish.

It had been necessary for him to begin at the beginning, which was tiresome but hardly difficult. The copy documents he had found hidden in Todd's filing cabinet made the chase simple. All he had to do was to go to the place at which the record was held, and there ask for and destroy the reference to Joseph Patrick Connor.

Strangely, the birth record held him up – until he discovered that the long-ago fire in the Irish record office had done the job for him.

Some people were, naturally, less trusting than others. The regimental museum at Enniskillen Castle was trusting. A lady with beautiful manners simply handed him the muster rolls and told him, 'Sit over there where you won't be disturbed.' Nor was he, as he unrolled the rolls, passed his pen over any entry relating to Connor, then rolled them up again, each one now burned through by acid at some point along its length.

At St Catherine's House, however, where access to records

of Births, Marriages and Deaths in Britain are housed, the visitor is not instantly struck by the trust on display. There is efficiency, there is assistance, there is much activity; but the seeker does not get his hands on the actual record. A duplicate is prepared, somewhere behind the scenes, and handed over upon receipt of payment. The prospect of trying to destroy records there had made Rabbett's forehead crease with anxiety as he lay brooding and planning in his bath. But a careful check of all Todd's copy documents finally convinced him that none came from originals lodged in St Catherine's House. And the Public Record Office, from which came papers had a general attitude which was a great deal more liberal. It also had a bespectacled viper in its dusty bosom in Rabbett's feminine catspaw, Miss Annette Hutchinson, whose known obsession with *Middle-Class Marriages of the Eighteenth Century* and the PhD it was intended one day to earn for her, provided sound cover for any kind of nefarious or destructive activity within the PRO.

But Annette was very deeply shocked – and not for the first time – by his suggestion.

'But Andrew,' she gasped, 'you can't!'

'I don't have to,' Rabbett said, 'because I know a lovely lady who'll do it for me, don't I?'

'But why?'

'Muns,' he said, rubbing thumb and forefinger together in a gesture so universal that even Annette Hutchinson knew it. 'Quite a lot of money, actually. Won't be a bit of bother for you, either. Now, drink up and we'll go somewhere nice – did I ever take you to the Trat?'

'No, Andrew.' The frown vanished. Annette was pleased, as well she might be – previously he had taken her to a Chinese restaurant in Euston, and that only once.

She rose and said, 'Really, I ought to go home and change, if we're going somewhere nice.'

Rabbett looked at her. She could change clothes a dozen times and it would make no difference. Only a miracle could affect enough of an alteration to make her attractive. He took the acid pen from his pocket and popped it into her handbag. 'No need to change,' he said. 'You look splendid as you are.'

He handed her the bag. 'I'll explain what that little gadget does while we're eating.'

'How's Madge?'

'Making progress, to everybody's surprise, including the neurologist's.'

'Champagne,' Todd said firmly. 'Best medicine for anybody, but Madge especially.'

Robin said, 'That thought's not original. Quite a lot has arrived from sundry sources. Madge could bathe in it. Where are you?'

'Suva.'

'You reckon J.P. left traces there?'

'I think he could have got married here. Haven't found him yet, but I live in hope. Another day will tell me yes or no.'

'Then home?'

Todd said, 'I'm flying on to San Francisco from here. Something I want to do – if I can. Then home.'

'What is it you want to do?'

'Tell you when I see you.'

'No messing about, now,' Robin said warningly, the Australian accent suddenly more marked. 'Somebody's playing rough, remember. Get home. Promise me.'

'I will.'

She laughed. 'That particular promise comes later, Mr Pom. What airline are you flying?'

'From here?'

'From San Francisco. I want to meet you.'

'All right. I'll fly the flag. British Airways.'

She laughed. 'Qantas is safer. Let me know when.'

He hung up grinning. Something about her seemed to make him want to smile all the time, and the prospect that it might continue in to the infinite future was wonderfully beguiling. On the other hand, she was a high-priced lawyer in a boom economy, on the other side of the world, and he was a record agent in a decaying one. She wouldn't want London, and he couldn't earn a living in Australia. Problems, he thought.

But the grin was in place as he went to sleep.

13

Todd had a friend who was given to saying that national stereo types were nonsense: that the French reeked not of garlic but of *le whisky*, that the Italians had the best manners in Europe and the English the worst, and, most particularly, that Americans were anything but free and easy. 'They're bureaucratic as Germans,' he'd say frequently, 'maybe more so. American rules aren't there to be broken or even relaxed.'

Upon this, on his first acquaintance with America, Todd felt bound to agree. He was on the ground, in transit, at San Francisco airport. He had a message he wanted to send. And he couldn't send it.

'Ain't one in the transit area,' said the Imm. & Natz. man, 'and you only got a transit visa. You stay right here till you board your flight.'

Todd went through it again, employing the word 'sir' frequently. 'Sir,' he said, 'at this moment we're standing in one of the world's greatest communications centres. Silicon Valley, I believe, is just down the road, right?'

'Right.'

'Somewhere on this airport, sir, there will be a facsimile transmission machine.' The man nodded. 'I must send a message by it.'

'Use the phone,' said the Imm. & Natz. man. 'Phone's right over there.'

Todd shook his head. 'Not good enough, sir, I'm afraid.'

'It's all you're gonna get.'

Inspiration: 'I'll bet you . . . say, twenty-five dollars eh? . . . I'll bet you you can't locate one before my flight's called.'

'I never bet small.'

'Fifty.'

'Pay me now.'

'How come?'

'There's one at Xerox you can bet.'

He telephoned Xerox and explained. Yes, they could take his message; yes. They could transmit it if he knew the number. But how would he pay?

Todd said he would put dollars in an envelope and the envelope in the post.

Not good enough – hadn't he a credit card? He'd sent it to the crook in Sydney, so no. And Xerox didn't like the other one, the English one.

Ah, but he still had a counterfoil from the VisitingCard. He hesitated, then. What if they traced him – the men who had found him before, probably through the VisitingCard? Well, by then he'd be in England, and they'd believe him to be in San Francisco. The flight was ten hours. They wouldn't trace him in ten hours or ten days.

He sent it to the number James Hamilton had given to him. The FT number allocated to Hampden & Bradford, the Wall Street law firm. All Todd knew was that it was a number. The message read, 'Saw published story. Have further information concerning J.P.C. Will respond, by telephone only, to message placed using those initials in the London *Times*. Todd.'

She had dismissed him from her mind. The message she had read once and promptly stuck in an out-tray. Zee Quist doubted that any further revelations about Joseph Patrick Connor had the power to harm either John Leyden or his thrust toward the Democratic candidacy. Recent public support for Leyden had been enthusiastic to a point close to idolatry. The day after what had become known as the 'I should have known' TV appearance, he had been greeted in the street by a yell of 'Here comes Honest John!' That cry had been taken up. It now greeted Leyden everywhere he went. With a week to go to the Convention, she thought him to be not bomb-proof, but certainly Connor-proof.

When William Crombie put his head round her door that morning, he waved at her a spiral-bound report.

Zee Quist said, 'I'm busy. Go back to your broads.'

'You'll want to see this, Zee.'

'What is it?'

'First digest of the new NYT/CBS poll. Taken Tuesday.' It was now Thursday morning.

She said, 'And?'

He laughed, a hard sound, rackety with triumph. 'Four points Zee. Four in the lead!'

'Over Jackson?'

'Over everybody! In particular over Jackson. Two horse race, Zee, and John's clear out in front.' He walked round the desk, opening the report as he did so, placing it before her with a flourish like a waiter with a big and elaborate menu card. 'See for yourself.'

He watched her absorbing it. She fumbled, without looking up, for a cigarette. He found it for her, and offered a match. While she read, his glance fell on Todd's message on the characteristically smudgy sensitized paper. 'Hey,' Brother Bill said, 'what's this?'

'Doesn't matter.' She barely glanced up.

'The hell it doesn't! When did it come?'

'Not long ago. Sent round from Hampden & Bradford.'

'What's the bastard got now?' It was almost a groan, and this time Zee Quist did look up.

'Forget it, Bill. What could he have?'

Brother Bill shrugged. 'This guy gives me the shakes. Always has – right from the start. Like there's a surgeon digging in your guts, looking for something wrong – that's how he makes me feel!'

She said, 'John Patrick Connor was a pig. Everybody knows it. What else is new – another prison sentence? Who cares!'

'I care. I'm gonna get to him, one way and another. Zee, we can't have him hanging over us like a goddam mushroom cloud!'

'Forget it – stick to broads, Bill. Leave the rest to people who stay with the job.'

He left the room angrily, slamming the door. She looked thoughtfully after him, brooded for a moment, then called her old secretary at Hampden & Bradford.

'Louise, I want you to get an ad in the personal column of the Times. Not the NYT, the London one, okay? Have the

171

account sent to H & B, but pass it on to me. Reads: Block capital letters J.P.C. colon, number seven four three three eight two converts to telephone zero one zero one dash two one two dash two seven four dash seven four one zero stop. Call collect? Read it back please. The numbers are important.' She listened, checked the numbers and said, 'Make that please call collect, will you, Louise? Thanks.'

Somewhere, Brother Bill would be concocting a message of his own, Zee Quist was sure of that. And building some kind of spider's web, too. And sitting in the middle of it, waiting for Todd. For Todd's sake, she hoped her ad was printed before Bill's. But it was a fleeting thought. With a Leyden triumph almost in her grasp, Zee Quist's mind was busy elsewhere.

Having solved the facsimile transmission problem at San Francisco International, Todd had booked himself on to the next London-bound 747. That done, he telephoned Robin at Madge's house to tell her that BA 286 arrived at Heathrow at one-thirty p.m. local time. 'If you're really going to meet it.'

'I'll meet it. What news?'

He said, 'Later.'

'Like that, eh? Okay, put it this way. Is there news?'

'Later,' he said. He could feel the smile pulling at the corners of his mouth.

She said, 'You're a sadist and I'm going back to Australia immediately.'

'Not you. Not until you know.'

'You're laughing!'

He said, 'So are you.'

'Hurry,' Robin said, and hung up.

But it was not either of the advertisements in the personal columns of *The Times* which attracted the attention of three women in three different parts of Britain that morning, for both the BBC news and the morning papers carried prominently the story of an explosion in a flat just off the Edgware Road, close to Marble Arch in London. Because London's explosions tend to be the work of either the Libyans or other Middle Eastern desperadoes, or the work of the Irish, there was a good deal of speculation. One person had been killed, a retired army captain named Andrew Rabbett, who was believed to have served in Northern Ireland.

Annette Hutchinson, who two nights earlier had stayed at that flat, went at once into an almost trance-like state of grief. Dressing-gowned, her hand still upon the coffee pot, she began to moan, and to rock backward and forward on her chair. She was temporarily enclosed in darkness; the one small human illumination that had entered her life, had now extinguished. The coffee pot grew cold as Annette rocked on.

The much anticipated happy smile of greeting was conspicuously absent from Robin van Geloven's face as Todd emerged at last from Heathrow's customs and saw her looking at him, grim-faced. As he moved towards her, she gave a tiny jerk of the head, then turned away. Understanding the movement but puzzled and disappointed, he followed her out of the terminal building, across to the car park and into the lift. At level six she got out. He followed. No one else did.

She had rented a little Ford, and not until his case was in the back and the car was on the move did she so much as greet him. At last he said, 'What is it?'

'You know a record agent name of Rabbett?'

'No.' Then he remembered. 'I know his name. He advertises to Americans. "I'll trace your –"'

She said harshly, 'He was blown up last night.'

'Blown –?'

'Newspaper's on the back seat.'

He reached over and picked it up. The *Telegraph*. Story on page one. So were two pictures: one of the wrecked building, the other of a face. 'Hey, I know him!'

'Do you?' she said it grimly. 'In general, or in connection with –'

'Connor. Yes, in connection with Connor. At least, that man came to my flat just before I went to Australia.'

'Why?'

'To sell me double-glazing, so he said.'

She wound down the car window and paid the parking

charge in silence. When it was closed she said, 'You're staying at Madge's until this thing's cleared up.'

Todd said angrily. 'I don't understand this.'

She glanced at him. 'Neither do I, but I can make a guess or two.'

'Go on.'

'I think it's a dirty tricks department like Nixon's years ago. This is Presidential year and you've pulled the nasty skeleton out of the cupboard.'

'That was me. What did Rabbett do?'

'Rabbett died,' Robin said. 'He's hamburger meat.'

'I mean –'

'I know what you mean. The answer is that we don't know.'

'But what could he know that I don't?' Todd demanded. And was silent for a moment. 'Except . . .'

'Except what?'

'Except what I got in Fiji.' He patted the document case.

'Which is?'

'He got married there, right enough. To –'

Robin said, 'Please wait.' She accelerated into the fast lane of the M4. 'We could be being followed, have you thought of that?'

'Somebody'd have to be slick about it.'

'Somebody cares enough to kill!' She had floored her foot and the little Fiesta was juddering now at over eighty miles an hour. 'How in hell,' she demanded angrily, 'do you know which of a thousand cars is on your tail?' As she spoke, she glanced in the mirror and suddenly careered across all the lanes into the slip road for Cranford. Behind her, affronted cars and trucks braked, wheels and tyres squealing, drivers honking angrily. At the foot of the slip road, she did two fast circuits of the roundabout, her own tyres protesting noisily, then darted off to the Old Bath Road.

Todd glanced at her. 'Who taught you that?'

She smiled but not much. 'I saw it on TV. Starsky did it. Or Hutch. Oh, Mister Pom, I've been standing round that damned airport just worrying! I got a map at the bookstall and worked it out. Now navigate me to Greenwich.' He reached for her hand. It lay on the gear lever and it was trembling.

174

He said, 'Park over there.'

'Why?'

'I want to kiss you.'

'Done.'

Several minutes later, she disengaged herself. 'We're being watched.'

'What?'

'Look!'

He looked up. The boy was about thirteen, and eating a hot dog.

She said, 'Let's get to Greenwich.'

The third woman to be shocked by the sight of Rabbett's face on the front of her morning paper was a bright young archivist at Chelmsford who had assisted Todd and would have assisted Rabbett, too, had he not preferred the crooked-crabwise approach. The local searcher whom Rabbett had abandoned in the Chelmsford pub, had described the incident to her in a rueful way, and when the name of Joseph Patrick Connor had later surfaced in the newspapers as Senator Leyden's miscreant grandfather, the whole incident had taken root in her memory.

She telephoned the police at once, gave them her name, and said, 'The man who was blown up. He came to the Essex Record Office. He was seeking information about . . .' She explained.

Another researcher also contacted the police in the course of that day. Mr Thomas said that Rabbett had once telephoned him, no, he didn't know Rabbett and the call was out of the blue, but the name of Connor had been mentioned.

In the course of the morning, these odd little developments in the case reached the Comissioner of Metropolitan Police, who happened to be having a routine meeting with the Home Secretary, to whom it was also mentioned.

The Home Secretary who had met Senator Leyden several times and privately thought him too damned innocent for any world but that of the nursery, laughed merrily at the notion that Leyden could be involved in murder however remotely. 'Senator Leyden,' he said to the Commissioner 'is clean, believe me. This is the boys from the bogs busy again!'

'Seen this?' Lady Madge van Geloven demanded. She didn't demand with much volume or with great clarity, because the stroke had, at least temporarily, affected both her speech and her left side. Her good right arm waved the *Times*.

Todd said, 'No. How are you?'

'Besser ever' day,' she muttered. 'Itza shambay.'

'I know it is,' Robin told her firmly. 'No more now, though.'

Todd took the paper, looked as directed, and passed it to Robin.

Madge let it be known there was a 'phone in the hall and another in her workroom.

'Hang about,' Robin said. 'What did you find?'

'He married in Fiji as predicted.' Todd opened the document case and produced a photo-copy. 'See for yourself. And look after it – I don't want to have to go back for another!'

Robin laughed. 'We'll go together. It's nice and safe in Fiji as long as you don't play rugby. And I don't. And won't! Now – let's see. Joseph Patrick Connor, right enough. Father general labourer. Did you know that? You didn't tell me about his father.'

Todd said, 'It's a marriage certificate. The most informative thing of all. Father's name and job for both bride and groom, address, job, age –'

'I was just looking at the address. It says "local bures!"'

'Native term. Native to the islands, anyway. I asked what it meant. Bures, apparently, are a kind of local thatched, or maybe tile-roofed shacks. Rough and ready – even more so, I expect, in those days.'

'Okay. He's listed as carpenter, the lying toad! She's a parlour maid. Or was. Okay, let's go on . . . Hey, this is a bit of a coincidence, isn't it?'

Todd said, 'There are two.'

'What – coincidences?'

'Yup. Which did you notice?'

'Where she was born. She was English. Father farm worker. Born – it's that same word again. Bures.'

Todd said, 'In Fiji they say Bure-ays. The other one is –'

'Bures, Essex.' She frowned at him. 'What's that, a village?'

'I expect so.' He looked at Madge for possible confirmation, saw she was dozing and took Robin's arm. 'Out.'

In the kitchen, with the kettle beginning to sing, Robin said, 'Madge is amazing. A week ago they'd given her up for dead. Now the doctor reckons she'll recover most of it – speech, movement, everything. Perhaps quite quickly.'

'Good. I'm fond of Madge.'

'Fonder of her niece, I hope!'

He laughed. 'In a different way, too.' He demonstrated. A minute or two later, he said, 'See if you can spot the second coincidence.'

'Do I have to just now?'

Todd said: 'It was on the plane that I saw it. Never struck me before that. I must have been blind!'

She examined the marriage certificate, reading each detail with care. Finally she looked at him. 'I'm looking for a coincidence?'

He nodded. A couple of minutes later, faced by a shaken head and a smile he found irresistible, he said, 'Try the name.'

'Jane Taylor, daughter of Samuel Tayl –' She looked up at him. 'This is his second wife, isn't it? Wasn't the first – the one who died at sea – wasn't she Jane Taylor, too?'

'That,' said Todd, 'is the coincidence. Odd, isn't it?'

'Important?'

'I don't see how it can be.'

'She was twenty years younger than he was,' Robin said indignantly. 'Yes, twenty-one. He was a dirty old brute of forty – what year was it? – yes, he'd be forty-five.'

'And well-worn merchandise at that.' Todd told her about the letter from Western Australia and Connor's time as king of the aboriginals, as she made some tea.

'Madge, too?' he said, pointing at his cup.

'With Madge, you fill up her glass,' Robin said. 'Doctor McKee says no, or not much and not often, but she's confounded Doctor McKee once.' She opened the fridge to reveal a dozen quarter bottles of Taittinger standing like chilled soldiers. 'What say if she's awake?'

'I say yes.'

They tiptoed in, and Madge at once opened her eyes and inquired indistinctly but comprehensibly whether that was a bottle she saw before her?

She wanted the whole story, and Todd told it, complete with coincidences. Madge sipped champagne; he and Robin drank tea. Twice he thought the patient had slipped into unconsciousness again; twice she opened her eyes as soon as he stopped speaking.

'And that's it,' he said at last. 'The whole villainous story, up to last night's explosion.'

'Last night's murder,' Robin corrected.

Madge tried a longish sentence and her lip muscles defeated her almost at once. She signalled right-handed for the notepad and pencil beside her bed, and scrawled quickly. She waved to Robin to give the pad to Todd.

She had written: "Bures strikes some kind of old chord. Bells ring in memory. Could be warning bells".

He looked at her and she nodded with surprising firmness, then almost instantly dozed off.

They left her sleeping, and retired to the pleasant solitude of the old kitchen. 'How old are you, anyway?' Robin asked. 'You a cradle snatcher like J.P.?'

'Not like J.P.' He reached for her.

She laughed. 'Rum kind of matchmaker, a larrikin like J.P.'

'What's a larrikin?'

'Someone who's up to no good. Like you right now. Time to make that call, like a good boy. Where's the paper?'

Todd wrote out the numbers as she dictated them: 743382. Well, he knew that number. He said, 'That's where the facsimiles go.'

'And the other?'

'Dunno. Read it.'

He wrote: 0101-212-274-7410. Then quoted the advert: 'The first one "converts" is that what it said?'

Robin said, 'It's no puzzle. You have actually used the first number. Now you phone the second. I'd guess it's New York City.'

'Why?'

'Two-one-two is the New York area code. I'm familiar with it. I'd guess oh-one-oh-one is direct dial here to America. That right?'

He checked the dialling code book. 'Right on both counts. You're handy to have about the place.'

She asked, 'How old?'

'Thirty something. You?'

'What's this "something"?'

'Somewhere round the middle. You?'

'Twenty-nine and a bit.'

'What's the bit?'

'Fifteen months.'

'It's a match,' he said. 'Thought so when I saw you in the shop window. Not sure I can afford you.'

'In a three act play,' she said, 'you meet the people in the first act, see the problems in the second and resolve 'em in the third. This is still, Act one Scene Two. Enjoy it – and make the call!'

The call was intercepted. Todd was asked by an American operator what number he'd called and then found himself swiftly connected with a flat, female voice which said, 'Hello.'

'My name's Todd,' he said.

'Mine's Quist. You probably don't know me or it, Mr Todd, but you've been sending all those faxed documents to me.'

'And was it also you,' Todd demanded, 'who had me followed, menaced and locked up?'

He heard a somewhat weary laugh. 'No, it's not. Nor did I kill Mister Rabbett. I've just been explaining that to a guy from your embassy in Washington.' She went on quickly to ask: 'Get any more on Grandpa Connor?'

'Not much.'

'Nothing deadly?'

'Not as far as I can see. Miss Quist –'

She interrupted. 'We have to be sure, Mr Todd. You know what this is all about?'

'The election, you mean?'

'That's what I mean. We've nine days to the Convention. Tell me what –'

This time Todd did the interrupting. 'Perhaps you'll tell me about Hamilton?'

She said, 'He was a campaign helper. I asked him to put a trace on Grandpa Connor. He hired you. I'm afraid he was killed in a car crash. Truth is, Mr Todd, you've always been working for me. Hamilton was really only an agent.'

'And he paid?'

Another tired laugh. 'That's politics, Mr Todd. But you don't have to worry about your fees. What else do you have?'

Todd hesitated. There was so little now to be said: but he knew nothing about this woman, and there was a murder inquiry going on, not to mention other assorted mayhem. He said, 'Who are you and should I know you?'

'Probably not. I'm a lawyer in New York, Mr Todd. My firm's Hampden & Bradford on Wall Street. Currently I'm running the campaign to elect Senator John Leyden next President of the United States. Now, what do you have?'

He said, 'the marriage certificate.'

'They were married, then? I wondered.'

'In Fiji.'

'Date.'

He gave it.

'His wife was –?'

'Jane Taylor. Born in Britain. Nothing known.'

'And you've now got all there is?'

Todd said, 'He was all kinds of a crook. I don't know what happened after he arrived in the United States, but that kind of leopard stays spotty.'

'Nothing happened here – not that we can find. And we've been looking! The fire in 1906 in San Francisco destroyed a lot of records, maybe including his. He's been an embarrassment, Mr Todd. But maybe that's all over. One thing, though, do me a favour, will you? Check out his wife, this Jane Taylor.'

'I was going to, anyway.'

'And if you want a little free legal advice, Mr Todd.' The flat female voice said, 'go talk to the cops before they come talk to you.'

He did, and the cops were fascinated. At Scotland Yard, Todd and Robin were whisked upstairs in a lift and interviewed, once-over-lightly at first and then in detail by a Detective Inspector Hair, red-headed, Glasgow-accented, patient and determined. Hair saw possible charges everywhere. At first, rivalry between Todd and Rabbett might, he plainly thought, have been a motive for murder.

'Mr Todd,' said Robin van Geloven, now Todd's solicitor, 'was in America at the time of death and had been out of the country for weeks.'

Hair moved on. He questioned Todd minutely about the detail of the genealogical search, about the incidents in Australia, the journeys, the credit cards, the payments. Every so often he sent his sergeant off to check something. 'You've not been to your own flat, Mr Todd, not yet?'

'No.'

'Aye, well.' Hair scratched his cheek. 'You'll find one of our laddies outside.'

'Will I? Why?'

'In case of bombs. Went in ourselves just to have a wee look.'

'You didn't find anything?'

'No, but I bet they had a damned good look,' Robin said. 'Right, Mr Hair?'

Hair smiled. 'It's good to be sure.' Then he said, 'Funny lot, these Americans, that ever strike you, Mr Todd?'

'Perhaps. Why, in particular?'

'Oh, it has a flavour, this does. On the one hand you've this Miss Quist – very important lady, she is, not a doubt about it. And on the other, you've violence and potential violence, and criminal activity. And you've the legacy of the Nixon business. You remember, do you, that the United States' Attorney-General went to prison! Yes, himself. To prison. Yet at the same time Nixon was making friends with China. All very statesmanlike and all very rum, very rum indeed.'

Robin said, 'I'm not sure what you're saying?'

Hair rubbed his chin. Stubble rasped against his fingers. 'That there could be a left hand here. And a right hand, too. And the one's not awful sure what the other's about.'

Asked to explain, to elaborate, to elucidate, Hair declined. It was a feeling he had, no more, and mentioned only by way of friendly warning. 'I've a feeling you're not out of the wood,' he said. And smiled for the first and only time as he added, 'Be like the wee Boy Scout – prepared.'

Todd and Robin smiled, too, and said, yes, and said thanks – they'd be prepared.

But they weren't. Not remotely.

14

How many days? Three months ago she could have given the number, snap, just like that, ninety-five, ninety-eight, whatever. Now it was close, so close. But how near – nine, eight, how many?

Okay, eight. Zee Quist tried to relax in her wheelchair, but one of the special properties of wheelchairs is that they are anti-relaxant. She held the infra-red switch box in her hand, not wanting to hear the music, the introduction. The rest of the hoopla. Tonight was Mercy Leyden on her own; a chance for America to see the most glamorous candidate's wife since Jackie.

It was a risk. Leyden himself had been heavily against, even when Zee Quist first had the idea and more so when she advanced it seriously. Waiting now, Zee Quist could rehearse that old argument word for word:

'Zee, that's crazy. Mercy's the most important asset I have, in every possible way. We can't hush her up.'

'No hushing-up, Senator.' She'd called him John for twenty years and more, but he was a candidate now, and maybe the candidate, and quite possibly the President also and for the moment 'John' was wrong and 'Senator' right. 'No hushing-up at all. She's with you all day every day, meeting the people, pressing the flesh, drawing the cameras. What she isn't doing is talking on TV.'

'Zee, I still say that's wrong! Mercy's a very charming and persuasive woman. When she talks, she wins votes, we all know it. Why waste an asset like that?'

'Senator, let me put it this way – your wife is pure magic. She's beautiful, she's good, she's talented, you know all that. Do we let her go on TV daily, till people start yawning and going to make coffee. She's an ace of trumps. What we do is keep her back as long as we can and then, when we need her, we get maximum impact!'

It was bold thinking. Zee Quist, initially, had seen Mercy as a shot in the locker in case the campaign had dipped. But it hadn't dipped; on the contrary, Leyden was out front: five points on both Gallup and Harris polls. Now Mercy wasn't the saviour she might have been. Now Mercy was the clincher.

The anchorman turned and Zee Quist pressed the button. Up came sound.

'Mrs Leyden, you've kept remarkably quiet all through the campaign. Why was that?'

'Well, I've six children to look after, and a barnstorming husband. I scarcely have breath for talking.'

'Nor have you allowed us to meet your children.'

'I grant you that's unfair. But TV exposure's dangerous for children. I don't want them turning spoiled and cheeky and I've seen that happen to kids in Hollywood. But they're lovely – I think so, anyway – and they're here tonight.'

Then they trooped in, all six, in clean jeans and tee shirts, hair washed and shiny and smiling shyly, and they were introduced and interviewed by mom, not the anchorman. It was smooth, easy, the war horror story behind each child shown only in type on-screen, not mentioned. Lim, the boat-child pulled from the sea, was hugely engaging and would, Zee Quist was certain, enchant mothers across America.

The kids then went to an on-screen bar where ice-cream and soda pop was available and refreshed themselves before the nation's eyes while Mercy answered questions. About her screen career – was it totally abandoned? She laughed. 'It never was abandoned. What it is, it's over!'

And so on. John, she said, was an ideal husband, his virtues obvious, his imperfections few. The children adored him.

On screen Mercy Leyden was, as she had always been, luminous. And the camera was kind, the interview kind, the whole ethos gentle and good-natured and human. No loaded questions, no tricks; all was according to Hoyle.

Until –

There were moments to go. Zee Quist reached for a cigarette, heard the interviewer saying: 'Your family's beautiful, Mrs

Leyden. But don't you wish sometimes that you had a child of your own.'

Bastard! thought Zee Quist.

Even Mercy Leyden flashed him a look. Visibly, she hesitated, then she said, 'They're all my own children. All of them.' She glanced briefly away, plainly upset.

'What I meant, Mrs Leyden –'

Mercy interrupted him. 'I know what you meant. You meant, how did I like being barren? Well, I'm not! I shall be having a baby in December.'

Zee Quist stubbed out her cigarette, looked at her telephone and waited for it to ring . . . eleven, twelve, thirteen . . . chirp, chirp: 'Why didn't you let us know, Zee?'

Private matter, she told them one after another. They'd all have been told soon.

What Zee Quist did not say as on-screen the Leyden kids grouped, waving, round their splendid, beautiful, pregnant mother, was:

How could I? I didn't know!

The doctor was sure that an interrupted day would do Madge more good than harm and the nurse was, after all, on the premises. Robin drove her rented Fiesta up the hill to Blackheath, and there on to the A207 road for Dartford. She gave a sudden little shudder.

'What's the matter.'

'That sign. Just the words – Shooters Hill. Spooky. Somebody jumping on my grave. London's spooky all round. We don't have things like that in Sydney. Just sunshine.'

'And sharks, I remember. We go through the Dartford Tunnel, then north.'

In half an hour the industrial horrors of the Thames's north bank lay behind them and now they headed north-east, bypassing Chelmsford, on good, new roads, and her mood passed. The countryside was clean, well-husbanded, but not manicured. The sun shone. Long before Colchester and the A133 for Bures, they were in serious farming country.

Bures. They parked the car by the church, got out and

looked around them. It was either a small town or a large village, hard to tell which.

'What a gorgeous church.' Robin walked up the path to the door. Inside all was cool and quiet and ancient. A little pamphlet about it was for sale for twenty pence: Church of St Mary the Virgin, serving two parishes. Robin, whispering though the church was empty, read out snippets, and splendid old names with the ring of chivalry: names like Fitzranulph, De Cornard, Mortimer of Clare. There was an ancient stone font and a strange, carved wooden figure of a knight in chain armour, spurred heels to the lion at his feet.

Above them the clock chimed and once again Robin shivered.

'What is it?' Todd asked.

'I'm being stupid. Just a bit cold, in here.'

Handsome houses ringed the church, one of them the Vicarage, but when Todd knocked, he learned only that the vicar and his wife were away that day.

'Post office,' said Todd, from experience of a score of previous searches. Three women were chatting in the shop. They turned and looked. Todd said, 'I want to find out something of the history of this place.'

'There's a booklet in the church.'

He held it up.

'Ah, well,' said one of the women. She might, he thought, be the post-mistress, but it was hard to know. 'There's Bures St Mary and Bures Hamlet, and they're separate parishes ecclesiastically, but not administratively, you understand?'

He nodded.

'And if you go up the road yonder, there's Chapel Barn, where King Edmund was crowned. Christmas Day, that was, in eight fifty-five or so. He was a saint – you've heard of Bury St Edmunds? That's him. Now let me see . . . there's always been a story that Boadicea was buried at Mount Bures.'

He glanced at Robin. The little frown was gone and she was smiling happily now. She said politely, 'It's old and very pretty.'

One of the women said, 'You Australian? I've a daughter in Perth.'

'I'm from Sydney – quite a way away.'

'It is. Still, you might run across her.'

Todd said, feeling oily with hypocrisy, 'The whole place must be full of fascinating things.'

They nodded at him. Certainly it was. Witch-hunters had passed this way in Cromwell's time, and Will Dowsing had desecrated the church. And only the other day – well, three Parliamentary constituencies met on the bridge, and the three MPs came to a little ceremony. Oh, yes, and the north bank of the river was in Suffolk and the south bank in Essex, so they had two policemen here, one from each county force.

Robin was positively grinning, drinking it in. She said suddenly, 'No dark secrets? No ghosts or buried treasure?'

One of the women said dismissively, 'Plenty of ghosts. Always are, so they say, wherever you go. But I've never seen one. Tell you what there is, though. At Chapel Barn, there's the Earl of Oxford's tomb – several earls, as a matter of fact. But the 11th one, he was commander at Agincourt. And there they are, him and his wife, and you should see her dress, my dear. It's lovely, even if it is carved in stone.'

Later they stood outside on the pavement, Todd making notes, trying to recall all that had been said.

'That's what rural England ought to be,' Robin said. 'All pleasure and pride and history.'

Todd laughed. 'Make the most of it when you meet it, madam. It's rare. Which earl was it – the 11th?'

The shop door opened behind them, a woman's voice said, 'There's Mr Green,' and called the name.

An elderly man, tweed-suited and accompanied by a pair of Airedales, crossed the road, raising his hat, to be told, 'This lady and gentlemen are interested in history.'

He smiled. 'If I can help. I don't pretend to expertise, but I'm a member of the local historical societies. I know a little.'

'My name's Todd, and I'm a record agent. This is Miss van Geloven.'

Mr Green raised his hat. 'Van Geloven. There was an admiral of that name.'

'A great uncle.'

'I served under him. *Trincomaleee* in the thirties. Splendid

187

man.' He turned to Todd. 'A record agent – that's genealogy?'

'Sometimes.' Todd looked at Green's face. Its expression had moved in a moment from one of interested kindness to something else. Suspicion, pity?

'The er – the malady, would it be?'

'I'm sorry,' Todd said. 'I don't understand. What malady?'

Green looked relieved. 'In the past there have been a number of chappies in your line come here to – you're not a medical genealogist?'

'No.'

The old man's manner was returning to its original gentle ease. 'I'm so sorry; rather misunderstood what you were doing. As I say, I'll help in any way I can. Care for a cup of coffee?'

He lived in one of the old houses by the church, 'A retired captain RN, now gardener, grandfather and amateur historian, if you list them in order of ardousness.'

Robin made him tell them. She said, 'The truth is Captain Green –'

'Mister Green.'

'The truth is we're on a trail that may possibly be very important.'

He cocked his head to one side, eyes widening a little. 'I read my papers. One tries to stay informed. Are you involved in this American business? Damn it, there was a murder!'

Robin said, 'Yes, he is. He's tracking a family history. You see how important it can be. What's the malady you mentioned?'

Green shook his head. 'Always said I won't talk about it. Thing like that, too much talk is a dangerous affair in a village like this. But I can put you in touch with a fellow at Addenbrooke's Hospital in Cambridge. He'll tell you, and nobody here will know. If you like, I'll telephone now.'

They could hear him talking, far off in the cool, quiet recesses of the old house, but not a word of what he said.

Robin asked, 'What do medical genealogists do?'

Todd shrugged. 'What I do, but they chase bloodlines for a different reason. Things that run in families – asthmas and cleft palates. I don't know very much about it.'

Green came back. 'I impressed on him that the matter was

of consequence and he can see you between one-thirty and three if he moves his lunch about a bit. You ought to manage to get there, just about, if you're quick. His name is Keighley, George Keighley. Ask for Dr Keighley at the reception desk. Sorry about the coffee.'

Keighley was a bulky man with a sandy beard, late forties probably Todd figured, with the gruff, authoritative manner often favoured by doctors. Robin thought it covered shyness. He took them upstairs to an office, and waved them to chairs.

'Can't be too long, I'm afraid. Borrowed this room from the ward sister and she'll need it soon. Nice view from the window, though.'

They looked out politely. The vast hospital was all glass and concrete and roads. There were low hills not far away.

Keighley laughed. 'Best thing is what you can't see. We've half a dozen Nobel Prizewinners on these premises sometimes. More than they can say at Oxford! You've come from Bures – where were you before that?'

'America,' Todd said. 'This trace has been a long one. Before that, Australia.'

'All right. Frank Green said it mattered. Am I allowed to know?'

'No reason why not. But better if it isn't passed on.'

Keighley nodded. 'Understand very well. What took you to Bures, a birth there?'

Todd nodded. Robin added, 'And then somebody said the name of the place rang a bell. A melancholy bell.'

'Quite right. You qualified?'

'Medically? No.'

'You?'

'A solicitor,' Robin said.

'The word is chorea.' Keighley spelled it. 'Not to be confused with career, because the one is liable to interfere pretty drastically with the other. It's a group of conditions, disease, what have you. St Vitus's dance is one of 'em. The Bures one is called Huntington's, after the doctor who described it.

Todd said, 'Where does Bures come in?'

'Good question. Bures is part of the story, because somehow or another chorea must have arrived there, centuries ago, possibly with the Vikings – there are pockets of it in Norway and Denmark and north Germany – and it stayed there for centuries. Then it went on. And the best known of the places it went to was New England.'

'To a particular place there?' Robin asked him.

He nodded. 'Several. One was Salem. Ring any bells?'

She said, 'You mean the witches?'

'Chorea is the noun, Miss van Geloven. The adjective is *choreic*,' Keighley said. 'And it is true beyond doubt that the movements described in the trials of the witches of Salem – the weaving motions of the arms and the strange gyrations which were thought to be devilish dances, are absolutely characteristic choreic movements. Involuntary movements, all of them.'

Keighley paused. 'I assume there is a name – you've found a direct birth-link with Bures?'

Todd nodded.

'Where did you find it?'

'In Fiji.'

'Did the person live in Fiji.'

'I don't think so. But it's not impossible,' Todd said. 'She certainly married there.'

'Oh, she did?' Keighley glanced up at him. 'Is she still there?'

Todd smiled. 'She died eighty-odd years ago. In New York.'

Keighley sighed. 'They certainly get about. I've sometimes wondered if it isn't one of the minor characteristics . . . what was the name?'

'Taylor,' Todd said. 'Jane Taylor.'

'And her parents?'

'Samuel Taylor was her father.'

'Mother?'

'Don't know. Should be easy to find out, though.'

Keighley gave a grim little laugh. 'With a name like Jane Taylor?'

'I have her date of birth. St Catherine's House will have it. Take half an hour.'

'Okay. But look, come with me, we may have something here.'

'Hallo. Who is it? Oh, Mr Todd!' Christ, she'd forgotten Todd in the chaos. 'Hi, how're you doing?' Zee Quist reached for a cigarette, the second pack of the evening half-gone, and the scrape of the lighter wheel drowned his reply.

'Say again, I didn't catch it.'

'Badly. We're doing badly, Miss Quist.'

'What's that mean?'

'I'm afraid it means unpleasant news.'

A stillness seemed to descend in her mind. 'What does that mean, Mr Todd? What kind of unpleasant news?'

'Information,' Todd said, 'that you will want to hear before anybody else hears it.'

'It's a private line we're on.'

Todd said, 'Have it your own way, then. I'm just trying to be helpful. And I expect you know much more about surveillance and phone-tapping than I do. If you really want me to go ahead, I will.'

'It's that bad? You're serious?'

'I think it's about as bad as it can be,' she heard Todd say. There was a harsh emphasis to the words and it carried conviction.

She said angrily, 'Give me some kind of a clue, for Christ's sake!'

The far-off, now-hateful voice said, 'I see no way of giving you a clue without giving it to anybody else who might be listening.'

'Hold it a minute.'

She sat and thought. What on earth could this goddamned researcher have found now? Something in Grandma? Grandpa was a general, all-round filthy thieving brute. So what was Grandma? A whore? A convict, too? Typhoid Mary herself?

Zee Quist put the phone to her ear. 'You still there, Mr Todd?'

'Yes.'

'You'd better come over here.' There was a pause. She said quickly, 'Don't worry. We pay your costs.'

191

Todd said, 'In Australia I was attacked. There were people on my tail. Here in London there's been a killing and my flat's been broken into. Will I be safe in New York?'

Zee Quist laughed harshly. 'Mr Todd, in New York City, nobody's safe. But yes.'

'I want to be sure. It's not particularly for my own sake, though obviously that matters. Suppose someone grabs me, as happened in Australia and gets it out of me.'

'Gets it out? You mean tortures you?'

'Pain. Pressure of whatever kind. I've thought about this carefully and –'

Zee Quist said, 'You're being over-dramatic. Okay, I'll even get you a guard, a bodyguard.'

'No,' Todd said. 'I don't think you understand, Miss Quist. I haven't any doubt at all that what I know is enough to change the course of your election completely. I think you should come here.'

She gasped. 'To London! Mr Todd, I don't think you understand. I'm in a wheelchair and I'm busy as hell. I can't come to London. Damn it, the convention's next week! Can't you send someone here?'

'No.'

'Why not?'

'If we talk, then we both know, just you and me. That's enough. More than enough. Third parties and fourth parties add to the problem, they don't solve it.'

'So nobody else knows?'

'One other person knows it all. Several know bits of it – that's inevitable.'

'Send the one person.'

'I'm not risking her.'

'Ah.' London, she thought. Could she? Zee Quist had been out of mainland America only once since the ski-crash, to Hawaii years back and it had not been comfortable. How could she go to London? The answer came instantly. In a Lear-jet, stretchered and sleeping, that's how. 'Give me your number.'

Todd said, 'No. I'll telephone you in half an hour.'

It wasn't difficult. There were three jet-rental outfits she'd used often, all in the Yellow Pages, and a Lear-jet, with distance tanks would have to make just two fuelling stops, Gander and Shannon, and was in Britain eight hours from take-off. So far, so good. But who took her to the airport. Who got her to the plane?

Bill, she thought. Bill would take her. Bill was perfect. She punched the telephone buttons.

'Hi, Zee. Great news about the baby, huh?'

She said, 'Marvellous. You busy?'

'Always. What can I do for you?'

'You can take me,' she said, 'to Teterboro' Airport.'

'You mean, over in Jersey? What's wrong with JFK or LaGuardia? Where are you going, anyway?'

She said, 'I'm going to Europe, Bill. And I'm going tonight. And –' she had a sudden inspiration – 'you, Bill, are going with me!'

'Me? I'm not going to any Europe, Zee.'

'It's Todd, again, Bill.'

'What's he got?'

'Bad news. Very bad,' he says.

'Oh, Jesus, I knew it!'

'So you're going.'

Brother Bill burst out, 'What is it? What's wrong? Damn it, Zee, there's a week to the Convention. We can't be away, either of us. Get him over here.'

'He won't come.'

'And you think this thing's important enough to –'

She said, 'He said it could swing the whole election.'

'And you believe it?'

'Don't just hate him, Bill. Think about it! Todd's been dead right every time. Every fact has been true. He's not a fool. He's not a Prodnose – he's a pro and we hired him. You've one hour to pack a bag and get over here!'

She hung up. Her own bag was packed already. There was always a packed bag in the closet.

The little Lear-jet swept like a silver dart through the dirty, grey overhang of Stansted Airport, north-east of London. Passengers in private jets receive attention unknown to the hoi-polloi packed into scheduled flights. Customs and immigration came to meet the Lear. The official van was waiting even before taxi-ing was complete. Nor were the formalities lengthy. As the van moved off, its place was taken by a VW Microbus with sliding doors. A girl got out.

'Miss Quist?'

'That's right. This is Mr Crombie.'

'Hope you don't mind a rented van,' the girl said smiling. The Australian accent made Zee Quist glance wryly at Brother Bill. 'You'll lift me aboard, Bill?'

'Right. Where are we going?'

'To meet Mr Todd.'

15

They had talked for four hours. Now they had been flying for five. Nine hours, and she still couldn't believe it, could barely catch her breath. The Lear-jet's seating was in its four-passenger configuration. Outside, the twin jets whistled softly and the thin pure air streamed by unseen. Inside were pale leather seats and cool drinks and black despair.

Zee Quist glanced across the narrow aisle at Todd, silent in the seat alongside, and said, 'Let me ask you again. I don't remember. There's so much to absorb. What possibility?'

He turned to face her. 'I suppose there must always be a chance. Certain things in genealogy always have to be taken for granted and it may be in this case that they're wrong.'

'Like?' Her voice held a small, clear ring of hope.

Todd shook his head. 'Trouble is, there's no way of finding out. Look, you get a birth certificate. Mother is Mary Smith, father is John Smith. We all take it for granted the facts are right and are stated correctly. But how do we know Mary Smith wasn't having an affair with a milkman, with the man next door, the choirmaster, the baker? How do we know John Smith was the father. Does he know?'

She said, 'Put it like that and everybody's legitimacy is suspect.'

'That's right,' Todd said. 'I know about my own parents. They were married nearly forty years. Devoted to each other. I don't believe for one second that I'm a bastard, but it's impossible to prove. What about you?'

'Much the same, if I have to make myself think of it.'

Todd said, 'In most cases it doesn't matter anyway. Even in law, where proof of identity is needed for an inheritance, it's enough to satisfy a court, isn't it?'

'Yup.'

'Whereas when it's medical . . .'

Zee Quist sighed. 'Yeah,' she said. A few minutes later she turned to him again. There was a solidity about Todd. He was a good wall to bounce a ball against. 'Fifty-fifty?'

He said, 'So they say.'

'So there's a chance there.'

'It's fifty-fifty over the generations, Miss Quist.'

'Call me Zee, for God's sake.'

'All right.'

'Maybe her father wasn't her father.'

Todd shrugged. 'No proof. You heard what Dr Keighley said.'

'How good is he –?'

'Addenbrooke's is one of the two or three top hospitals; it's attached to Cambridge University. Keighley is a consultant neurologist there. He must be high-grade.'

'And he says no marker.'

'That's what he said. Not yet, perhaps soon.'

'But not now.'

'No.'

She hesitated. 'Did you understand that stuff – dominants and markers.'

'Most of it, I think.'

'Not sure I did.'

He said, 'You understand. You're looking for a way through. I fear very deeply that there isn't one.'

'So do I.' Minutes later. 'If Jane was pregnant when they left Fiji, how long to New York?'

He said gently, 'It doesn't matter. In the finish John Patrick Connor doesn't matter. It doesn't matter a toss whether he was the father or not.' He laughed a little bitterly. 'After all these weeks on his slippery heels, that comes hard. But it's Jane who counts.'

She was tired beyond bearing, and now almost beyond logical thought. Hammer-blow after hammer-blow had knocked the stuffing out of Zee Quist that day. But the fight hadn't been knocked out; the fight was still boiling around inside her. It was futile and would achieve nothing, but it was there and when she slept, it would nourish itself.

Her eyes didn't want to close. But they did. Behind the closed lids, Dr Keighley repeated his lecture.

Keighley, a man long-practised with medical horrors, had taken things carefully to begin with. They sat round a small circular table, with hot coffee poured, and he said, 'Anybody a relative?'

Bill Crombie said, 'I'm his half-brother.'

'Mother's side or father's?'

'We have the same mother. John's father was killed before he was born.'

Hair smiled gentle reassurance at him. 'Well, then, I don't think this is a problem for you, Mr Crombie.'

'But it is for John – you're sure?'

'It looks that way,' Keighley said. Before him on the table lay a diagram; it was a family tree drawn up in colours. He added something to it, then pushed his chair back and rubbed bis eyes. After a moment he pulled a folded sheet from a file beside him, and spread it out.

'Map,' he said. 'And you can see the way the thing has moved over the years. First in Europe.' As Keighley held up the map, they could see the red arrows that crossed the North Sea from Norway, Denmark and Northern Germany to Britain.

'Angles, Saxons, Vikings,' Dr Keighley said. 'We don't know where it began, or who with. But as you see, it came over here, centuries ago. And I must emphasise, because you'll certainly have questions I can't answer, that there is a great deal we do not know.'

'But here are two pockets. One is, as you see, in the fishing port of Lowestoft on the coast of North Suffolk. Lowestoft is a curiosity, in that it is the most easterly town in England and that it has a natural arrangement of waterways that have acted to preserve the so-called old town intact, more or less. The Lowestoft pocket is there, in the old town. As far as we know it has not spread widely from there, and certainly not in the way the so-called Bures pocket has spread.'

Brother Bill stirred impatiently. 'Look, doc, I'm sure this is fascinating, and ordinarily I'd be happy to hear it. But we have a problem here, and it's damned urgent. We told you. My half-brother is a candidate for the Democratic nomination as President of the United States. You appreciate that?'

Keighley nodded. 'I do.'

'And now he may have this disease, that's what you're telling us?'

'Yes.'

Brother Bill sighed. 'Doc, John Leyden is healthy. I'm here to tell you he's fit, in mind and body. If you ever saw *mens sana in corpore sano*, he's it. He had a whole parcel of doctors go over him at Walter Reed Hospital in Washington before he started campaigning. They said he was in great shape – and they said it unanimously! So tell us, will you?'

Hair looked at him. 'I understand your impatience. You want to know what the disease is.'

'That's right. If he's got it, let's get it treated before –'

Keighley interrupted swiftly yet softly. 'I'm afraid there's no treatment.'

'No treatment!'

'Palliatives, that's all. And there's no way to be sure if he has it or not.'

'What?'

Zee Quist said, 'Surely there must be tests?'

Keighley spread his hands a little helplessly. This moment always came with Huntington's – the abrupt transmission of the news that nothing could be done. He said, 'No. There are hopes that a test may become available before long. But no, no tests now. There are symptoms. But it's extremely unusual, indeed almost unknown, for it to appear in a family with no previous history of the chorea.'

'What are these symptoms?' Brother Bill demanded.

'Well, at first you get irregular muscular movements, out of control, weaving motions.'

'John has first-class co-ordination!'

Zee Quist blinked, and said, almost to herself, 'The water.'

Keighley turned to her. 'I'm sorry – what did you say?'

Her face, always sallow, had turned almost gray. 'He knocked over a water glass. On TV.'

Bill Crombie laughed, dismissively. 'Oh, come on, Zee.

Everybody in this room has knocked over a glass. Maybe not on TV, but in the last six months, I'll bet!'

Hair said, 'You're probably right. How did he knock it over?'

'Reaching for it. He told me later he'd hit it on the button with a long, looping left.'

'You see it?'

'Yes.'

'Accurate description?'

'I think so.'

In Bill Crombie, impatience was turning to restlessness. 'Look, this is crazy! We're talking about a guy who's visibly fit, who's going for the world's top job and has a good chance of getting it, and all because he knocks over a glass of water – you're saying he has this, what-is-it, chorea?'

'The water's not the reason, Mr Crombie.'

'Then what is?'

Hair said, with patience, but flatly, 'The genealogy. The family history that Mr Todd has produced.'

'Damn the guy!' Crombie said. He swung his big body round to glare across the table at Todd. 'Why in hell –'

'Shut up, Bill,' Zee Quist ordered harshly. 'We have to know about this. We have to know.'

He said rudely, 'Know what? John's grandmother had spots on her ass so maybe we're gonna get us a spotty-ass President – is that what we get to know?'

Zee Quist looked at him savagely. 'You're behaving like a kid, Bill. A real dumb kid. Keep quiet and listen.'

Dr Keighley watched the exchange. News of Huntington's was always brutal, and this was far from the first time he'd had to pass it on. Some were tough in the face of it, like the woman in the wheelchair. She'd had to learn to be tough. Others it damaged. Keighley was neither much interested in politics nor a newspaper reader on an extensive scale, but he'd read, like everyone else about John Leyden, the clean and balanced candidate. He said, 'It can be distressing, Mr Crombie, I know. That's why it's best to take the talk slowly.'

Brother Bill's jaw was clamped tight. He said, grinding out the words, 'This guy's genealogy is conclusive – no doubts and no appeals? He says so and John Leyden has to stand down? A man who's going to win the Presidency! I ask you, does that make any kind of sense?' He rounded on Keighley. 'Tell me, doc, how long's John had this thing, this chorea?'

Keighley said, 'All his life. It's a genetic inheritance, like blue eyes. That means from birth and from pre-birth, from conception, in fact.'

'Well, let me tell you this: after four decades and more of living, doc, he's still a class games player, skier, runner. He copes without strain with all the intellectual pressures of the campaign and the Senate. He's quite a man.'

'And forty-how many years old?'

'He's going on forty-nine.'

Dr Keighley pursed his lips. 'A little old, perhaps. Trouble is, Mr Crombie, that if it's there it comes out, and once it does that, it kills.'

But now Brother Bill had spotted a chink of light. 'So it kills okay! How long does it take – days, weeks, years?'

'Years,' the doctor said. 'A long time. Up to twenty.'

'Twenty years!' There was triumph in Crombie's voice now. 'Presidents are only elected for four!'

'A man can be re-elected,' Zee Quist said. 'And if he's FDR, he can be re-re-elected.'

'It's okay isn't it?' urged Crombie, his tone now sweet with reason. 'Four years. He'll be fine.'

Dr Keighley frowned. 'Not so easy. Mr Crombie. I'm afraid it can produce profound personality changes: ill-humour verging on mad fury, a terrific querulousness, a kind of permanent anger. There can be physical violence. It's a very –'

'Slow process, were you going to say?' Crombie demanded.

'No. It's an inevitable, unstoppable, downward road. Who's going to tell him?'

'I will,' Zee Quist offered. She thought: God, how can I? But better me than Bill.

'No, I'll do it,' Crombie said. 'It's a brother's job.'

'He'll want to know how,' Dr Keighley said. 'You'll have to explain that the thing is without doubt genetic. It came to him through his grandmother and his father.

200

'Oh, Jesus Christ!' Zee Quist said softly. 'Mercy's pregnant . . .'

'His wife?'

'Yes.'

Crombie slowly lowered his head into his hands. 'Is there no end to this? You mean the baby'll get it?'

'The baby,' Dr Keighley said, 'has a fifty-fifty chance.'

'Can anything be done?'

Hair rose and walked to the window. He stared out for a moment, then turned. 'Huntington's could be wiped out if – and only if – the people who suffer from it could be persuaded not to have children.'

'You mean abortion?' Zee Quist asked, after a stunned moment.

Reluctantly, slowly, he nodded.

'Abortion?' Crombie repeated. 'A Presidential candidate with an election campaign ready to start and you talk about abortion!'

Keighley said gently. 'If there's a chance – and I'm afraid there is – that he has Huntington's, then he should withdraw. It destroys the brain, Mr Crombie.'

Brother Bill was on his feet. 'Maybe, in twenty years! Maybe none of us will live twenty years – you, me, none of us. I'll take my chance on John for the next four!' He banged his fist on the table. 'I've had enough of this. John's A-okay. I know, I've seen a lot of him all my life. He can fight and he can win and he can govern! You coming, Zee?'

She said quietly, 'I want to hear the rest, Bill. So should you.'

'What's the name of that airport?'

'London-Stansted,' said Todd.

'I'll be waiting there.'

As the door closed behind him, Dr Keighley said, 'Do you know Mr Crombie well?'

'Me?' Zee Quist's tight grin appeared. 'Yeah, I know him.'

'Is he – well, er –'

She helped out. 'Is he unusually touchy today, that what you mean?'

'Something like that.'

'Then yes. He can be touchy, but today's exceptional. This hurts.'

'It always hurts,' Keighley said softly. Then, 'If you're an old friend, it would probably be better if you told Mr Leyden.'

'I'm an old friend,' she said wearily.

'But I should warn you,' Keighley said, 'that the friendship may not survive the telling. News as bad as this engenders hate in anyone, let alone people with Huntington's.'

She nodded sadly. 'Another of Life's cheerful pats on the head. Just explain to me what I tell John, will you, doc?'

And on top of everything, there was another doubt, in Todd's mind, at least. He was mindful of the Immigration officer who'd been so truculent when Todd was in transit at San Francisco. Now here he was in mid-Atlantic, still without a visa, and once more America-bound.

'Don't worry,' Zee Quist had said levelly – there was an almost heart-turning crispness about her manner, now; a means of holding the lid down on her feelings about Leyden. 'What's lined up on your side may not look much, but there's a Presidential candidate, who's also a US Senator, and one of the top six law firms on Wall Street, all ready to give guarantees. You're in. They'll be waiting at Newark with visa stamps!'

Todd's passport was in his pocket, simply because since returning from Australia, he hadn't yet been back to his flat to put it away. Robin had left hers at Madge's house and returned there from Cambridge to collect it and to ensure Madge's welfare for a few days. She would fly on to New York on the evening scheduled service later that day.

Small, administrative problems in their minds, then. But the big problem, the real problem, everywhere – in minds, in hearts, in the scrubbed and refrigerated air they breathed:

John Leyden.

And Huntington's Chorea.

Todd glanced across at Zee Quist. She wore a suede jacket over a sweater and tweed slacks, all expensive, all designed for bulk, because there was nothing of her. Twenty immobile years had made a matchstick woman of her. It seemed to Todd that the bones and the wasted flesh were held together by only spirit, by courage, by determination. He said, 'You've given yourself a terrible job.'

She turned her head. 'I know it.'

'How will he take it?'

She seemed to flare briefly. 'How do you imag –' Then she stopped, and thought for a moment. 'He'll take it like a gentleman, Mr Todd.'

From the seat behind, raised above the engine's damped whistle, came Bill's voice. 'Damned if I see why he has to take it at all!'

Todd and Zee Quist turned.

'What the hell!' Brother Bill said. 'There's an even chance he hasn't got the damn thing. If he has, there's maybe years before it shows. If it develops while he's President, he can resign. That's why we have vice-presidents!'

'And the baby?' Zee Quist said.

'Look, Zee, it's fifty-fifty with John, right? And then it's fifty-fifty with the baby. You're down to a twenty-five per cent chance there. And that doctor said there was progress in development work. Maybe in a year or two . . .'

Todd saw her eyes close wearily. In front of his seat, built into one of the Lear-jet's beautifully compact fittings, was a small bar: whisky, brandy, gin, all with little pump mechanisms, and mixer cans stacked in a slide. He said, 'Have a drink. You need it.'

'Whisky,' she said, eyes still closed. 'And water.'

He made it for her, and she said, 'This is on an empty stomach. What I really ought to have is food.'

Bent-backed, Todd went forward and spoke to the pilot. 'Yes, sir. There's a tray of assorted sandwiches and a big thermos of coffee. I'll get it.'

Todd got it out himself, and returned to the passenger seats. Bill Crombie was asleep across the rear seats, collar undone, snoring. Enviable gift, Todd thought. A couple of minutes earlier Bill had been wide awake and arguing.

'Soup.' he asked her.

'What is it?'

'Chicken, I think.'

'So chicken I'll have. My favourite. Always was.'

He poured it into a beaker and gave her a roll, then served himself.

Forty minutes later. Bill Crombie thrust a worried face through the flight-deck door.

'Yes, sir.'

'Captain, I'm worried. The others are being violently sick, both of them.'

'Oh, Christ. Did they eat?'

'Dunno. I was asleep. But Captain, you have to do something!'

The captain glanced at his watch. 'Three hours to Newark.' He thought for a moment. 'Let me have a look.'

One look was enough. Both Todd and Zee Quist were on the edge of unconsciousness, wracked with violent abdominal spasms, both breathing stertorously.

In a little more than an hour, the Lear-jet was landing at St John's in Newfoundland. By that time both had lost consciousness. The plane had radioed for an ambulance. They went straight into hospital.

There were a number of consequences. The six p.m. British Airways flight from London to New York landed at 6.50 p.m. local time, disgorging more than three hundred and fifty passengers. They spent an hour or more in customs and immigration, and then emerged into the night. They were tired. In London by now it was nearly three in the morning and they had had a long day. Among them was Robin van Geloven, expecting to be met by Todd.

But Todd, naturally enough since he was literally on the edge of death and a thousand miles away to the north-east, was not there. Nor was Zee Quist, for identical reasons.

William Crombie, who similarly was absent, was also far away. As Robin van Geloven stood looking about her hopefully in the arrivals hall at Kennedy airport, Crombie was in another aircraft crossing the continent.

16

Todd should have been there to meet her, and it took time for Robin van Geloven to convince herself that he was not. She first searched through the crowds of meeters-and-greeters waiting at the arrivals gate, then had Todd paged.

No Todd. No message, either.

Nothing – the drongo!

Characteristically resourceful, she took herself to a payphone to set about tracing John Leyden's campaign headquarters. The time was ten p.m. but she reasoned that at this stage of the campaign, the HQ would have to be manned round the clock in a land of several time zones, where the west coast was three hours behind the east.

Since Kennedy airport also has round-the-clock manning, she was able without difficulty both to change currency and to obtain a pile of quarters for the phone.

Information gave her the number.

'Leyden campaign,' said a girl's bright voice.

'I want to speak to Zee Quist, please.'

'I'm sorry,' said the smooth voice, 'but Zee Quist is no longer connected with the campaign.'

'Not at all?'

'That's my information.'

Robin said, 'Did she resign, or what? Where can I reach her?'

'I have no information on that.'

'When did this, this lack of connection begin?'

'I have no information on that. I'm sorry.'

'Who's taken her place?'

'The operation is in process of moving out to San Francisco, California. All the staff are engaged in that. The Convention opens tomorrow.'

'And no name?'

'I don't have the information, caller.'

'Okay, thanks.'

'Don't forget to vote Leyden in November!'

She hung up. Not difficult, she thought, to guess why Zee Quist had gone. But where was more important, for whither Zee Quist had gone, there had Todd gone also. How to find out? She sat for a moment on the little, triangular corner seat of the phone booth, trying to work out some way of locating Todd among America's teeming millions yearning to be free. The question why could be answered later, she thought, and the answer had better be good!

Leartaxi – the name on the little jet they'd used. And there was an airport – what was it? Began with a T . . .

No difficulty. Yellow Pages listed Teterboro' under Airfields and Leartaxi under Airplane Hire. She called, expecting an answering machine at this hour, and got a fully human voice.

'I want to get in touch with people who came in today on a flight from England.'

Momentary silence, then the news. They were in a hospital in St John's Newfoundland, with what was said to be serious food poisoning.

'All of them?'

'The hospitalized passengers were Ms Quist and Mr Todd.'

She asked quickly, 'There were three. What happened to Mr Crombie?'

'He returned here on the airplane.'

'When?'

'About two hours ago.'

'Where did he go?'

'I'm sorry, I have no idea. We called a cab for him.' A pause then: 'But Mr Crombie's bound to be at the Convention, I guess. He's John Leyden's brother, you know.'

'How do I get to St John's?'

'Air Canada flight from Kennedy, you connect at Halifax.'

'More questions,' Robin van Geloven said. 'First how ill are they?'

'We called when Mr Crombie arrived. He wanted that information also. We were told they were still seriously ill.'

She swallowed. 'Question two. What did they eat?'

'We don't know. It may be food was brought aboard in England.'

'Third question. What's that number in St John's?'

They were undoubtedly seriously ill, both of them. And this was the second day; Robin had had to stay overnight in Halifax because the Leartaxi lady had been wrong. There wasn't a late connecting flight to St John's.

'It's a word, like backache,' the doctor told her. 'Two words, anyway. What we call food poisoning comes in various ways. There's dysentery, which this isn't, and staphylococcus, which I think it isn't, and salmonella, which I think it is. I doubt very much it would be botulism, because that attacks the central nervous system, where this is classic: pain in the gut, diarrhoea and vomiting.

'They'll be okay?'

'Maybe in a week. At the moment we have them both on glucose drips.'

'Can I see Mr Todd?'

'Who are you?'

She stretched the point. 'We're engaged.'

He nodded. 'He's still comatose – or was a few minutes back. No waking him. You can just peer in through the glass.'

He remained more or less comatose all day. Robin van Geloven was in the waiting room, watching the evening news on CBS, and when a nurse came to tell her Todd was awake, she had just been watching an item on John Leyden. Looking at that healthy, vital man, it was hard to believe that in him a malign gene might be destructively at work. Leyden was in Detroit, burnishing his image with America's blacks, meeting the kids at the Joe Louis auditorium. He squared up to one youngster, threw a left, and missed by a long mile. He smiled, but he looked surprised.

Either Todd was plugged into a variety of tubes, or they were plugged into him. His grin at the sight of her was weak and ghastly, but it was unmistakeably a grin, and she felt reassured. But it was Monday evening.

Todd didn't know what had happened. He remembered

only a sudden gripe and the churning in his stomach on the plane, and nothing afterwards. She explained.

He said frowning, 'Crombie?'

'Perhaps. If it wasn't native.'

'Has reason.'

She said, 'I saw Leyden, just now – on TV.'

'Was he okay?'

'Something odd, I thought. Nothing, much, but something all the same. Movements not quite . . .'

'Poor sod.'

She smiled, 'Look who's talking!' And added, 'You're going to be here a week.'

Todd shook his head. 'Not me. How's Zee Quist?'

She went to find out. Zee Quist, far weaker to start with, remained in a serious state. The doctor's expression seemed to Robin van Geloven to indicate doubt.

Robin spent the night at the Hotel Newfoundland, and returned to the hospital early. Morning television had discovered nothing strange about Leyden's missed punch. Maybe they thought the black kid he'd sparred with was another Louis.

Meanwhile Todd was stronger. Not to the point of getting up, or even sitting up. But there was more strength in his voice. On inquiring Robin learned that Zee Quist was awake but weak.

'Can she talk?'

'Not even for a second!'

On the second day of the Democratic Convention, therefore, the future of one possible – indeed probable – candidate lay in the hands of two people: one English, and incapacitated, flat on his back in a hospital as far away from the convention city of San Francisco as it was possible to get and still be in North America; and the other an Australian woman. Both were wholly unfamiliar with the American political process. Yet the Nixon episode and its criminal aftermath, plus their own adventures in Australia, not to mention food poisoning, had given both, by now, a feeling of deep suspicion. John Leyden might be the Man in the White hat/suit/shoes/shirt/ tie, but there was somebody close to him who wasn't. There

208

was somebody close to Leyden to whom nothing, not kidnapping, not assault and battery, not deliberate poisoning, not even murder, was too extreme if it cleared John Leyden's path to the nomination and ultimately to the White House.

A sudden thought had Robin van Geloven summoning a nurse. 'Any calls this morning about Mr Todd's condition or Miss Quist's?'

'I'll find out.' The girl went away and came back a couple of minutes later. 'Yes, there was. A gentleman called early, about seven.'

'That's all?'

'Yes, ma'am.'

Crombie, she thought. Now he'd know they'd survived the night. And he knew, also that at this hospital in remote Newfoundland were the only people in North America who knew about the horrific potential in John Leyden's genetic heritage.

She said to Todd, 'Your brief-case?'

'Don't know.'

She looked in the locker by his bed. No brief-case. She called the nurse. No brief-case.

Simple. It had stayed on the plane. So Crombie had it. There was therefore now no readily available documentary evidence outside Crombie's hands, and Crombie could and perhaps would continue to get all the originals destroyed *in situ* in their assorted archives.

Suddenly she had no doubts. So may figures pointed directly at Crombie. And Crombie's finger would inevitably point at Todd, because Todd was the man who could destroy a dream.

She knew at once that Todd must be removed from the hospital! Immediately her mind battled against the idea. Todd was still seriously ill. He was safer in hospital, than he'd be anywhere else with her.

But while she was in London, three IRA men had entered the Royal Victoria Hospital in Belfast to murder a patient, had done so, and had then escaped. The story had been big in the newspapers and on TV.

She must get him out – and be quick about it.

They were appalled. It was crazy. His condition was still very serious. He needed the glucose drip, he needed the hospital's resources behind him; there could easily be a severe relapse . . .

She fought them off. Todd was in danger, she said, actually in danger of his life. More so, maybe, they said, if you take him away.

She looked at him in abrupt indecision.

Todd said weakly, 'I'll sign myself out.'

And he did. She'd called a private ambulance and a private medico, both from the blessed Yellow Pages, and it took less than half an hour to transfer him to the Airport Hotel and rig up the drip. Would the doctor stay with him for a while? The doctor would, but the price was high. Here, Robin thought, goes my quarter share in the Piper.

It was one of those modern motels with a phone in the bathroom. She closed the door and applied herself to it.

They were matters of friendship, favours. They were things rich and important men in positions of influence could ask of others in like positions. Crombie had flown into Teterboro' with a variety of useful items: Quist's handbag and Quist's wheelchair; Todd's briefcase. He had their passports and both were on foreign soil.

From San Francisco he made calls. Useful to the Leyden campaign if Todd and Ms Quist were detained a few days, incommunicado if possible. Shouldn't be hard to arrange: both were pretty damn sick. And the favour would be remembered, maybe by a President's brother! How about a Mountie outside the door of the hospital room, ha, ha! Yeah, Zee Quist would be mad as a pitsnake when she recovered, but old Zee had some funny ideas lately, and it was really for her own good.

The funny ideas he later explained to a frowning John Leyden, angry at Zee Quist's sudden removal from his campaign HQ.

'You had absolutely no authority, Bill,' Leyden said.

'It had to be done.' Crombie went straight for Zee Quist's jugular. 'It must have been the pressure, John. Too much and too long. She's cracked right across.'

'I doubt it.'

'Let me tell you how bad she is. She's got this tame Limey researcher says you're syphilitic.'

'That I'm *what*?'

'You heard right the first time. He says you have congenital syphilis. Says he's got documentary proof. Your father had it and so have you.'

'Not true,' Leyden protested. 'Simple fact. Not true.'

'It is to Zee. And it gets worse. According to Zee now this disqualifies you from the Presidency.'

'It does, if it were true. But it isn't. Medically, I'm clear.'

Crombie piled it on. 'This researcher is the same guy who dug up Grandpa Connor, John. Zee's had him on your tail for months, digging for any dirt that can be found.'

Leyden's frown deepened. 'It's so hard to believe, Bill. Especially of Zee.'

'Not if you'd seen her the last few days. She's nuts, John.'

'Where is she?'

'Hospital in Canada. On top of everything else she went and got food poisoning. She'll be okay physically, I hear. Mentally's another question. She had a bad shock, that's my guess.'

'What kind of shock?'

'Mercy's baby. Your baby. She was raving about the transmission of congenital syphilis to the innocent unborn. Also she must have been crazy with jealousy.'

'Jealousy?'

'Of Mercy. Zee wanted your child, John.'

'My child? But she couldn't!'

'Oh, she knew that. Of course she did. And as long as Mercy didn't have your baby, either, only other peoples', it was bearable. But your baby, and diseased, I think it was just more than she could take.'

Leyden stood up. 'I'd better go see the poor kid!'

'Sure you must. But not today.'

'It's the right thing, Bill. She's been my friend most of my life. If she's sick, I have to go.'

Crombie said, 'It's Wednesday, John. Convention week.

Your name's going to be put in nomination tonight. You-are-going-absolutely-nowhere. Except the Convention Hall.'

'But – okay, maybe you're right. But I'll call.'

'You'll stay off the phone, John.'

'Why?'

'Because everything's nice and quiet. It's all organized. There isn't a word in the papers. But if some reporter gets to Zee and she starts yelling syphilis – how about that, brother?'

'I haven't got it.'

'The word alone would destroy you. For ever. Two days from now, when you've got the nomination in your pocket, we can drag the skeleton out of the closet and bury it in public – false evidence, malice, medical reports and all. But not today, John, and not tomorrow!'

There was a pile of Air Canada timetables in the motel foyer, and Robin unfolded one and stared at the route map with a growing feeling of helplessness. San Francisco was four thousand miles away. No arguing about it, no altering it, certainly no defeating the problem the number presented. She finished her coffee and returned to Todd's room.

'How are you?'

'He's picking up,' the doctor said. 'That's the way it goes. It's like with kids. One second they're healthy, the next they're at death's door, ten seconds after that they yell for ice cream and bicycles. He's picking up.'

'Does it feel like that?'

Todd smiled. 'I can manage without the ice cream.'

'Me, too,' said the doctor, 'but coffee would be appreciated.'

'He's fit to be left?'

'Fitter by the minute. I'll be back in ten.'

John Leyden talked daily to his mother or communicated in some way: letter, cable or telex. In the Leyden/Crombie family such contact was habit more than obligation.

'Heard from Bill today, mother?'

'Half an hour ago. He told me.'

'About Zee?'

'I find it difficult to believe, John. You have no better friend than Zee Quist. There isn't an ounce of malice in her, and above all, she doesn't gossip.'

'Bill tell you what she's been saying?'

'No. Just that she was spreading dangerous rumour?'

John Leyden said, 'If she's been doing it, then it's far worse than that. Seems I have congenital syphilis.'

'You have what?' Helena Crombie was not easy to shock, but she was shocked now.

'Remember the researcher who dug up Granpa Connor's criminal record? Apparently the same man has found –'

'He has *not*!' said Helena Crombie.

'Bill says the strain of the campaign has broken Zee. Hard to believe, but well, she's carried a big bag of burdens.'

His mother said, 'Bill said nothing to me about this hereditary syphilis nonsense.'

'He probably thought,' Leyden said, 'that it wasn't suitable teatime talk between the boy and his ma.'

She said tightly, 'If it's congenital, his ma's in on it already, I'd say. Still, never mind. Is Zee still in Newfoundland?'

'So Bill says.'

'Who's replaced her?'

'Hurst Kilgallon. Safest hands in the hemisphere.'

'But not too much imagination. It's not a good trade, John.'

'I know it. But it's temporary.'

'Your idea, or Bill's?'

'Bill asked who. I said Hurst.'

'My love to Mercy and the children.'

''Night, mother.'

As the door closed behind the doctor, Robin said, 'Strong enough to listen?' He nodded. 'As far as I understand it, John Leyden gets proposed for the nomination tonight. So do others – this man Jackson, for one. Tomorrow they have a kind of roll-call in which the various states declare their votes for each candidate. Okay?'

Todd nodded again.

'Leyden's leading. There was a poll published this morning and it put him five points ahead of Jackson. But between the state delegations' votes, it's apparently a great deal closer. All the same, it seems to be a general view that Leyden will get the nomination.'

Todd said, 'Unless we stop him.'

'How can we? We're four thousand miles away. We couldn't get near him even if we weren't.'

'Miss Quist could.'

'She's too sick.'

'Is she conscious?'

'She wasn't earlier. And I don't like leaving her where she is, unguarded. She knows too much – we all do!'

Todd said slowly, 'She's the key. She actually knows Leyden. That's more than we do!'

'It's impossible. She's too ill.'

He lay still for a moment. Then, 'There's more than one way.'

'What do you mean?'

'One: we tell him quietly – he does the decent thing. We assume.' He spoke slowly, the words visibly a strain upon him. The doctor might be right about a swift recovery, Robin thought, but the evidence wasn't really visible to the untrained eye. 'Two,' Todd said after a moment, 'is we tell the world.'

'The world. You mean the Press?'

A nod. 'Television, the lot.'

'We can't prove a thing, Mr Pom. Crombie's got your papers.'

'More where they came from. And there's Dr Keighley.'

She said, horrified, 'He can't do that!'

'Might have to.' His expression changed. 'Unless . . .'

She waited, but no more emerged. 'Unless what?'

He said slowly, 'Women.'

'What do you mean, women?'

'Wife. Mother.'

'Leyden's? They'll be guarded, too.'

Todd's eyelids looked heavy now. He was tiring fast. Hardly surprising, Robin thought. He'd had a hard morning for a man who ought really to be in hospital for another week. He said, 'But Zee could get through, even if the barriers are up.'

A moment later his eyes had closed and his breathing became even.

'Asleep? Good,' the doctor said, returning.

Robin van Geloven telephoned the hospital. Miss Quist was sleeping.

'Sleeping or unconscious?'

'Who is calling?'

She rang off. Probably Todd was right and Zee Quist could get through.

Robin van Geloven looked at him thoughtfully. He wasn't, after all, simply a doctor. The man worked locally and would know the local ropes, the legalities, the practicalities – everything necessary.

She said, 'Doctor Newton, I'm going to have to tell you something you'll find hard to believe.'

He laughed. 'Listen, you wouldn't believe even half the things I hear! Go ahead, though, I'm at least as secure as the confessional.'

'To put it at its simplest,' Robin said slowly, 'I have good reason to think we're in considerable danger.'

'Danger? Well, he was, your pal over there. But he's out of danger now, take my word for it. But, you said "we", didn't you? Must be I'm getting slow!'

She said, 'Three of us. We're all in danger. The other one is a lady in the hospital. Now look, I'm not raving crazy, but to some important and powerful people it would be very convenient indeed if we didn't exist – if we ceased to exist.'

He regarded her steadily from behind his wide framed glasses, then said, 'You think somebody's going to try to kill you?'

'That's what I think. What's more, they know the other lady's in that hospital. I think we have to get her out, ill as she is. I'm shocking you, am I?'

Dr Newton smiled. 'You're not shocking me, ma'am. I was raised in New Jersey, and I don't mean Princeton. I worked as an intern in a hospital in Newark. I know people kill people – they do it a lot. That's why I came to Newfoundland, for

215

the peace and quiet, but sometimes there's a little too much. Okay, you want her where?'

'Here. Under your care.'

He rose. 'I'll fix it. Won't make me popular, but that's okay. And I hate to sound mercenary, but my time gets expensive when there's personal hazard involved. Two and a half times more expensive. Somebody will pay?'

Robin said, 'I will, if necessary.'

'And your work is . . .?'

'I'm a lawyer.'

'But Australian?'

'That disqualifies me?'

'Let's say,' Newton said, 'that it's a long way off.'

'In that case, let's also say,' Robin replied, 'that the lady in the hospital is a partner in a very big Wall Street law firm. Closer to home. And, at a guess, a lot richer.'

'Now that,' Dr Newton said, smiling, 'is what I like to hear.'

'So it'll pay you to keep her alive.'

'Don't worry. I'm just like all the other American doctors, greedy but good. Coming with me?'

She nodded towards Todd. 'Will he be all right?'

'Him? He won't make a move.'

Dr Newton's flip manner evaporated at the hospital. They knew him, knew he was responsible, and so stood only briefly in his way. Robin waited, first while Newton obtained his copies of the case notes and then for the private ambulance to arrive. By the time it came, Zee Quist had been readied and her stretcher lay on a trolley. It was a matter only of moments to put her in the ambulance and drive off.

The car was a Chevrolet, green, far from new. She'd spotted it first parked in the roadway outside the hospital and she could see it now, a couple of hundred yards back. Following? It certainly seemed so.

Was so.

The ambulance made a right turn, so did the Chev. Yes, following.

Robin looked at Zee Quist; at the drawn, pale, haggard face

216

with its yellow-parchment skin and eyes like ink blots.

Dr Newton thumbed an eyelid open. 'She's healthier than she looks. Breathing nice and easy, too.'

Robin nodded, wondered for a moment whether to tell him about the green Chevrolet, and decided against it. He'd only jack up his charges, her sense of humour told her. Plain sense told her the man might walk away. Newton was a volunteer, after all.

But the fact was clearly that they were under surveillance, and equally clearly there was no escaping it – not with two hospital cases on her hands. She had made the best attempt she could and it had already failed. So what now?'

Robin van Geloven had no idea. Brother Bill seemed to have them where he wanted them. Brother Bill would, presumably call a tune and in due course they would have to dance it. She watched through the rear window; watched as the green Chevrolet drove on when the ambulance turned into the motel car park. The driver didn't even glance to his right; but then, he had no need.

They could do nothing with Zee Quist comatose. Doubtfully, Robin asked Dr Newton, if she could be awakened.

He said,'Just a minute. The name is Zelda Quist, is that right? It says so right here.'

'Yes.'

He looked at her sharply. 'Zelda equals Zee, is that right? I mean, that's Zee Quist lying there?'

She hesitated. But there was no point in dissembling. Brother Bill, if Brother Bill was the enemy – and she was no longer in any real doubt about that – knew well enough who everybody was and where everybody was; at that moment he was merely sitting in his lair considering what best to do about them.

'That's her,' Robin said.

'Jesus. You know, I saw her once on the big slalom at Sun Valley – oh, years back. I tell you she was a poem, a real light floater. Weightless. Beautiful. Oh, boy – Zee Quist!' He turned suddenly, 'Say, who are these hoodlums?'

She said, carefully and with emphasis, 'Better not to know. Just look after her.'

217

'Believe me, I'll look after her. You Australians know what a crush is? Well I had a crush on her then that lasted me years. Tell the truth, maybe there's still a little left.' He laid his hand on Zee Quist's forehead. 'You awake and listening?'

There was a tiny nod, and Dr Newton laughed delightedly. 'I'm going to wake you up a little so you can meet your number one fan, Ms Quist.' He took a tiny amount of some clear fluid into a syringe and injected it into her arm. 'I'm not too sure how wise this is.'

But in a few minutes her eyes were open. She could speak a little, but it was a light whisper, and she was very weary indeed. Yet her memory appeared to be in good order. She offered names and numbers and Robin, listening hard, wrote them down as Newton, conscience-stricken and worried about the stimulant he'd injected, hovered near. After five names and numbers, his nerve broke. 'Enough talk,' he barked.

Robin moved to the telephone, got an outside line and went to work, punching the digits to call John Leyden's own suite at the Fremont Hotel in San Francisco. It didn't ring. Swiftly she tried again.

This time an operator fielded it. 'What number are you calling?'

Robin told her, and was asked to hold. Rapidly the operator's voice came back. 'I'm sorry. The number you called is now out of service.'

'You mean it's faulty?' Robin asked.

'It is not on allocation,' the operator said. 'Nobody is using that number.'

'But –' Robin stopped then and didn't go on. No use going after the operator, who couldn't help anyway. Better to call the next number. She said, 'Thanks,' and cut the connection.

Who next? She had Bill Crombie's number, but there could be little point in trying him. Brother Bill already knew the entire story detail by detail – nobody better. There was a joint number for Leyden's sisters, sharing a suite at the Mark Hopkins Hotel as they awaited their brother's great day.

That number, too, was now out of commission, the intercepting operator said.

Brother Bill, she thought, had moved quickly. She asked

information for the Mark Hopkins number, pressed the digit buttons and after a few moments was answered by the hotel switchboard.

'I'd like to speak to Mrs Henry Lodge Duke,' Robin said. This was Leyden's sister Jane.

'Sorry, ma'am,' the hotel operator said. 'The hotel line to the suite is disconnected. Do you have the private number?'

'No.'

'Then I can't help. Sorry. It's the security system. No outside calls are allowed through the hotel board.'

'What about Mrs Crawford Whitley?' Robin demanded. Mrs Whitley was Leyden's other half-sister, Alice.

'One moment.' Then: 'Same suite and same answer, caller. I'm sorry.'

'How long will all this go on.'

'Until the convention's over,' the operator said. 'Till then, nobody gets to talk to anybody unless they have a private line number to call.'

Robin rang off. John Leyden's mother, Helena Crombie, once Helena Leyden, had a house in San Francisco, and Zee Quist said she had insisted on staying there all through the Convention. Perhaps the security teams hadn't bothered too much with an old lady who was also a local resident.

But they had. Robin's call was answered by a man's voice: soft, polite, infinitely impersonal. It said merely that Mrs William Jerome Crombie was currently unavailable, but if the caller would care to leave her name, it would be listed and Mrs Crombie would be informed.

Robin said in sudden exasperation, 'This is damned important!'

'I'm sure it is, ma'am. Importance will be indicated.'

Robin felt her temper rising and controlled it. One of America's foulest contributions to twentieth century life, she thought savagely, was the mechanically polite voice wrapping unpleasant information in soft polysyllabic jargon. She imagined a computer print out sheet listing all the calls, and a small star beside those claiming importance or urgency. She doubted whether Leyden's mother would bother with lists like that – why should she? What she'd do, when the Convention ended, would be to wait for the telephone to ring again. As ring it would.

Nevertheless, Robin pressed ahead. 'This concerns Ms Zee Quist, head of campaign staff for Mr Leyden. It's very important Ms Quist speaks at once to Mrs Crombie.'

She might as well have pressed a switch. Back came the voice: 'My information ma'am, is that Ms Zee Quist's connection with the campaign was severed as of two days ago.'

'Who's in charge now?'

'I do not have that information.'

'Bill Crombie, is it? Brother Bill's taken over?'

'I do not have that information.'

'Do you have a number for campaign headquarters in San Francisco?'

'I do not have that information, ma'am. You should contact operator information for the information you require.'

'My God!' said Robin, 'you worked the word information into that little speech three times!'

'Because we were speaking of information. You should now call the information operator.'

Silence. He didn't hang up. His voice was pleasantly pitched, his tone always neutral. Discourtesy lay in the eye of the beholder, or so he'd say, and the system would always support him. He was waiting with patience for her to continue. She listened hard to the silent line. Nothing. He didn't even appear to be breathing.

So she hung up. Quite violently. Victory again, she thought, for the Impersonal Approach. And for Brother Bill. Churchill's words, Robin van Geloven reflected, could well be applied to the Leyden clan in their various San Francisco fortresses: an iron curtain had indeed descended.

It might have descended also, she suddenly thought, here in Newfoundland, with the old green Chevrolet – neutral as the impassive telephone voice, acting as scout for the main force. She'd been wondering, briefly, who to try next. With the thought of the Chevrolet, she had an answer now: call the police.

She called, and was asked to hold. She held. A long time

220

later, a man came on the line and began to take down details. He was very slow, and in her mind's eye a picture grew of an old man licking a stub of pencil between each word he wrote. She told him – slowly because there was no other way – about the predicament: three lives in danger; dangerous people with much to lose; the acute vulnerability of two invalids. Robin even became a little embarrassed in telling the story at a rate of about one word a minute, that it must sound like a particularly bad episode of a tenth-rate TV series.

Finally she said, 'What will you do?'

'Do?' The voice said. 'I'll report all to this to my superior officer.'

'And what'll he do?'

'How do I know, ma'am?'

She said, 'We need protection. There's nothing false or phoney about this. We need help from the police. Are we going to get it?'

'Give me your number.'

'I've already done that. You took it down twenty minutes ago.'

'I did? Can't see it. Give it me again.'

Who next? Well, there was John Leyden himself. Zee Quist had given her the candidate's number for the Convention week. Maybe he answered that one phone himself, though she doubted it. In any case, Brother Bill would have sealed that avenue off first, before he turned to mothers and sisters. Brother Bill would make absolutely certain that the security ring around his brother was inpregnable. The last thing he'd want was Zee on the phone to John Leyden.

All the same . . .

Bill might have forgotten, he just might. Or left the number untouched for other reasons – perhaps because John Leyden insisted.

Robin thought: worth a try, yes; well worth a try.

She picked up the phone. No tone sounded. It was dead. It remained dead.

There was a chill inside Robin as she rose and went over to Zee Quist's bed. The eyelids were closed, but flicked open as Zee Quist sensed her presence. 'Well?'

Robin said, 'Nothing. Nobody. All the numbers have been changed.'

Zee Quist nodded slightly. Her voice had perhaps a shade more strength as she said, 'My name's poison. Do no good now.'

'So what do we do?' Robin demanded. 'Go to the press? Do you want me to go to the desk in the lobby and phone this man –' she glanced at the list '– this man Drew Turnbull of the, what is it, the *Atlanta Constitution*?'

Todd, gaining vitality quickly now, spoke suddenly. He was sitting on the edge of his bed, barefoot in pyjamas. He said, 'Robin, it's no business of ours. The more I think about it, the more I'm sure.'

Robin van Geloven turned her head. She walked quickly across to him, planted a kiss on top of his head, and said, 'I love you. I'm damned glad you're recovering, and you're talking rubbish.'

'Rubbish, eh?'

She nodded.

He said, 'Robin – think about it. This is a great big process. Goes on for years. People get elected to small jobs, then bigger ones. Leyden's a Senator, has been for several years. People see him and they like him and they vote for him in primary elections. Then delegates gather from all across a nation of two hundred and thirty million people –'

'How do you know?'

'What?'

'That number?'

'Read it somewhere.' He gave her a strained grin. 'Look, it's a serious point. They gather to pick him by acclamation. What gives us the right to stand in the way, you and me? When we're not even Americans.'

She looked at him. 'It's clear enough to me.'

Todd said, 'Suppose it wasn't Huntington's Chorea. Suppose it was cancer.'

She said: 'There's a difference.'

'They both kill.'

'They do.' She nodded. 'But first, before it kills, Huntington's makes mad. Whose finger on the trigger, eh?'

Todd said, 'The man who's elected.'

'By people in possession of the facts,' she demanded tartly. 'When were they ever?'

She began to say, 'They know more now that they used to –' but from somewhere the roar of an incoming jet seemed to drop on them like thunder. They listened as it faded and died to a distant whistle, which, as that too, faded, ceased to blot out Zee Quist's whispered words from the depths of her bed.

She said, 'A wrecked body is one thing and I know it. But a wrecked mind shouldn't be on display. Not ever. And certainly not –'

The sound of a key in the door lock interrupted her. The door opened and a man stepped into the room.

'Yes, what is it?' Robin van Geloven said glancing at him.

The man looked at her, then at the doctor, at Todd and finally at Zee Quist. He turned his head to speak to someone behind him: 'We have the right room,' he said.

17

Bill Crombie came in wearing his nice-modest-man-who's-the-candidate's-brother smile. He gave a polite little nod and crossed the room to Zee Quist's bed. 'How are you, Zee?'

'I've felt better.'

'Most unpleasant thing, food poisoning.' He looked round the room. 'And you, Mr Todd, you okay?'

Todd nodded.

'Glad I didn't have any of the chicken soup,' Crombie said.

'But then, you wouldn't,' Todd said, 'would you?'

'In other circumstances, perhaps I might,' Crombie said. There was about him a curious politesse; he stood in the motel room like the Ambassador from Ruritiania, Todd thought, all little nods and inclinations of the head. Now he went on: 'I feel I have a duty to explain.'

'To explain what?' Robin asked crisply.

'My case.'

'Case,' said Robin, 'is a good word. Yours will come up. An American-registered aircraft is technically American soil.'

He smiled. 'Oh, I forgot, you're a lawyer, too, aren't you? Let me see, there's one, two, three of us in this room. Perhaps more if this gentleman –?' He turned an inquiring glance to Dr Newton, who said, 'Me, I'm just a doctor.'

'Still, the professions are well represented,' Bill Crombie observed.

Robin rose. 'I should think there'll be plenty more professions in court.'

'Please sit down.' She remained standing facing him. 'Miss van Geloven – or perhaps you prefer Ms? – those two gentlemen by the door whom we lawyers outnumber, are not members of any of the learned professions. If they follow a profession at all, it is the profession of arms, though they follow it in an informal way. Please be seated.'

She looked across at them. The two men stood side by side, their backs to the door. Neither fitted the conventional picture of the gunman, as the men in Australia had. These two were youngish, fresh-faced, intelligent-looking.

'Under the Constitution,' Crombie said, 'there is a right to bear arms, and they do. Sit down.'

She shrugged and obeyed. 'Why do they bear arms, Brother Bill?'

Zee Quist whispered something, and Crombie bent to hear. 'Zee,' he told them, 'seems to think it is for offensive purposes. I myself would say the purpose is one of control.'

'Of two invalids, their doctor and an unarmed woman?'

Once again he made the small, mannered inclination of the head. 'Only in part,' Crombie said. 'I was thinking, more specifically, of control of a country.'

'You have my brief-case, of course?' Todd asked.

He nodded: 'I have it, yes. And it's very useful to know the source of all the documents. I'm indebted to you.'

'The originals are still in place.'

'Not all. And certainly not for very long.'

Todd said, 'You'll find some are beyond your reach.'

'In no way. Oh, for the immediate moment, perhaps. But you can't have been listening to me a second ago, when I spoke of control of a country. Listen to me now, please. John Leyden is unstoppable. The roll-call vote will give him the nomination. When he makes the acceptance speech, he becomes the officially-adopted candidate of the Democratic party. In November he'll walk all over that tired, sick old comic in the White House. Do you seriously imagine that all the small restrictions which apply to you will apply also to the President? Or to the Democratic candidate for President? He's only to pick up the phone. His staff have only to pick up a phone. Prime Minister? I'll put you through, sir. Home Secretary? Likewise. Say come to Washington and they'll come running. Go to hell, they go. And you think a few pieces of paper are out of reach! If I didn't know where to find everything, a threat might still exist. But I do know, so it doesn't.'

'Which just leaves us?' Todd said.

Bill Crombie nodded. 'It leaves you three, and the doctor we saw in Cambridge, plus the old navy captain you talked to in Bures.'

'That's why you're accompanied by armed men?' Robin said scornfully.

'What's that, Zee?' Crombie bent to listen. Her whisper was too weak even to cross the room. When Crombie straightened it was to say, 'Quite right. Zee says they're my bodyguards, which is true, because as an inevitable holder of high office, I'm a potential target for homicidal madmen.' He grinned winningly. 'And she flatters me by saying I'm too subtle for guns. That, also, is true.'

'So what,' Todd demanded, 'will you do with all this power?'

Crombie studied him for a long moment. Finally he said, 'I shall preserve a secret. What did you say, Zee?' Again he bent and listened. 'Yes. Zee always sees the realities, it's her particular gift. Her precise words were: by destroying all knowledge of it.'

Zee Quist went by stretcher – if she'd yelled for help at the top of her voice, the sound wouldn't have been heard ten feet away. Todd, in his hospital dressing gown, followed with Robin van Geloven supporting his arm perhaps unnecessarily. Immediately behind them was one of Brother Bill's goons. Last in the little procession was Dr Newton, with a goon to himself. The motel's lobby was empty, but for a man behind the reception counter who gave a small nod as they passed.

Immediately outside on the parking area, stood an ambulance, a big one, rear doors gaping and inside a rack for Zee Quist's stretcher and seats for the others. The whole efficient operation, room to ambulance, ambulance to airport, was carried through in minutes: ten, no more, before the vehicle was halted at the foot of the already-positioned boarding stairs up to the Crombie DC9, itself parked on an isolated pad well out of reach of casual observation. They were loaded like so many packages.

'Where are you taking us?' Robin demanded as, inside the

aircraft, brother Bill Crombie moved with an almost regal confidence past her seat.

He paused. 'I'm afraid,' he said, 'that all you get now is sustenance for the body. As to the mind –' he shrugged and moved on.

Sustenance for the body turned out to be pre-prepared, bland, lukewarm slop: baby food.

'Why this?' she demanded of the goon who brought it.

'For invalids,' he said. And moved away.

When she turned her head she could see Dr Newton in the rear of the plane already spooning the goo into Zee Quist. Eight rows ahead, Todd sat. Thinking what? she wondered. Did he feel, as she did: dazed by the scale of things, the available army of Brother Bill's men, the big jet used casually and privately, the efficiency that pre-planned aeroplane meals of baby food for recovering hospital cases? She yawned, surprising herself. A yawn? With this damned aircraft taking them all to their . . . She yawned again! She closed her eyes tightly and shook her head in exasperation, hoping to clear it. Damn it, she might be, and probably was, being transported to her death! And Todd's death. And Zee Quist's. And the doctor's – he'd have to go, knew altogether too much. Come to think of it, so did that doctor in Cambridge, Doctor . . . what was his name? Yawn.

Something in the food, she thought. She'd read once, somewhere, that there was no such thing as a knock-out drop; that all the films and books, in which a tablet dropped into a drink produced instant unconsciousness, were false. How long since they ate? Her eyelids were heavy. Half an hour. More . . .

She forced herself to sit up. Todd's head wasn't visible. The doctor's was; in a seat far back, mouth open, head lolling. It was hard to keep her own head upright. Big slugs of some sleeping drug. Putting baby to sleep. Her eyelids drooped, and she willed them open. One of the goons was grinning down at her.

He said, 'Why fight it?'

She woke in a room, sitting in an armchair. All of them were there, together.

But no-one else. No guards, no Bill. And the others still sleeping: Todd and Dr Newton in armchairs, Zee Quist's stretcher on a couch. Robin was disorientated only for a moment. Reality came crashing back. She got to her feet and looked around.

The room was big, square, maybe thirty by thirty. Walls of wood planking, a rustic air. But comfortable, even luxurious. Good thick carpet, heavy curtains – drawn. They opened on a drawcord to reveal sealed windows and no light, because there were heavy outside shutters. There were doors in each of two walls, both doors locked, both heavy timber. But maybe they could be forced. There was a big, decorative stone fireplace with a set of horns (moose, caribou?) mounted high up out of reach. But no fire irons. Nothing metal at all, anywhere in the room. Only the chairs.

She went to Todd and kissed his forehead. He stirred and grunted. She kissed his lips and he came awake with a splutter, eyes focussing slowly. 'You all right?' he said.

She nodded. 'You?'

Todd stretched. 'I've felt stronger, but not recently. Where are we?'

'Some kind of luxury cabin, that's my guess.' She pointed up at the antlers. 'Very macho. We're locked in. The windows are shuttered. There's nothing to hit anybody with.'

'No visitors?'

'Haven't seen any. What do we do, Mr Pom?'

'We wait, I expect,' Todd said.

They waited the better part of an hour. By that time Dr Newton was not only wide awake, he was kicking one of the heavy doors and yelling to the bastards to bring a guy a cup of coffee. Zee Quist, too, was conscious, her voice much stronger now. She felt better, she said, Dr Newton, hearing her, came over, pointed a finger and said, 'Grip it.'

She obeyed.

'Squeeze.'

She squeezed.

'Hundred per cent improvement,' he said. 'You're strong as a week-old mouse. I guess we're in trouble here, right?'

'Right indeed,' Todd said. 'And we're not the only ones.'

'How's that?'

'You really want to know?'

'You mean,' Dr Newton said, 'that these hoods'll kill you for what you know, so I'm better off ignorant?'

'Yes.'

'You imagine they'll believe me when I say I don't know? If I'm going to die let me be at least well-informed!'

Todd told him, in swift sentences. Dr Newton listened, and watched him. At the end, Newton said, 'So why have we lived so long? Where are we? How many hours did we fly?'

Nobody knew. Zee Quist said, 'They have homes all over the place.'

'Like?' Newton said.

'Like Minnesota.' At the sound of Bill Crombie's voice all of them turned. Crombie stood beside the open door, watching as a trolley was wheeled into the room: a trolley that jingled and clanked. On it, a coffee pot was visible, and plates, and deep dishes. He said,'Eat. Enjoy yourselves,' and turned to leave. Then he paused. 'I shall leave this door open to allow access to a bathroom. But another stronger door will be closed.'

Todd demanded flatly: 'What do you intend to do with us?'

'Feed you,' Brother Bill responded, still speaking in his ambassadorial mode, 'as you can see. And leave you for a while, too, I'm afraid.' He smiled. 'But I'll be back, I promise and meantime you'll be looked after.'

The breakfast on the trolley was lavish: juices and fruit, eggs fried and shirred, ham, steak, bacon, waffles, hot cakes, syrup, toast rolls. Coffee and tea. But paper plates and plastic cutlery.

The prisoners, all hungry, fell on it like wolves, and over it, began discussing their plight.

'Why the hell Minnesota?' Dr Newton said disgustedly, 'of all –'

Todd said, 'I don't even know where it is.'

'It's where de Mississippi rises,' Newton said. 'It's a whole damn state full of Norwegians and dull politicians. The worthwhile things are the trout fishing and the Canadian border. We're at the western end of Lake Superior. You could call it Limbo.'

Robin said, 'So Brother Bill brings us here. How many miles?'

'Close to two thousand, I guess.'

'Brings us here to kill us?' she pursued.

Todd said, 'You mean, why not kill us in Newfoundland?'

'That's what I mean. And why all these calories? Why's he feeding us like this?'

'Hold on,' Todd said. 'There has to be sense in this.'

'There is,' Zee Quist said wryly. 'And I can give you a good guess where we are. Maybe even how we got here. The DC9 must have put us down at Thunder Bay on the Lake and we came on here by seaplane. Bill has a shack in the woods for when he wants the simple life; six bedrooms, seven bathrooms and diesel generator for the freezer room.'

'All right. But why?'

'Easier to dispose of us here, I suppose,' Robin said.

'Hold on,' Todd raised a finger. 'We can't just disappear. We were registered in that motel, and there are people – the Learjet rental people for instance – who know where we were. Agreed we've left there, but there'll be someone who wonders, surely!'

'Don't bet on it,' said Zee Quist. 'You're English, she's Australian; any inquiries will take weeks to get started. I've been at death's door, maybe still am –'

'You're up to maybe C3 now,' Newton said encouragingly.

'And the doc is American resident in Canada and he's gone for a holiday, gone on the lam, who cares? But all this food is something else. You fatten pigs, you fatten cattle, but nobody's going to eat me!'

Todd said, 'Been here before?'

Zee Quist shook her head. 'This place is strictly for the boys. Rifles and cookouts and lots of beer. That's not to say a few girls don't get up here once in a while, because they do, but they aren't the girls he's going to introduce to Momma.'

Todd said, 'Zee, it's completely foreign to me, a set-up like this. Too big, too costly, too remote. Can you tell me any more?'

'Well, there's his plane. Seaplane for the lake. Last I heard it was some kind of Caribou aeroplane made in Canada. He'll

230

have a few boats, too. Rowboats for fishing, maybe a couple of speedboats for water-skiing. Oh, and I did hear he had a Chriscraft, li'l ole toy, you know, forty feet, twin GM diesels, that kind of thing.'

'All on a lake. Which lake?'

'Who knows! There's a million lakes in Minnesota.'

'To drown us in,' Robin said gloomily.

'There's another million of 'em in Newfoundland,' cut in the doctor. 'And just as much privacy. You'd drown there just as quick.'

'So why here?' Robin said.

They were still speculating hours later, and no nearer the solution, when once more a trolley loaded with food was brought swiftly into the room. Just as swiftly, its bearer disappeared.

Dr Newton inspected it morosely. 'Ribs of beef, handsomely carved,' he said. 'Mustard and horseradish, you name the vegetables. Pecan pie and cream. Coffee. I do not understand!'

None of them did. They lunched, quietly now, because what there was to say had largely been said.

But afterwards, Todd murmured, 'Escape?'

'You reckon?' asked Zee Quist.

He said, 'Out there is what? – water, woods, planes, boats?'

'Sure, and starvation and bears and wolves. This is America, sonny. Not all the killers are on two legs.'

Todd said, 'There are certainly armed men in here and locked and bolted doors. But we haven't even inspected this place yet!'

So the inspection began. It was very thorough. It ended with Todd, stripped to his pants, trying to climb up the inside of the chimney, and finding it impossible.

By then it was dinner time and on the trolley was salmon, a selection of salads, apple pie, a cheese board, a plastic jug of chablis. Plus coffee. Plus paper plates and plastic cutlery.

'I suspect,' Robin said, when she'd finished, 'that I might just as well apply all this direct to my hips, without going to the bother of eating it!'

'What it is,' Dr Newton offered, 'is it's the modern way to go. Murder by obesity. Like all those geese in Strasbourg.'

'Nobody, said Todd, 'is going to die laughing. That's certain. There must be something we can do!'

If there was, they couldn't think of it. For one thing minds did not seem able to stay focused. At last Dr Newton yawned and said, 'They got to us. It was the apple pie. Good pie, I thought. Aromatic, you notice that? I thought it was cinnamon, and all the time it was chloral hydrate, goddammit!'

The dosage must have been heavy. Todd first to awaken, checked his watch: ten o'clock, though a doubtful ten o'clock, based upon putting the watch back two and a half hours, first on an assumption this actually was Minnesota, and secondly on a further assumption – that Minnesota was two and a half hours behind Newfoundland. It could have been three and a half. Or one and a half – no one was quite sure which time zones enclosed Minnesota.

He smelled coffee. The trolley stood there; its arrival must have wakened him. He wakened Robin with a kiss and then turned to shake Dr Newton.

'Me, I'd as soon have the kiss,' the doctor said. He slid out of his chair to look at Zee Quist, and whistled softly. 'The whipcord kid,' he said to Todd. 'Boy, is she tough! Colour's come back!'

To all of them the situation was weird and quite unreal. Their prison, while undoubtedly a prison, gave the illusion of being something else: a comfortable, not to say a luxurious living room, or perhaps a big sitting room in a good hotel, one with an efficient kitchen and good room service.

Forty minutes or so later, Dr Newton had just poured his fourth cup of coffee. He said, 'I'll say this for the bastard, his coffee's good.'

'I'm glad you like it,' said Crombie's voice suddenly from the doorway. As they turned to look at him, it was clear to all of them that something about Brother Bill had changed.

He seemed now to exude a vast pleasure as though there was so much of it inside him and under such pressure that he couldn't prevent its leaking through his skin in a hundred places. But it was more than pleasure, there was a visible excitement about the man, and an energy that almost seemed to give off sparks.

232

'You sure you're feeling okay?' Newton asked sourly. 'You look kinda run-down to me. Need a blood tonic, maybe.'

Brother Bill grinned at him. 'I've had my tonic, doctor. And how!' He paused. 'But I'd value your professional opinion all the same. How's Zee?'

Zee Quist spoke for herself. 'Better every minute.'

'And Mr Todd, how's he?'

'He's okay,' Newton said. 'Give him another hour or two, he'll be back to normal.'

'Pity I can't,' said Brother Bill.

'Can't what? Give him another –'

'Let me ask you something else. Have they been eating well, Zee and Mr Todd?' Newton nodded. 'Plenty of good food inside them?' Crombie pursued the matter. 'And keeping it down – no sickness, no diaorrhea?'

'Listen, I'm the doctor here,' Newton said. 'They're okay.'

'But I'm puzzled, Bill,' Zee Quist said, 'by your concern.'

'Are you,' he said. 'That's interesting. Have you worked out where you are?'

She said, 'Minnesota. Your lodge.'

Crombie nodded. 'And you're still puzzled? You must be slipping, Zee. But it doesn't matter. We've got it.'

Newton said, 'You sure have and its name is paranoia.'

'Got what?' Zee Quist demanded. 'The nomination?'

He beamed. 'Roll call of the states went on till two. You never saw such demonstrations! We swept it, Zee! John's now the officially adopted candidate of the Democratic Party, for the office of President of the United States.' Pride was bursting from him. 'It's a pity, Zee. A real pity –'

'Welcome, Hugh!' Dr Newton said sharply.

Crombie stared at him. 'What do you mean, Hugh?'

'Hugh Bris,' Newton said, '*Hubris* – the other thing you're suffering from. Remember, pal, those gods don't care to be taken for granted.'

It made Crombie scowl.

'And anyway,' Zee Quist reminded him, 'technically the job's still open until the acceptance speech has been made.'

'That,' said Brother Bill, 'is tonight.' He gave a jerk of his head. 'I want you all outside. Doctor, you and Todd will take Zee's stretcher.'

Todd felt himself swallow, even heard the sound. That was it, then he said, 'Where are we going?'

'Out.' Two of Brother Bill's goons were in the room now, pistols in hand, though not pointed; each was held loosely by the man's side, though the threat of them was enormous. Todd picked up the rear two handles of Zee Quist's stretcher and followed Newton.

The morning air was warm and clean as they emerged into the bright sunlight. Ahead twenty yards or so lay a lake, a big one, nothing but water clear almost to the horizon in three directions. Before them lay a wooden jetty, where a big motor cruiser was tied up by the stern.

Brother Bill, walking beside them, said, 'All aboard.'

Newton halted. 'You actually going to do it?'

'Nobody will miss you, doctor,' Crombie said. 'Nobody.'

Once more it was easy and efficient. They boarded the boat by the stern, and, again on Crombie's instructions, moved from the stern well into the cabin just forward. The pistols, never much in evidence, were never far away, as the little group negotiated the three steps below.

They laid Zee Quist's stretcher on the wide bench seating, and Todd could see Crombie standing in the hatchway, looking down at them.

'Here.' Crombie tossed him a plastic bag, taped into a parcel. 'Now this is your present.'

Todd sank his fingernails into the thin material and pulled. Assorted bundles of brightly coloured material fell out, one or two to the deck.

'Swimsuits!' Robin van Geloven said.

'We tried to guess the sizes,' Crombie said in mock apology. He turned around. 'Okay, get them on. Let's go!' He closed the hatch-door. Inside the twin diesels' throb was immediately damped. Zee Quist said quietly, 'Why swimsuits, for God's sake?'

Todd thought he could guess, but said only, 'We'd better turn our backs, Doc, while Robin gives Zee a hand.' He looked at a door leading from the after cabin, forward to . . . to what? Must be locked, surely, he tried it. It opened inward.

On the other side lay a galley. He stepped in quickly, glanced round the thing at once, turned the switches, and withdrew fast. Just in time. Abruptly, Crombie opened the hatch and called, 'Make it fast. You can change for yourselves, or we can change for you! Five minutes.'

The hatch closed noisily, and expensively, mahogany against mahogany, brass mortices clicking into place.

Todd went hurriedly round the small after cabin, lifting cushions, raising the lids beneath. He found plenty, but nothing he wanted. That left only . . .

'Lift Zee,' he instructed Newton.

The doctor obeyed. Todd pulled aside cushions, lifted the bench seat. There was a plastic box, an old ice cream tub. Opened, it contained what looked like small, coloured truncheons. He took a red one, flicked the lid closed, put the cushion back.

'Better change, doc.' He pushed open the door to the galley. 'In there, Robin. Be quick.'

'Australians,' she said, 'are faster into swimsuits than anyone else on earth.'

'Prove it.'

She did. She was back in a moment and assisting Zee Quist. Todd and Newton, backs turned, were also swift.

'But where in hell,' Todd demanded, 'do I hide this?'

Robin grinned. 'This is a big bra, and I'm not a size ten. Give it here, Mr Pom.'

He'd just pushed open the galley door when Brother Bill opened the hatch. 'Come on out. Leave the stretcher. You carry her, doc.'

Newton lifted Zee Quist in his arms and carried her up the stairs. Todd and Robin followed, looking round them, blinking at the bright sunlight reflected blindingly off the rippling water. The big cruiser was slowing, its engines down to a low throb.

'Death by drowning, eh, Bill?' Zee Quist said contemptuously. 'Four of us. One genealogist, one Australian lawyer, one doctor and me! You're starting your own Watergate, Bill.'

'You're underestimating me, Zee: you always have,' Crombie said. 'We have a scenario here. It's real sweet.'

'Do us a last favour,' Todd said. 'Tell us.'

Crombie frowned. 'Waste of time. Won't do you any good.'

Zee Quist said: 'If it's so brilliant, let's hear it. You can't say it's not our concern.'

'Trying to put off the evil moment, huh? Well, why not. Here's old Zee, the great international athlete, and the only sport she's good for now is a little gentle swimming. Also it's good for her. Well, she's been ill, old Zee has, but she's better, and she gets herself taken down to the lakeside at her old pal Bill Crombie's lodge in the woods.'

'What in hell's she even doing there?' Zee Quist demanded.

'You're recuperating, Zee, what else?' He added evenly: 'Eating well, too, as the autopsy will demonstrate.'

'So that's why we got the food.'

He nodded. 'Well, Zee, off you went swimming. But of course you're still a little weak and you got in difficulty. So you yelled, and the doc came after you. But the water's damn cold – you'll find that out in a minute – and the doc must have got the cramps. So he yelled.' Crombie paused. 'What have we now? Icy water. Two drowning. Enter Miss Australia, the life-saving queen – powerful stroke to the rescue, but she sure as hell isn't used to water temperatures under fifty. More cramps. Three struggling, one to go. Who's left. Why the gallant British fiancé of the life-saving queen. Naturally, he plunges to her aid. Equally naturally, since he's only just out of hospital, he's too weak. *Four die in Minnesota Lake drowning tragedy*. Saw those very words in the Saint Paul paper last summer. Only question now is, who's first?'

236

18

'According to your scenario, I'm first,' Zee Quist said challeng-ingly. 'You going to toss me in yourself, Bill? Got the nerve for that, have you?'

'You doubt it?'

'Yeah, Bill. I doubt it.'

'Always doubted me, haven't you Zee. Maybe that's been the problem.'

'I never had doubts about you, Bill. I've always known what kind of low life creep you are.'

They saw the fury blaze in Crombie's face. He suddenly grabbed for Zee, wanting to tear her from Dr Newton's arms. Newton, anticipating, turned his back swiftly. Crombie instantly seized his shoulders, trying to spin him, stepping close, as he did so, and wrenching at Zee Quist. Newton's knee came up like a piston.

It was done in a second. The two goons had stepped forward. The two pistols were levelled. Newton faced them defiantly, holding Zee Quist firmly cradled. Brother Bill Crombie lay on the deck, clutching his groin, whimpering.

Newton grinned down at him. 'There are advantages,' he said, 'to even a rudimentary knowledge of simple anatomy.'

Crombie looked up at him, hatred smeared across the pain-filled face. 'Kick them over.' He grunted the order. 'Kick them all over.'

The two goons manhandled Newton roughly up on to the bathing platform of the stern, and there was nothing the doctor could do to resist, as one of Crombie's men hacked with the edge of his hand at the back of Newton's knee. The sudden stagger on the collapsing joint pitched him forward and, with Zee Quist's weight pulling him outward, he stood teetering, struggling for balance.

Todd hurled himself forward, arms grasping at the waists of the two goons, his thighs pushing hard, like a sprinter driving forward from the start. They didn't go over, but both crashed in a heap and he was past them, stepping on to the platform, hand outstretched to Robin.

She jumped neatly over and past the three sprawling men. Crombie, staggering to his feet, made a grab for her, but she was gone before his lunge came near her.

'Want this?' As she came on to the platform, she handed the miniature truncheon to Todd.

He took it and looked at it, for a brief moment doubtfully, but then Crombie was up roaring towards them, lashing with his big fist at Robin.

'Yes. I want it. Now dive!' He took the truncheon from her, twisted fast at its plastic handle and then, as the scarlet incandescence flowered, tossed the now-blazing flare towards the open hatchway, and then was diving for the water himself while it was still in the air, and feeling something pluck softly at his feet before they plunged beneath the water.

He stayed under while his breath lasted, but when he surfaced, half a minute later, the air was still filled with falling debris, and the big Chriscraft was in two parts, the after half ablaze, the forward half filling fast and about to sink.

He looked anxiously for the others. Newton, at least was alive, his head bleeding a bit, thirty yards or so away. And Zee Quist – now he saw her, too, clinging to a chunk of wood a few feet from Newton.

Where the hell was Robin? Todd forced his body out of the water, looking round for her.

No sign.

He did it again. No Robin.

The water was very cold, but now nowhere near as icy as the desperate fear that now grew deep inside him.

She'd dived first! She must have been safe! She'd actually been entering the water at the instant the flare touched off the bottled gas that had leaked from the cooking stove he'd switched on in the forward cabin.

238

So where was she? Could a piece of flying debris have caught her?

He was still groaning at the thought when she surfaced beside him and said: 'You okay, Mr Pom?'

'Yes,' he said faintly. 'I'm fine.'

'Well come on!' Robin van Geloven said, 'we won't be okay for long if we stay in this freezing bloody oggie. This here is Froznograd!'

The flukes and peculiarities that accompany explosions are many and well recorded. The massive blast of one V2 rocket in London in 1945 picked up a woman in the street and put her down again three streets away; she was unharmed but she was naked.

The exploding gas had smashed up Crombie's big cruiser, but left intact the two inflatable dinghies in their stowing place beneath the seats of the stern wall. To get at them, Todd had to run something of a gauntlet of fire, but finally he got them out.

The next two hours were nightmarish. Both parts of the Chriscraft sank while Todd and Dr Newton struggled to inflate the dinghies. A few small remnants of the cruiser, now floated where she'd been, and one or two other things: a foam cushion, a glass coffee jar, a sponge. Zee Quist, her exceptional thinness and absence of body fat making her particularly vulnerable to the cold, clung to the bobbing cushion, teeth gritted, looking bluer with every passing minute. When Newton had the first dinghy blown up, the urgent priority was to get her into it. Once that had been achieved, Newton assembled the paddle and set off for the shore, without waiting. There was miles to go and it was killing work.

As soon as Robin van Geloven, first into the remaining dinghy, had helped Todd haul himself aboard, she rose to an unsteady crouch and, turning slowly, looked carefully at the water around them. Then she looked down at him. 'Nobody,' she said flatly, her Australian accent suddenly more pronounced. 'There's nobody at all!'

Todd grimaced. Three dead, he thought. Maybe more than three. The Chriscraft could have had an engineer, or crew –

it had been big enough. He'd killed, actually killed three men! He said, 'Maybe I ought to try a dive? Somebody could be trapped in the wreckage down there.'

'Yeah. Try that and maybe it would be you!' Robin said unsentimentally. 'They got what they deserved. You did exactly the right thing. Come to that, you probably did the world a favour.' She bent and kissed him. 'Do me a favour, Mr Pom and let's get ashore!'

Todd's head, as he screwed the bits of the flat-pack paddle together, still whirled with the violence and speed of it. How long, he thought, had that gas tap been on? Ten minutes at the outside. He said dazedly, 'I thought the explosion – if there was one – might just disable the boat, or even attract attention. Not that it –'

'There must have been gas down in the bilges,' Robin said. 'It's heavier than air, so it just lurks about forever unless a strong draught of air clears it out. Those bazza's weren't just crooks – they were sloppy boatmen and that's worse! Now paddle.'

He paddled. The only habitation in view was Crombie's lodge on the lake shore, small in the distance. To his left no shore was in sight; behind him, miles away, lay pine forest; to his right, also several miles off, were more pines. It came to him suddenly that as they approached the house, the little rubber boats would be ludicrously easy targets for a man with a rifle. He said so.

Robin said. 'Like who? The big boss has gone. Crombie's dead! Nobody else wants to kill us. Probably there's nobody else there.'

'There's a cook,' Todd said. 'It wasn't Crombie and his thugs who did the six course meals.'

She managed a grin and a nod of agreement. 'Cooks can be dangerous, and don't I know it! Look at the one who did the chicken soup.'

He didn't smile back at her. Todd, she thought, would bear the scars of this morning for a long time. Whereas she . . . well, what? she asked herself. She could work up no guilt about the end of Brother Bill, who would have killed so lightly, or of his men, who had been ready to obey him, however foul his instructions. No guilt at all. She shivered as the light airs that swirled over the water touched her skin. It had been like a scene from a TV film: clear and visible but unreal. Maybe its brutal reality would hit her later, like shock, and as it had hit Todd.

She glanced at him with a great welling of affection. He was hunched, concentrating, beginning to sweat with the effort.

Then he stopped and yelled to Newton to stop, too.

She said, 'What's up now?'

'We're nuts,' Todd said. 'This is wasteful. We need to put both paddles in one dinghy and tow the other.'

'Right, Mr Pom!'

Even then it took more than an hour of back-aching, shoulder-punishing work to reach the shore, with Robin van Geloven taking over Todd's paddle for a couple of brief spells. The food poisoning had entirely drained his reserves of strength and they were far from fully restored. But he struggled on and finally the leading dinghy struck the lake shore's pebbles a hundred yards or so from the lodge. Todd had insisted. 'A hundred yards isn't much to a good shot,' he said, 'but to a bad shot, it's a hard target.'

Leaving Dr Newton to look after Zee Quist, Todd and Robin van Geloven moved quickly but cautiously through the surrounding trees towards the back of the lodge. It looked empty, as they approached, and empty it was. There was nobody there, indoors or out. The garage building was empty of vehicles.

'Goodbye, cook,' Robin said.

They found blankets and Robin ran with them to meet Newton, as he carried a near-frozen Zee Quist towards the lodge.

Todd, meanwhile, had found, and turned on, the boiler, and was hunting for a telephone. One room's door stood locked. Unhesitatingly he smashed it open, and saw with relief the rows of books, the desk – and the radio set.

Crombie's study.

And on the desk – Todd's own thin document case! Todd was trying to operate the radio when Robin found him. 'Move over, Pom,' she said. 'I was raised on bush wireless. Let the dingo see the rabbit.'

'It's not a bush wireless,' she said, 'this is a radio telephone . . . Switch is yes, here –' Far off, they heard the diesel generator kick into life. '– and this here . . . what was that number?'

'Which number?'

'The mother, Mrs Crombie. Look, he may be no great loss to you and me, but she's just lost a son.'

'Zee carries it in her head.'

'So do I. I can remember numbers.' She passed the San Francisco number to the operator, and asked for the patch. A moment or two later, from the radio's little loudspeaker, came the familiar, implacable, relentlessly polite voice of the man who guarded Mrs Crombie's privacy; the voice said simply: 'Hello.'

Robin said, 'I'm on the radio phone from Bill Crombie's lodge in Minnesota. Tell Mrs Crombie there's real trouble here. Bad trouble. Get her to call back quickly. She'll have the number. Over.'

'Excuse me, who is calling, please?' There was anxiety in the voice. 'And what is the nature of –'

'Tell her,' Robin said, her hand-switch interrupting him. 'Tell her. Over and out.'

She sat waiting. 'If she's out somewhere they'll have to get it patched in' she told Todd. 'It's no great trouble. A few minutes.'

'Don't you think,' Todd said, 'that that's a bit brutal? She must be pretty old.'

She shook her head. 'The code words are there. Real, bad trouble at her son's lodge, that's what I said.' She smiled. 'I'm a solicitor, darling. Don't forget that. In my game we have plenty of experience of handing out the bad news.'

'Hello?' The man's voice came hissing from the speaker. 'Is that Steelhead Lodge?'

'Yes.'

'I have – er – your caller.'

'Right.'

'Is this bad news of my son?' It was clearly the voice of an

242

old woman; equally clearly, it was a voice accustomed to command. 'Over.'

'I'm afraid,' Robin said gently, 'that it is very bad news, Mrs Crombie. Over.'

There was a pause. 'He's dead? Over.'

'Yes. I'm sorry. Over.'

'May I ask, who are you? Over.'

'I'm calling,' Robin van Geloven said, 'on Zee Quist's behalf. Over.'

The old woman's voice shook a little as it responded, but it was under control nonetheless. More than under control, Todd thought: dominating. 'Please stay there, if it's possible, until I arrive. Can you do that? Over.'

'Yes. Over.'

'And Zee, also? Over.'

'Zee's here. Over.'

Newton, with the lodge's considerable resources available, cocooned Zee Quist in warmth. She was exhausted and very badly chilled and he was terrified of circulatory problems arising in the bloodless extremities, specifically gangrene.

'Is that a possibility?' Todd asked.

'Always a hazard in circumstances like these.'

She was packed round with hot water bags and fed hot soup laced with brandy, and after a while she slept, leaving the others to face the problem of Mrs Crombie on this unimaginable day in her long life, a day on which one son was violently dead and the other about to accept nomination as candidate for the Presidency.

Todd set about checking his document case, expecting to find that the papers in it had been destroyed. But all were there – retained no doubt, as sources. Once the originals had been destroyed *in situ*, these would quickly have followed.

There was a two-hour time gap. As Robin spoke to her, the clock in Crombie's study showed a few minutes before one p.m. – it would therefore be eleven in San Francisco. They found a Rand McNally road atlas containing a chart showing distances. Mrs Crombie would have to fly almost exactly two thousand miles. There was no way of knowing how she'd do it, but equally no doubt that she could demand any and all available services: jet to Duluth or St Paul, Dr Newton reckoned, then a float plane in direct to the lake.

About five p.m. they heard an engine, faint at first, but coming nearer, standing on the grass outside they saw the Caribou making a low circle and then turning into an approach and taxiing toward the wooden jetty. The pilot's familiarity with the place was demonstrated by the neat way he placed the plane so that its passenger could simply step over from the float to the jetty.

Todd offered his hand as Mrs Crombie made the step, and was surprised by the nimble way she did it, considering that she was a lot nearer eighty than seventy. She straightened at once and faced him. Pale blue eyes examined him from above a very straight nose. Her hair was snow white and stiff as a hairbrush. Her head was altogether Roman, he thought, and it surmounted a slim, upright body that was still lissom for all her years.

'Who are you?' she asked, her voice was pleasantly low, her tone courteous, her air of command unmistakable.

'My name is Todd.'

'Is Zee Quist here?'

'She's in bed. I think she's still sleeping.'

'She's ill?'

'Zee got very cold. The doctor is worried.'

'You have a doctor here?'

'We have.'

'And he couldn't help Bill?'

Todd said gently, 'I think it might be better if you come indoors, and I explained there, Mrs Crombie.'

She blinked. 'Yes, of course.' As he turned towards the lodge, she fell into step beside him, 'If I'm right, Mr Todd, you must be the genealogical expert who discovered Grandfather Connor's unfortunate history.'

'I'm afraid I did.'

She stopped. 'You evidently deal in facts, Mr Todd. Are there others apart from Zee, in the cabin?' He nodded. 'Then tell me here, please, not in front of the others. How did my son die?'

244

Todd swallowed. 'His motor cruiser blew up. Out there –' he pointed '– in the lake.'

She frowned. 'Blew up? Was it an accident, Mr Todd?'

He hesitated. 'There was a good deal more to it than that, Mrs Crombie.'

'It was not an accident?'

This time Todd did not hesitate. About this woman there was a level clarity that made dissimulation seem impossible, and a degree of control that made it necesssary. 'No,' he said, 'it was not an accident. Please come indoors, Mrs Crombie, and I'll explain.'

She placed a detaining arm on his arm. 'He was killed, Mr Todd, I understand that now – but by whom?' The pale blue eyes were on him.

'By me,' Todd said flatly. 'I'm afraid that there was no alternative.'

Her hand still held his forearm. 'Mr Todd, was it because you know something enormously important? I know that you were working with, or for, poor Zee. I know that someone had telephoned a few days ago when I was in San Francisco, on Zee's behalf, with an urgent message. You had discovered something more – and perhaps worse – about Grandfather Connor?'

Todd said, 'No. Not about Joseph Patrick Connor. Please come inside.'

19

Days ago – years it now seemed – Zee Quist had agreed to it. She would take the baleful tidings to John Leyden; she would explain, would stay with him as he absorbed first the knowledge and then its fearful consequences.

But it was not John Leyden who was to be told or not yet. Facing them now was an elderly woman who, for all the obvious strength in her character and bearing, had lost her youngest son that day. She sat lance-straight on an upright chair. No, thank you, no coffee. No, nor tea. Brandy? – thank you, she would not touch alcohol now.

'Perhaps you would all be kind enough to leave me alone with Mr Todd?'

Dr Newton was disposed to help and offered; he would not be required. He withdrew and Robin van Geloven went with him, looking back over her shoulder at Todd. 'Call me if . . .'

'I will.' He turned and faced Mrs Crombie.

She said, 'Tell me about William. Tell me how he came to die. Tell me where his body is.'

Todd had been trying frantically to think of a starting point. The whole story was brutal – and far from ended. There was no soft entry to it, no easy way along.

Perhaps sensing it, she helped him. 'If not Connor, then who? What is this knowledge?'

Todd said, 'Does the name of Jane Taylor mean anything?'

'Of course it does. She was his wife.'

'How do you know her maiden name?'

'She lived, you know, after the accident. Just a few hours, and then the child came and she died. Apparently it was one of the things she said.'

'One of the things?' Todd prompted. 'There were others?'

'Not really. Or very little. She mentioned San Francisco

246

and Australia and their journey, but I believe she was barely conscious and rambling.'

Todd said, 'She was his second wife. It was knowledge of her that led, I'm afraid, to your son's death.'

'Something you had discovered Mr Todd, and William knew? And you killed him?'

Todd said defensively, 'He was going to kill me. And not only me.'

She closed her eyes tightly, as though at a spasm of pain, and to Todd her face seemed in that moment to dissolve into age. But it was only for a moment. Then the blue eyes were upon him again, and the composure was back. 'May I ask you two questions, Mr Todd?' He nodded. 'First, by what means did William intend to kill you?'

'He was going to drown us. A boating accident was how —'

'And, forgive me. By what means did he . . . did you . . .?'

Todd said, 'A flare. There was gas in the boat and it exploded. When it sank, I'm afraid his body —'

She held up a hand, interrupting him. 'Thank you.' And paused. 'It is a strange situation to me to be sitting here talking to the man who killed my son. You are an intelligent man and, I rather think a sensitive one, so you too must feel it.'

Todd moved uneasily in his chair. She seemed to be looking at him in an odd way: hate, anger, pain — any of them would have been natural to her at this moment on this day. But her look seemed almost of benevolence. She said suddenly, 'In a curious way, Mr Todd, this moment, and this meeting has about it, for me, a kind of inevitability.'

Todd frowned. 'I don't follow, Mrs Crombie. My researches led towards your family, of course, but —'

She said reflectively, 'And we are even in Minnesota!'

Todd didn't see at all. 'Minnesota?' he said, thinking: is it shock, has grief unhinged her? Should Dr Newton be sent for?

Somehow she seemed to intercept his thoughts. 'Don't be alarmed, I'm very sane.' Helena Crombie was crisp now. 'Your knowledge threatened my other son, John, did it not — at least in William's eyes?'

It would have been easy to nod, to duck away from the

reality behind the question. Todd was tempted; but he said, 'Not just in William's eyes, Mrs Crombie. The threat is there.'

'To John?'

'I'm sorry, but yes.'

She said, 'You probably think me heartless, Mr Todd, and that a bereaved and grieving mother should be prostrate and tearful. I tell you I have wept already and I will weep more. If this talk of ours is difficult and disjointed, it is because I am not strong enough to tackle everything direct and at once. I have to take it a piece at a time. Because take it I must, and take it now, today, because tonight my son . . .' she stopped. A tremor went through her, and Todd half-rose but she waved him down.

Then Helena Crombie was speaking again. 'I have – no, I had – two sons. You will have seen John, I'm sure, perhaps on TV? I can tell you without any false pride at all that he's a credit to himself, to me, to his father, to humanity itself, if you like. William was my failure, even my fault. He lived all his life in John's shadow –' The corners of her mouth were abruptly drawn down by her grief; he saw her swallow and fight for control; then she went on, 'John, from babyhood, was a golden child to whom everything came easily. Yet he was never spoiled, his character was fine, his emotions steady, his brain and body first-class. William, poor child, always wished to compete, and never could. He always hero-worshipped John, and yet was deeply jealous of him. Where John has always been serene, William was always a little off balance. Yet William had many virtues. He had made far more of his life than I ever expected. Until this. But in some far corner of my mind, Mr Todd, I have often thought I heard a timebomb ticking. Now, I suppose I know what it was.'

Todd said hurriedly, 'What is the significance of Minnesota?'

'Ah that was something else. There is a town in this state by the name of Rochester. Does it mean anything to you?'

He shook his head.

'Rochester is the home of the Mayo Clinic, which is a celebrated centre of medical education and research. My first husband, John's father, was on his way there when he was killed in a plane crash.'

'Do you know why he was going to a clinic?'

Helena Crombie said, 'No. After his death I learned that he had consulted his own physician and later a specialist. He was a very fit, active man, Mr Todd, and he never mentioned to me that anything was wrong.'

Todd hesitated. As the doctor in Cambridge had said, there was no tactful way, no easy entree, no emollient or sideways approach to the subject of Huntington's. But could she already have a hint . . .? He said, 'And was anything wrong?'

She gave a sad little shrug. 'My husband died in an aeroplane crash, Mr Todd. The plane burst into flames. His body was never even identified. But –' and the shrug was repeated '– the doctors told me what he had complained of. He felt his temper was getting bad, and that he was becoming clumsy.'

'Had you noticed any of this?'

'Me? Not for a second.'

He couldn't let it go now. Todd said, 'Did the doctor speculate?'

She smiled. 'He said it was probably fatigue. That or imagination. I worried because I was pregnant. And then when John was born, he was perfect as could be.' She paused. 'Even then I wasn't satisfied. I hired an expert in England – someone in your profession, Mr Todd – to investigate the background of my husband's parents. He did not get very far. He found Grandfather Connor, of course, because of the regiment's number in the line and he learned of his repeated wickedness and imprisonment. He even discovered the record of his marriage to Jane Taylor. Then he lost track and couldn't find it again.

'I was terrified you see, that my beautiful baby son might in some way be contaminated by that terrible grandfather. I was fearful, you see, of heredity itself . . .'

Bitterly he recognized the moment, the opportunity to speak. Let it pass and another such moment would have to be sought or manufactured.

He said, trying to be gentle, but hearing in his own ears the harshness of his word, 'You were right to be afraid, Mrs Crombie.'

She frowned, and the china blue eyes were puzzled. 'I don't follow you –'

He said, quickly because now anything less than speed was torture, 'The second Jane Taylor carried a disease in her genes – a very severe one.'

Her hands flew trembling to her face. She blinked rapidly several times, fear and pain widening her eyes. Todd, hating himself, trapped as Dr Keighley had said the informer was always trapped, forced himself on. 'She came from a family in England. A family afflicted with a disease called Huntington's Chorea. I can call in Dr Newton to explain . . .'

She was gaping at him. 'Huntington's,' she whispered. Her eyes closed tightly and her head turned from him.

Todd repeated a little desperately, 'I can call in Dr Newton to explain . . .'

The white head shook. She whispered 'No.' For a long moment she sat motionless, and then to Todd's astonishment she raised her head; her back straightened. Helena Crombie faced him and said, 'I was a girl in East Hampton, Long Island, Mr Todd. It was there that Huntington first studied it. I have seen sufferers. And you say that John . . .?'

Her voice trailed off. There was only so much courage and all of it was in use.

'He comes of choreic stock,' Todd said. 'I understand the odds are roughly fifty-fifty.'

'My husband – John's father?'

'May have had it and died before it showed.'

She was staring at him, struggling to keep some degree of composure in the face of the barrage of disaster that his words, and his work, represented. Then, abruptly, the control departed. Helena Crombie suddenly wailed, 'Oh, my God, Mercy! John's child!' and the straight back sagged; her face seemed to collapse and Todd, afraid she must fall, leapt across to take her shoulders in his hands.

She clung to him weeping, and now that the dam had broken, Todd found tears coursing down his own cheeks, too. Through them he looked down at the bowed head with its fine, proud hairdo, and thought: she woke this morning with two living sons, the elder perhaps to be President of the United States, the younger his aide in the battle for election. And now . . . one was dead and the other . . .

He knelt beside her chair, arms round her, muttering, 'I'm sorry, I'm so very sorry,' as she wept, her head turned now against his chest. A few minutes passed. He had no idea how many. Still, he held her, but he could sense the determined straightening of her body. Soon she shrugged him away. Her voice, when she could speak, had a tremor in it. 'All this is true – it can be proved?'

'Yes.' Todd said. 'I have the papers.'

She nodded. 'I shall need them, Mr Todd, when I tell John. Will you be so kind as to accompany me to San Francisco and bring them with you.'

20

——◆——

There was no spotlight – all the lights, the colour, the clamour, all the rejoicing lay on the other side of the barriers of brick and wood and fabric that stood between John Leyden and the colossal greeting that awaited him. There was no spotlight here, at the bare junction of corridors and passageways, where the impatient jubilant army of his campaign staff stood at increasingly reluctant distance from their hero, obedient but puzzled, desperately anxious to claim him now, now and forever, as the new White Knight of the Democratic Party. No spotlight, except that John Leyden looked always as though a light was on him: some compound of the fair hair and the open face, the paleish suit and the upright stance, always picked him out.

He was to speak at midnight. Midnight here, in California . . . ten in Minnesota where Zee Quist would be watching and Newton caring for her . . . eight in New York where the network directors sat facing their banks of monitors, waiting for the moment of his appearance, of his acceptance.

And still he stood, unmoving and unwontedly grave, with the little group to whom he had been talking for exactly thirteen minutes, a time that dozens of stop-watches had already recorded. All the watchers knew one of the group. In her way, Helena Crombie was almost as famous as her son: one of America's famous mothers, herself prominent in business, in politics, in charity work.

She'd come hurrying in, calling his name, intercepting him as he strode with a group of his aides towards the heavily curtained doorway that led to the speaker's podium and the place of honour.

The aides and the watchers knew Helena Crombie well enough, but who were the others? Who was the man in his thirties with the dark beard and the briefcase? Who was the attractive fair girl with the deep sun tan who stood with them? Staffers asked one another, with ever-increasing urgency, who was who – and what was happening!

And still the talk went on. Once or twice Leyden aides came forward. 'Senator – the time! You're due up there now!' But he waved them away and the urgent conversation continued – its urgency plain to see in the assertiveness of the speeches.

And then the bearded man was opening a flat document case, handing papers to Senator Leyden, and the Senator was reading, looking up from them, asking questions.

A TV director, observing the scene by chance from a gallery thirty yards away wept for a zoom lens, a close-up and a good directional microphone. 'What in hell's on the papers – what do they say?'

And then, quite suddenly, it was over. Senator Leyden summoned an aide. 'Peter, take my mother and my – er – guests back to her car.'

'Isn't your Mother going to be with you for the acceptance speech?'

'Take them please,' Leyden said, 'to the cars.'

He kissed her cheek, and turned away, striding athletically down the corridor towards the curtained entrance and the cheers . . .

At the Lodge in far-off Minnesota the diesel generator chugged softly, providing the pulse of power which lit the lamps and heated the water and fired the electrons down the cathode ray tube.

Zee Quist lay propped against a bank of pillows; Dr Newton was in a chair by her bed. On the TV screen a heavy man with a heavy southern voice was saying:

'. . . my privilege to introduce to you the junior Senator from Connecticut, the elected Candidate of this great Democratic Party of ours and –' the voice paused dramatically and then rose to the traditional shout '– the next President of the United States: JOHN LEYDEN!'

There was a pause. Five thousand delegates and alternates happily set out to cheer themselves hoarse in an ovation extending over several minutes. But it began to go awry, at the moment when it should have peaked. John Leyden had entered down a small flight of stairs and past a dark drape. But he did none of the things traditional for the occasion: there was no wide grin, no Eisenhower salute. The embrace from Lewis Jackson, newly-endorsed vice-presidential candidate, was made brief, to Jackson's clear dismay. Above all there was present no mother, no sisters, no Brother Bill, no family to stand happily united in the spotlights, arms round one another's shoulders in a great public demonstration of family pride. 'Even Mercy Leyden,' Dan Rather said, his voice raised in astonishment, 'is absent from her husband's side at this – the most important moment of his life!'

The surprise of Jackson and the commentators spread steadily into the great hall and the ovation began to falter. The great cheers were diluted into mere applause, then the applause thinned, soon turning to no more than scattered hand-claps.

Then these, too, died away and there came the sweeping sibilance of a thousand gasps, for Mercy Leyden had slipped past the curtain and now appeared beside her husband and her distress was plain to see. Under the bright lights and on monitor screens throughout the hall, tears could be seen, glistening upon the fragile face. In all the tumult it was a moment before Leyden even saw her. When he did, he embraced her instantly. A few in the puzzled throng tried to raise a half-hearted cheer at that but it died at once as Leyden stepped forward, one arm raised for silence, the other tight round the shoulders of his wife. The handsome, boyish face was changed now. The nation was accustomed to seeing this man alight with fun and energy, happy in all of his life and sharing his happiness.

Now, a single glance was enough to prove all of that had gone. Here was a handsome man turned haggard with stress.

'Ladies and gentlemen . . .' the familiar, pleasant, low-pitched voice began, 'I owe to you all, to this great party, to millions of Americans, the most prof –' his voice cracked and he stopped to clear his throat several times '– the most profound apology it is possible to make. I have sought your help and your support and they have been given to me – overwhelmingly. By

254

giving me your faith, you have honoured me far beyond anything a man could expect or even hope for. I ask you to believe I have campaigned with an equal belief in the essential rightness of our cause, of our party and of our people. You merit the victory, all of you, for the wonders you have worked, and the new opportunity you brought into being for all Americans.'

Five thousand in the hall stood unmoving and unsmiling. If they were breathing, it would have been hard to tell. In a faraway box something scraped and the small sound was audible everywhere.

Leyden's hand passed across dry lips. He went on sombrely, 'At this final moment, I have learned that it is impossible – now – for me to accept the great trust you have placed in my hands. I cannot accept the honour you have done me. I can not be the Democratic candidate for the office of President.'

From somewhere in the hall, a voice yelled, 'Why?' and the question was taken up in an instant. Why – why – why? became a chant. In tight close-up on twenty million screens, John Leyden's face now seemed to be actually aging. Wearily he raised a hand for quiet, and when the noise died, he said, almost gently. 'The reason is good. It is important to America. I can not and will not say any more, now or at any other time. Except this: my country, my family, and I myself, are all in the hands of God.'

He and his wife went at once, vanishing behind the hanging drape, before the clamour of anger and disappointment, of defeat and frustration began to rise to the level that would keep feeding upon itself for days to come; that would extend into weeks and probably years. Behind him the crowd bayed, the commentators yelped, and the enduring Leyden Mystery began to take root.

Zee Quist's eyes did not leave the screen. She seemed not even to blink until, as Leyden left the platform, her eyes did close and she murmured: 'Over. All over.'

Somewhere the car still waited. Helena Crombie had stayed to see. Now she was leaving. She switched off the TV set, from which her son's image had just faded, and straightened her suit. Tears streamed down her face but she made no attempt to hide them, or even to dab them away. She was half-way to the door when she stopped, turned and looked at them. 'You two intend to marry?'

They looked at each other. Nod followed nod.

Helena Crombie achieved a smile. It was not much of a smile; just effort and generosity forcing movement into muscles that resisted. 'Thank God that something good comes out of this awful day. I must go to John.'